HEART'S LANDING

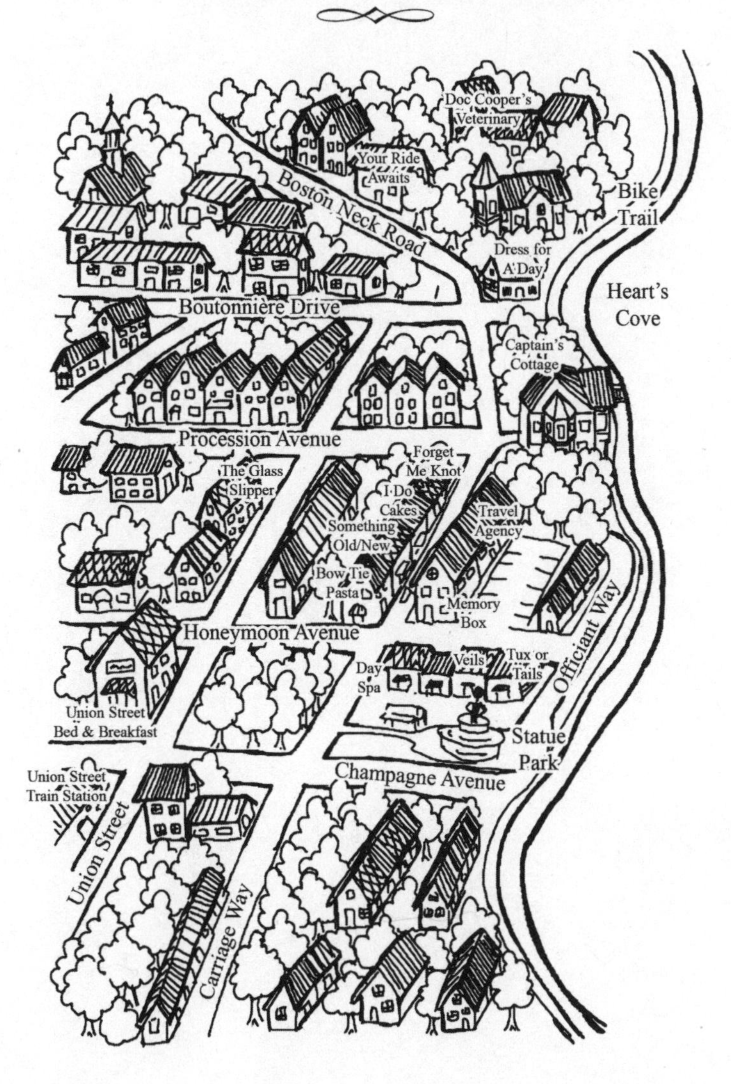

A SIMPLE Wedding

LEIGH
DUNCAN

A Simple Wedding

Print: 978-1-947892-38-5
eBook: 978-1-947892-47-7

Hallmark
PUBLISHING

www.hallmarkpublishing.com

Table of Contents

Chapter One

The tires of the delivery van brushed the curb at the corner of Bridal Carriage Way and Procession Avenue.

"Easy does it," Nick Bell coached his young assistant. He cast a quick glance over his shoulder. The momentary jump in his heart rate returned to normal when four tiers of the palest pink confection barely wobbled. "We have plenty of time—two hours till the reception. Trust me when I say neither of us wants to answer to the bride, or the rest of Heart's Landing, if anything happens to this cake."

"You got it, boss." Though sweat beaded on his upper lip, Jimmy nodded dutifully from behind the wheel. The young man slowed the van to a crawl.

Turning to peer out the windshield, Nick traced the hedge-lined drive that curved toward one of the most photographed sights in the state. The rays of the setting sun reflected off the white masonry of the Captain's Cottage, giving the turn-of-the-century home a golden aura. With its wide verandas and stately architecture, the manor stood as an elegant reminder of simpler times. No wonder brides from across the country chose this spot to exchange their vows.

The slight tension between his shoulder blades eased

while the tires rolled past the meticulously maintained "cottage" that would have been called a mansion if it had been built anywhere but on the coast of Rhode Island. Situated not much more than a stone's throw south of Newport, where the uber-rich had once summered on sprawling estates with names like The Breakers and Rosecliff, the house Captain Thaddeus Heart built might have faded into obscurity if his granddaughter hadn't married into the Rockefeller clan. But when she'd glided down the circular staircase of the family's summer home in a wedding that had turned the socialites of the day all misty-eyed, brides across the country had declared Heart's Landing *the* place to get married.

It had been ever since.

"Turn there." Nick pointed to a discreet sign directing deliveries around to the rear of the three-story cottage and away from the arched openings of the wide veranda, the porte cochere that protected arriving and departing guests, and the tall, mullioned windows flanked by towering black shutters.

He forced himself to relax. He didn't need to second-guess his assistant. Though Jimmy was freckle-faced and barely sported enough peach fuzz to require shaving on a daily basis, the young driver had been born and raised in Heart's Landing. He, along with the good citizens for miles around, knew the importance of getting each detail right in a town that had staked its reputation on providing "a perfect wedding for every bride." From Forget Me Knot Flowers on Bridal Carriage Way to the Perfectly Flawless Day Spa on Honeymoon Avenue, from Tux or Tails to the Dress For A Day bridal salon, businesses in town catered to every whim of brides, grooms, and their guests. They were so good at what they did, in fact, that the village had been repeatedly named one of America's most sought-after wedding destinations by none other than *Weddings Today*.

A standing Nick and Jimmy would do their best to uphold.

This time, when Jimmy took the fork onto the pathway that looped around the Captain's Cottage, the van's precious cargo barely shimmied. Nick lowered his window. In the distance, the green ocean glistened. The sound of breakers crashing against the rocky shore rose above the crunching sound the tires made on the pavement. In the cooler temperatures of a late afternoon, the heady scent of blooming azaleas mingled with the air's salty tang. The flowers were direct descendants of the original stock Captain Thaddeus Heart had brought from Japan for his wife's twenty-fifth birthday. Rumor had it, the plants had survived the long voyage carefully wrapped in burlap bags and stowed in the captain's own quarters, where his cabin boy had been tasked with keeping the roots damp with precious fresh water. Now, the flowers dotted the grounds of the family home. Though Nick always enjoyed his visits here, he especially liked making deliveries in late spring, when clumps of brilliant buds colored the landscape and perfumed the air.

The van rolled to a stop. Behind the house that had been passed down from one generation of Hearts to another for well over a century, panel trucks and other vehicles crowded a wide asphalt apron. Through his open window, Nick waved to Mildred Morrey, the owner of Forget Me Knot Flowers. The spry senior citizen hurried past, her ready smile and silvery hair barely visible behind an immense spray of roses the exact same shade of pale pink as the buttercream frosting Nick had spread over each cake tier. Next came Roy Rolland. Lugging a tri-pod and an oversized shoulder bag, the videographer gave Jimmy a jaunty wave before darting across the road in front of them. Closer to the house, a bevy of assistants and staff toted items ranging from trays of crystal wine goblets to photos of the lucky couple up a wide incline and through the double doors at the back of the house.

"Is it always like this? Where are we supposed to park? There's no room left." Jimmy's jaw hung open.

"Yeah. We'll wait here a minute." Turning away from the blur of activity, Nick felt a smile tug at one corner of his mouth. When he'd caught his first glimpse behind the scenes of the Cottage in full wedding prep mode, his reaction had been much like Jimmy's. It hadn't taken long before he'd figured out the system beneath all the bustling about. In the distance, the few who didn't mind a bit of a walk hefted bins from the trunks of cars parked on the far side of the lot. Those with heavier or more fragile loads patiently waited their turn for a spot closer to the back entrance. Nick ran his fingers along the crease on one leg of his crisp white pants while, with a tip of his cap, the driver of a truck bearing the Food Fit For A Queen logo pulled away from the house.

"Okay, now it's our turn." He pointed to the open parking spot. "Think you can back us in there?"

"Sure." Despite Jimmy's confident tone, his fingers on the steering wheel tightened until the tips turned white. Cautiously, he eased the van into the place.

Nick raised his window. *So far, so good.* "Once we get the cake and our equipment inside, I want you to come back out and move the van so the next in line can use the space. Got it?" He nodded to the delivery truck from a local winery idling on the driveway behind them.

"Yes, sir." Jimmy shifted the gears into park and set the brake.

Moments later, Nick held his breath while he and Jimmy gently guided the cake onto a rolling cart. The duffel bag he'd packed to the brim with the tools of his trade, along with tubs of icing and marzipan, came next. He tucked it onto a shelf beneath a pleated white skirt. After straightening the edges of a decorative pink bow, he added the box containing a dozen cupcakes to the rest of the gear. He smiled down at the miniature copies of the wedding cake, his surprise gift for the bride and groom.

Always give them more than they ask for, his dad had coached. It was a tradition Nick intended to pass along to the next generation, if he was ever lucky enough to have a son or a daughter of his own.

A quick scan of the cargo area satisfied him that they'd left nothing behind. He signaled Jimmy. Moving in tandem, they slowly rolled the cake up the ramp.

"Okay, come straight back after you park the van," he told his assistant once they'd reached the airy rear foyer.

The boy's shoulders slumped, and no wonder. A big wedding reception like this one required a cast of hundreds. With so much motion and color and noise in play, Jimmy probably wanted to explore a little. But there'd be time enough for that once they'd done their job. Nick threw the young helper an encouraging smile. "You can take a break after we get things set up in the ballroom."

As for himself, he wasn't budging. Someone had to stand guard over their masterpiece from the moment it left the delivery van until every guest had received a slice. In the ten years since he'd inherited the bakery from his dad, the founder of I Do Cakes, Nick had broken that rule only once. It was a mistake he wasn't likely to make again. Though he'd only stepped away for a minute to take an important phone call, sixty seconds had been long enough for a young ring bearer to make a mad dash through the kitchen, helping himself to a handful of icing along the way. Only the grace of God and a half-dozen strategically placed wooden dowels had held that cake upright instead of letting it cascade onto the floor. Nick had counted his blessings and repaired the damage. Still, it had been a close call, one he never wanted to repeat. From then on, either he or his assistant watched over their treasure like a mama hen hovered over a single chick.

"I'll wait here until Alicia calls for us," Nick said to Jimmy's retreating back. He stole a glance down the long hallway filled with people who, in one way or another, would ensure the reception went off without a hitch. When he didn't spot Alicia Thorn's matronly figure moving through the crowd, he propped one shoulder against the wall and settled in to wait.

Somewhere behind him, a wheel squeaked. Nick quickly stepped into the space between his cart and an overloaded one that lumbered the last few inches up the ramp and into the foyer. Behind a monstrous pile of boxy frames and sheeting, he spotted JoJo Moss's sparkling green eyes and chestnut hair. Wearing an impish grin, the girl reached out a finger as if to steal a taste of icing.

"You stay away from my cake, JoJo, or I'll tell Aunt Doris on you." Nick tempered the warning with a smile. His cousin took weddings as seriously as everyone else in town. She wouldn't damage the cake any more than she'd risk upsetting her mother. "Need some help?"

"Nah. I got it. Sally's already inside." Both hands back on the cart's push bar, JoJo moved forward. "Stop by when we get everything set up, and we'll take a picture together."

"If I have a chance. We're cutting this one a little close." He tapped his watch.

"Oh, you always say that." Looking at the cake, JoJo whistled softly. "Nick, I think you've outdone yourself this time." She licked her lips. "Chocolate?" she asked, her voice full of hope.

"You'll have to wait to find out along with everyone else." The flavors chosen by the bride and groom were such closely guarded secrets he didn't even share them with his family.

"Well, whatever it is, save me a piece." JoJo wiggled her fingers and moved along, intent on erecting the photo booth in one corner of the reception hall before the first of the guests arrived.

Through the kitchen's swinging doors, Nick spied Janet Hubbard, proprietor of Food Fit For A Queen. The tall chef gave instructions to a dozen or so young people decked out in tuxedoes. "Remember, you're here to serve our guests. Not huddle in the corners talking to one another. Smile and circulate, that's what I want you to do. Any questions?"

In the pause that followed, she and Nick traded amused glances. He and Janet had worked dozens of weddings together, and she always gave the same little speech. Most of her servers were students from the local college who'd worked a reception or two before. They rarely asked questions. This time was no exception.

After half a beat, Janet continued. "Tonight's appetizers include mushrooms stuffed with sage sausage, skewers of roasted vegetables drizzled with a balsamic demi-glace, bacon-wrapped scallops, and shrimp cocktail shooters. I've laid out a selection on the table behind you. Try them, and don't be afraid to recommend your favorites to our guests."

Nick spotted Jimmy's lanky form striding through the entry and checked his watch. The kid had hardly been gone long enough to move the van, much less go on an unauthorized tour. He gave the young man the thumbs-up sign. With more and more brides planning their weddings in Heart's Landing, he'd been looking for a dependable helper to train as his apprentice. Someone who took the responsibility as seriously as he did. So far, Jimmy gave every sign of filling that slot.

"What now, boss?"

"Relax for a minute, but keep an eye out for Alicia Thorn. You know her?"

Solemnly the boy nodded. "She goes to our church."

"She'll be along any second now to say they're ready for us. Once we get everything set up inside, you can take that break I promised."

While Jimmy thumbed through texts on his cell phone, they waited for the signal to move to their table in the ballroom. Barely ten minutes passed before Nick spotted a familiar figure moving toward them at a brisk pace.

"Sorry for the delay." Alicia's words rang throughout the wide hall. As she closed the gap between them, her voice dropped to a whisper. "The MOB insisted on changing the seating chart at the last minute. It took a moment to work out."

Nick grinned. Mothers of the brides were well-known for last-minute requests. No doubt Alicia had handled this one with the same grace and professionalism she'd applied to every situation during her thirty-year tenure as the Captain's Cottage event coordinator.

Alicia's mouth formed a small O as her gaze shifted over his shoulder. "I swear, I've gained two pounds just looking at that cake, Nick. It's exquisite, and each one you make is lovelier than the one before it. I can't wait to see what you bake for your own special day." She arched one finely drawn eyebrow. "Any idea when that might be, hmmm?"

"Not anytime soon." He paused to let his lips shift into a slight grin. "Unless you're back on the market. I'd whisk you away in a red-hot minute."

Deep and throaty, Alicia's laughter rang out. "I think Mr. Thorn would have something to say about that. But all kidding aside, any prospects?"

"There's not exactly a wealth of possibilities." His cheeks warmed. He didn't really want to discuss his love life within hearing of his young employee.

Not that there was much to say. Sure, he'd had his share of girlfriends. Even one relationship that had gotten pretty serious before he'd discovered she wasn't the person he'd thought she was and broke things off. He'd tried online dating services, had even gone out on a couple of blind dates arranged by friends. None of them had panned out.

Lately, it seemed like most of the women he met had already found their Mr. Right. He glanced through a nearby window at the flowers. The odds of him finding a likely candidate hidden among the azalea blossoms were slim or next to none. So, no. He'd never found the right woman, the one he wanted raise a family and spend the rest of his life with. Now, with his thirtieth birthday a scant year away, he often wondered if he ever would.

"Well, let me know if you meet someone special. I'd love to reserve the grand ballroom for you before I retire." Alicia paused, her lips straightening into full lines as her gaze returned to the cake. "But are you sure *this* bride wanted pink? Doesn't it clash with the rest of her color scheme? Everything else is blue and yellow."

"No way!" Having lost interest in his phone while Nick and Alicia talked, Jimmy voiced a quick protest.

"Hang on there, bud." Nick held one hand like a stop sign when his young charge would have argued the point. Tut-tutting, he turned to the event coordinator. "You shouldn't tease the boy. You'll just get him riled up over nothing. He doesn't know you like I do, and he'll think you're serious." It had taken a few years, but he'd grown to appreciate how Alicia's humor helped everyone stay relaxed during the harried preparations.

"Yeah, Jimmy, relax." Beneath a stubby nose, the thin lines at the corners of Alicia's mouth deepened into a grin. "It's all good." To Nick, she added, "You gonna stand there all day?"

"No, ma'am!"

Though he was perfectly capable of wheeling the cart with its delicate cargo across the hardwood floors and into the main ballroom, Nick handed the honor off to his young protégé. Instead, he walked ahead, setting the pace and warning his assistant of the bumps and rough patches that gave the hundred-twenty-five-year-old house its character.

At the threshold to the grand ballroom, they lingered long enough to let Jimmy drink in the atmosphere of a room where the elite of America's society had once danced to the music of the Original Dixieland String Band, Benny Goodman, and Louis Armstrong. Glossy hardwood floors stretched half the length of a football field from the entry to the fireplace at the opposite end. In recent years, the hand-crafted wainscoting had been carefully restored to a lustrous finish. The dark wood contrasted with the pale-green walls. Ornate, carved crown molding circled a vaulted ceiling that boasted not one, but two crystal chandeliers the size of small cars.

Beneath them, garlands of roses in the bride's chosen shade of pink draped the arched entryways.

Vendors and their assistants circulated through the large space. At one table, a thin figure straightened the corners of a dark bow on the back of one of the two hundred chairs draped in white linen. Another young woman plucked imperfect blossoms from the low centerpieces and dropped them into a miniature dust pan. Here and there, waitstaff adjusted the placement of crystal, china, and silver that glinted atop linens in the bride's signature colors. The dark violet tablecloths topped by china and napkins of the palest pink weren't what Nick would have chosen, but then, planning a wedding didn't factor into his immediate plans. His long-term plans either, for that matter.

He nodded and turned to face Alicia. "This looks amazing. The bride and groom are sure to be pleased." He waited a beat. "But they're probably going to want this cake." He thumbed a finger at the towering layers covered with his legendary buttercream icing and dotted with a thousand painstakingly carved marzipan flowers. "Where do you want us?"

Over the next hour, he and Jimmy worked side-by-side at the display table, nudging a fallen bit of almond paste into place here, repairing a small gap in the frosting there. By the time they finished, every inch of the cake had been examined and glistened under a fresh dusting of edible gold flecks. Finally, Nick stepped away and snapped a photograph of their handiwork. Alicia was right. This was one of his best designs. It deserved a place of honor on the bulletin board in the shop.

Squaring his shoulders, he summoned a bright smile for the guests who began streaming into the room.

Chapter Two

Jennifer Longley pressed the key on the intercom. "Kay, the car will be here any minute. Are you almost ready? You know how the director hates it when you're late."

No answer.

She didn't leave while I was getting coffee, did she?

Jenny lowered her mug to a coaster on one corner of her desk. Two quick steps took her to the doorway of her alcove office in the Beverly Hills mansion. Beyond the sleek leather couches and rich Oriental carpets, a rosewood-and-gilt table stood by the front door. Perched atop the glossy surface, Kay's shoulder bag was exactly where Jenny had placed it fifteen minutes ago, filled to overflowing with every conceivable item one of Hollywood's hottest stars might need over the course of a day's shooting. The script, complete with highlights so Kay could study her lines during the hour-long commute to the set. A pair of designer sunglasses immediately available in the side pocket. A dozen copies of the star's latest head shot, exactly six felt-tip pens, and her signature pink, sequined flip-flops to slip on the instant a pair of pricey shoes with four-inch heels pinched her precious toes. Check, check, and double-check.

Confident that everything was exactly as it should be, Jenny nodded. All she needed now was the star herself. But, as far as she knew, Kay had yet to emerge from the master suite. When she did, she'd most likely breeze through the house, slip the strap of the trendy bag over one arm, shove the sunglasses over sparkling blue eyes, and step from the air-conditioned luxury of her house into the town car that idled not five feet from her front door.

But first, Jenny had to discover the reason for today's delay and fix it.

"Karolyn, are you feeling all right?" Patting her pockets for the supply of over-the-counter medications she kept on hand, she trotted down the hall. Though head and stomach aches didn't plague the star often, Jenny prided herself on being prepared for every crisis, no matter how big or small.

When there was no answer to her knock at Kay's bedroom, she pushed the door to the master suite ajar. The rumpled bedcovers on the king-sized bed had been pushed aside, and Jenny breathed a relieved sigh. America's leading lady had rolled out of bed on time, at least. Jenny's bare feet sank into the deep pile carpet as she padded toward the dressing area, where she sometimes found Kay standing in the immense closet, fretting over which of the hundreds of options she should wear. But the closet, like the spacious bathroom beyond it, stood empty.

Jenny's brows knit. Where to next? Heading back the way she'd come, she eyed doors that opened onto the theater and a library, the hallway that led to the servants' quarters. The house was too large for a room-to-room search. She tugged her cell phone from a back pocket and punched a few keys.

Where R U?

Kitchen.

Jenny's lips thinned at the immediate reply. What on earth for? She stifled a laugh at the thought of the thin brunette scarfing down eggs and bacon, or the utterly improbable pancake. The newly hatched chicks on her aunt's farm enjoyed a heartier breakfast. In the two years she'd worked as Kay's assistant, she'd never known the mega-star to down more than a cup of coffee before leaving for the studio.

Cutting through the immense living room with its two-story glass walls overlooking an Olympic-sized pool, lush gardens, and guest house beyond, Jenny skidded into the kitchen on bare feet. She hastily skimmed over built-in appliances cleverly hidden behind white panels, the acre of pale gray granite that stretched into the distance, the breakfast nook that offered comfortable seating for up to a dozen. Her focus landed on the woman who'd pulled a bar stool up to the center island. Cool and calm, Kay sat there, munching on a slice of toast as if fixing her own food was an everyday occurrence.

The butter dish and a pot of imported jelly she must have pulled from the massive Sub-Zero refrigerator lay among the crumbs scattered across the countertop, along with several loose papers. Steam rose from a pot of water on the stove. Damp leaves spilled from a discarded tea strainer near a heavy, white mug. The comfort food stirred memories of the tea and toast Jenny's aunt used to fix for her when she was little and had an upset stomach. An awful flu bug had been making the rounds, but Kay, like most of the celebrities she knew, carried an industrial-sized bottle of hand sanitizer with her wherever she went, and she wasn't afraid to use it. Was she feeling the effects of a late night out with her leading man and current beau?

"Are you okay? You aren't sick or anything, are you?"

Jenny searched flawless skin for a touch of green or any symptom of a queasy stomach.

"Nope. I'm right as rain. Better, even." Her hair swept back in a sleek ponytail, America's reigning movie queen calmly spooned another dollop of jam onto her toast. She held out an uneaten slice. "Want to share?"

Jenny fought past an urge to stare. Because the cameras added at least ten pounds to even the tiniest figures, studios insisted on having weights and measurement clauses written into multi-million-dollar contracts. Which explained why Kay counted every calorie and carb that passed through her lips and why she insisted on only eating farm-to-table produce supplemented by certified organic meats and cheeses. She certainly didn't eat starches and never, ever, something concocted out of white flour, drenched in butter and slathered in jelly.

"Who are you, and what have you done with Karolyn Karter?" Jenny gasped.

The dark-haired beauty looked over her shoulder. "I think she's left the building. The only person I've seen this morning besides you is the future Mrs. Chad Grant." Kay tapped her ring finger against her mug of tea.

"You and Chad are getting married?" Jenny's voice scaled the register at the exciting news. In the same breath, she told herself she shouldn't be surprised. Thanks to the reporters who tracked Kay's every move, everyone in Hollywood knew it had been love at first sight when the co-stars had met for the first time on the set of *Two Hearts on the Run*, their current blockbuster-in-the-making.

Dashing forward, Jenny snatched the other woman's hand and held it up. A brilliant cut diamond sparkled in the ray of sunlight that streamed through a plate-glass window overlooking the pool. She peered closer at the elegantly worked metal around a rock the size of a hen's egg. "Are there two bands?"

Nodding, Kay beamed. "Chad had the jeweler line the platinum setting with rose gold. Isn't that the sweetest thing?" She sighed. "He knows me so well."

In the scant six weeks since shooting had started, how had Karolyn and Chad gotten to know each other well enough to fall in love, much less get engaged?

Jenny ran her fingers through her hair and gave a strand a tug. This wasn't the time or the place to raise questions. Or to point out that marriage and family weren't in the plan Kay had laid out for her life. The one that called for adding two more Oscars to the collection in the den before the star allowed herself a serious relationship or to start thinking about white picket fences and babies. Adjusting the plan could wait. This was the time for congratulations.

"I'm so happy for you!" Leaning down, she gave Kay a fierce hug, all the while taking care not to brush her cheek against the plain white T-shirt that had probably cost more than her own salary for a week. She stole a quick glance at the kitchen clock over the star's shoulder. "I want to hear every detail. Where did he pop the question? Was it romantic? Were you surprised? But first, we need to get you to the studio. You can't be late, not even on the first day of your engagement."

"Relax." Kay took a dainty bite of her toast. "I have the morning off. Guzman texted to say they were working on a problem with the lighting and wouldn't be ready to shoot the next scene till after lunch."

Jenny drew in a relieved breath. She and Kay might both be brunettes and, without heels, they each stood precisely five feet, two inches tall, but the similarities ended there. Her own dark brown eyes were far less commanding, her shape a touch rounder, her features more girl-next-door than Kay's. Sitting in the kitchen with slicked-back hair and without a speck of makeup, her boss was easily one of the most beautiful women in the world. Heads turned whenever she walked into a room. But without her standard two hours of hair and makeup at the studio, Kay would look like a pale and sickly image of herself beneath the hot camera lights. With the schedule pushed back, they had at least an hour before Kay needed to head across town.

Sliding onto an empty seat, Jenny cupped her chin in her hands. "Tell me everything," she gushed.

"It was magical. We drove down to Santa Monica. Chad had reserved my favorite booth in the back of La Bon Chance. Louis, the maître d', is so good to us there. He always makes sure we're left alone."

Jenny nodded and quietly jotted a mental note to add to the maître d's Christmas bonus. Ever since Karolyn's latest film had broken box office records across the country, guaranteeing the star's privacy had become harder than ever. Not even a pricey, five-star restaurant was safe from camera-toting reporters.

"We had drinks and appetizers." Obviously reliving the moment, Karolyn's eyes filled with a soft glow. "I don't have to tell you what I ordered."

"Mmm-hmmm." The soft, poached egg stuffed with caviar, topped by a lemony sauce, had always been Kay's favorite.

"I hadn't planned on dessert—have to watch the figure, you know." Kay took a second bite of toast before abandoning the rest to her plate. "But Chad insisted on ordering one of those chocolate things where they pour caramel over the top, and the outer shell melts to reveal a hidden yummy treat. Well." She took a dramatic breath. "When they did, there was the ring, nestled in the most beautiful raspberry soufflé. Chad got down on one knee and asked if I'd make him the happiest man alive. It was incredibly sweet. Of course, I said yes! Louis opened a bottle of Cristal, and the entire staff applauded." Her eyes sparkled as she clasped her hands over her heart. "I'll treasure that moment forever."

"That sounds perfectly dreamy," Jenny said with an exaggerated sigh. "You two make such a beautiful couple." But the statement led to other, less pleasant thoughts. The merger of two of Hollywood's biggest stars would prompt reporters from every tabloid in the nation to camp out on the grounds beyond the front gates. Some of the more obnoxious ones might even try to scale the ten-foot fences. As Kay's personal assistant, she'd need to beef up security first thing. Was she already behind the curve? She drummed her fingers on the counter. "Who else knows about the engagement?"

"No one yet." Karolyn pushed her plate out of reach. "I'll call Shelly and Mara this morning, of course. They'll probably arrange a press conference. I'm sure we'll hit the talk shows this week. You know how it is."

She did, but letting Karolyn's publicist and agent in on the news hadn't exactly been what Jenny had in mind. "I meant, have you called Aunt Maggie?" The phone call to the star's mother needed to be placed before some reporter shoved a mic in the woman's face and splashed her reaction all over the internet.

"Oh!" Karolyn snapped her fingers. "Oh, you're right. Mom will be so excited!" A faraway look crept into her eyes. "But first, you and I need to talk."

Jenny swallowed. What was it about that last word that

sent a chill down her spine? "You aren't firing me, are you?" she asked, hating the tentative note in her voice. But the question wasn't that far off base. If the two lovebirds were going to combine households, it stood to reason they'd make some adjustments.

"Goodness no! Quite the opposite, in fact. I need you to plan my wedding."

"Me?" Jenny reeled back in surprise.

"Of course you, silly. Who else would I trust? After all, you are my cousin, aren't you?"

Well, there was that.

Actually, having grown up in the same house, she and Kay were closer than most cousins. They were practically sisters. They had been since that awful day Jenny's parents had died in a train wreck on their way into the big city. At seven, she hadn't had a clue what was to become of her. Where would she live? Who would take care of her? Would she go to an orphanage like the one in Little Orphan Annie? Her whole world had become a series of questions, each more frightful than the last. But then, Aunt Maggie had draped one arm around her shoulders and told her not to worry, everything would be okay.

She'd never forget her aunt's kindness that day, or everything Aunt Maggie had done for her since then. Two years ago, she'd had a chance to repay at least a little of what she'd been given when Aunt Maggie had called with the news that Kay had landed her first big role. When she'd followed that up with a request for help, Jenny hadn't hesitated. She'd boarded a plane the next day and flown to California. In a matter of weeks, she'd straightened out her cousin's chaotic schedule, had ensured her timely and prepared arrival on set, and had put an end to far too many brushes with the paparazzi.

Thanks to Kay's tendency to wait until the last minute to plan anything, Jenny had learned how to throw together a soirée for twenty with ten minutes' notice, stage an elegant birthday bash with the snap of a finger, and she no longer batted an eyelash when her cousin needed a last-minute reservation at one of L.A.'s trendiest restaurants.

But a wedding, even a small one, was something else. And planning the ceremony and reception for two of the biggest names in the entertainment industry was something else entirely.

"Oh, I don't know…" Jenny hesitated. She wasn't quite sure where to even begin. "Don't you think you need a wedding planner?"

"Ordinarily, yes, but Chad and I talked it over, and we agreed. Neither one of us wants to turn our wedding into a media circus. We just want to slip away someplace where the reporters and camera crews won't find us. We'll say our vows in front of our family and a few close friends. Fifty guests, maximum. That sounds doable, doesn't it?"

"Fifty? You're sure?" How was that supposed to work? On any given day, it took a small army just to get Karolyn from the house, through makeup, hair and wardrobe, and onto the set.

Her cousin leaned forward and took Jenny's hands in her own. "We're absolutely certain. Something small and intimate. Honestly, it won't be as hard as it sounds. I've already done most of the work." With a dramatic flourish, Kay snagged a few pages off the kitchen counter and held them out.

"What are these?" An uneasy feeling shifted through Jenny's midsection.

"It's everything I want for my wedding, from my gown

right down to the cake. With these notes, you shouldn't have any trouble making the arrangements. Right?"

The papers rattled in Jenny's hands. She stared down at them, trying to decipher her cousin's scribbles. "So your colors are pink and gray? Any particular shades?" There had to be a hundred different variations.

"Just pink." Kay lifted one shoulder in a casual shrug. "Like in my ring." She tapped the band. "And the gray shouldn't be too dark."

"Good to know." Taking a pen from a drawer under the phone, Jenny carefully added "rose gold" in the margin. "What's this about your gown?" She frowned at an illegible mark.

"Oh, that." Kay waved a hand through the air. "You don't have to worry about the dress. I'll fly Mom out from Pennsylvania. We'll go shopping together. Can you make her flight reservations today? And get us on the schedule at Madame Eleanor's for the week after next?"

Getting Kay an appointment at L.A.'s most exclusive bridal salon, even on such short notice wouldn't be a problem. But why the rush? "You two have set a date, then."

"That's what I'm trying to tell you." A giddy excitement rippled across Kay's face. "We're getting married in six weeks, as soon as we wrap up shooting on *Two Hearts on the Run*."

"Oh! That's awfully soon." Allowing herself one small sip of air, Jenny pressed crossed fingers into her lap. "Most brides allow themselves more time to plan, don't they?"

"We have to get married now or wait at least eighteen months. You know how tight my schedule is."

Jenny nodded. Kay lived a luxurious life, but she worked hard. By the time her current film appeared in theaters, her next one would be in post-production, and she'd be shooting a third.

"The only time we both have off is right after this movie wraps up. But..." When her cousin's voice trailed off, Jenny felt her stomach tighten. "I need your help. You're the only one I can trust to get everything right. Can I count on you?"

The pleading look in Karolyn's gaze melted Jenny's resistance. "Of course you can," she answered. After all her aunt and cousin had done for her, how could she say anything else?

"Oh, that's such a relief," Kay gushed.

Glad to see her cousin's posture soften, Jenny nodded. Maybe planning a simple wedding wouldn't be as difficult as she'd thought. After all, she'd put together larger parties with even less notice. Plus, living in the same house, she'd be able to run any decisions past Kay each morning on their way to the set. "I suppose the first step is to pick a venue," she said, getting down to business. With only six weeks to pull this off, they'd have to take advantage of every second. "Did you have a special place in mind?" Jenny turned one of the pages over, prepared to take notes.

"I know just the place!" Kay's mouth twisted into a sly smile. "Actually, it was your idea."

"Oh?" Confused, Jenny pursed her lips. She and Kay hadn't discussed weddings in years, probably not since they'd played dress-up in grade school. Back then, her cousin had insisted she'd only get married on the white sandy beach of some faraway tropical isle. Jenny, though, had dreamed of walking down the aisle in the one town that consistently received a five-star ranking from *Weddings Today*. She glanced at Karolyn. Surely, her cousin hadn't chosen *that* spot for her own wedding.

Apparently, she had.

"We've decided on a Heart's Landing wedding. It's the perfect place because everyone will expect us to choose an exotic destination. Even better, I called this morning and spoke with the event coordinator. She's had a cancellation. A bride and groom who'd rented out the entire Captain's Cottage for their wedding had a change of plans. I was able to snag the reservation for the last week in June. Isn't that fabulous?"

The tiniest spark of frustration burned in Jenny's stomach. She quickly squelched it. What did it matter if Karolyn had stolen her choice of wedding venues? It wasn't like she planned to get married next week, or next year. She didn't have anyone special in her life, a situation she didn't see changing anytime in the foreseeable future.

Not that she minded. Even though her hours were long and her schedule as capricious and hectic as a hummingbird in flight, she enjoyed her job as an assistant to one of Hollywood's leading ladies. But it was definitely not the kind of job that allowed for much of a personal life. She could hardly remember when she'd last been out on a date, much less had gotten involved in something serious. So no, she refused to be mad at her cousin for jumping at the chance to get married at one of the top ten wedding destinations in America.

Besides, she knew just about everything there was to know about Heart's Landing. Thumbing through the latest issue of *Weddings Today* would fill in any gaps. Given that Karolyn and Chad had decided to keep things small and intimate, she really didn't know what she was worried about. Why, she'd probably have this wedding wrapped up within a week, two at the outside. She rubbed her fingers together. "When do we get started?"

"Well, that's the thing." Karolyn heaved a sigh worthy

of the stage. "*We* don't. Between my shooting schedule and the rest of my commitments"—maintaining her position in the top echelon of Hollywood's leading actress required daily workouts and weekly pampering at an exclusive spa, not to mention the nights Karolyn spent hobnobbing among the industry's movers and shakers—"I won't have time to even think about it. I need you to handle everything. But not here. You know how good the paparazzi are at sniffing out details. To throw them off track, you'll need to go there and pretend you're arranging your own wedding."

"But…" Jenny sputtered. Fly to Rhode Island and plan a wedding that wasn't hers? She could think of a million ways that could go wrong in a wedding that was growing more complicated by the minute.

Karolyn's warm hands wrapped around her cold ones. Leaning forward, her cousin pinned her with a laser-eyed stare. "Can you do that, Jenny? Can you help Chad and me start our lives together with the wedding of our dreams?"

Nodding, she took a deep breath and reminded herself that Karolyn wanted a minimum of pomp and fuss. Just her and the groom and fifty or so of their closest friends and family. An event that size shouldn't be difficult to pull off without anyone finding out the real identity of the bride, should it?

There wasn't even that much left for her to do. The venue had already been nailed down. According to her notes, Karolyn had chosen the flavor of the cake, the flowers for her bouquet, and her wedding colors. Jenny only had to get everything to the church—or, in this case, onto the veranda of the Captain's Cottage—in time for a simple wedding.

Chapter Three

After six hours crammed into an economy seat on the flight from LAX to Providence, followed by the time it had taken to wrestle her luggage from the baggage carousel and into the trunk of a very sensible rental car, Jenny breathed a happy sigh of relief. Her hands maintaining a light grip on the steering wheel, she darted a quick glance at a pair of adorable lambs frolicking in a hillside's emerald-green grass. The sheep and cows in their pastures reminded her of her aunt's Pennsylvania farm and filled her with the oddest sense of coming home. Especially when traffic turned out to be lighter than she'd expected on the scenic back road that hugged Rhode Island's coastline.

She'd grown so used to L.A.'s clogged highways and surface streets that she'd imagined there'd be more of the same on the East Coast. Once she left Providence, though, the oncoming cars had slowed to a trickle. She trailed the truck ahead by at least a half-mile and, unlike on the West Coast, no one here rode her bumper. She surfed one hand through the open window. A cool breeze filled the car with moist air. The humidity would probably make her hair curl, but after spending much of the past two years in Southern California's arid climate, a little dampness felt good on her skin. She eased her foot off the accelerator as she took in the view.

The stacked stone fences that lined the roadway were unlike any she'd ever seen. Who had built them, and how long had they been here? Had early settlers constructed the knee-high barriers using the rocks they'd unearthed as they'd sawed down trees and pulled up stumps? Like a calming blanket, a rich sense of the area's history settled over her shoulders. She pictured herself, clad in Colonial garb, digging each stone from the ground and piling them along the edges of the land where she and her husband planned to raise crops and a family. At a spot where several of the fences came together, she rubbed her eyes. She could practically see militiamen taking cover among the rocks, their rifles aimed at approaching redcoats. That silly tune about feathers and macaroni whispered through her head. Driving past another set of low fences, she hummed the melody.

When the road climbed again, the ground dropped precipitously on the other side of a metal guardrail. Below it, the ocean pounded against jagged gray rocks. A shiver passed over her when she imagined how many ships had been lost on the unforgiving, rocky coast. She was glad when the land angled down toward a postcard-perfect inlet, where white sailboats bobbed at anchor. Here, flocks of sea gulls soared on air currents above the dark green ocean. Occasionally one spied a fish and dove, straight as an arrow, into the water. Seconds later, it emerged, dripping and carrying dinner.

Trees crowded the highway up ahead. Her lips parted when the land on the other side of a sharp curve opened up just like someone had unrolled the red carpet at a Hollywood awards ceremony. But instead of ending at a stage, the road headed through the center of a quaint New England village.

She spotted a sign welcoming visitors to Heart's Landing and smiled. Her heart happily skipped a beat as if it, too, knew she'd arrived at the place she'd dreamed of visiting ever since she'd leafed through her first bridal magazine.

Just beyond the city limits sign, she giggled when the name of the road changed from Boston Neck to Bridal Carriage Way. The speed limit dropped to a sedate twenty-five, which was fine with her. She slowed, enjoying her first long look at the town thousands of brides had chosen for their destination weddings. She sensed a theme in the cross-streets that bore names like Boutonniere Drive and Procession Avenue. As she approached the center of town, she half expected the gingerbread trim that dripped from Cape Cod-style houses to disappear. But if anything, it increased until the shops and stores practically bowed beneath layers of gilt and heart-shaped frills. Romance hung so heavy in the air, it might as well be fog. She placed a hand over her chest.

Her pulse fluttered as she passed shops she recognized from bridal magazines and websites. An array of bouquets, each more luscious than the next, filled the windows of Forget Me Knot Flowers. At Bow Tie Pasta, a dark green awning stretched from the main entrance to the street, offering its guests protection from nasty weather.

A surprising number of couples walked hand-in-hand beneath the shade trees that lined the village streets. Seeing them stirred an empty feeling in her chest, but she did her best to squelch it. She was still young. She had plenty of time to find her own someone special. Once she wrapped up every detail for Kay's wedding and returned home to California, she might put more effort into finding Mr. Right. As long as she was in Heart's Landing, though, she needed to focus on the job at hand and nothing else.

With time to kill before she could check in at the bed and breakfast, she turned onto Honeymoon Avenue. She rolled past buildings with intriguing names like Step In Style Shoes, Ice, and a dance studio aptly named The Right Moves. Another turn took her to Officiate Circle and more restaurants, a large fitness center and a line of storefronts offering wedding services. The street ended in a cul-de-sac. There, a statue of a seafarer stood in the center of a small park. The rakish tilt to his hat piqued her interest. She sensed there were stories in the deep lines carved into his weathered face.

Outside her two-story bed and breakfast on Union Street a few minutes later, she sighed contentedly as she studied cedar siding that had aged to a burnished silver. She hadn't known quite what to expect when she'd made her reservations. Of course, with Kay picking up the tab, she could have stayed at a luxury hotel, but she knew herself well enough to know she'd feel guilty about spending so much money on a place to sleep at night. The inn had a nice website, and a healthy discount had practically made the decision of where to stay for her. Still, she'd fretted just a little. In the past, lower prices had sometimes meant compromises in quality. Thankfully, that didn't seem to be the case this time. From the white picket fence surrounding the house to the red and white blossoms that spilled from boxes under each window, the bed and breakfast looked every bit as inviting as it had on the internet. If it was even half as pretty inside, she'd have no problem making it her home-away-from-home for the next two weeks while she tackled the details of Karolyn's wedding.

Suddenly as nervous as a hummingbird, she pressed a hand over her fluttering stomach. Everything she'd seen since she'd driven past the welcome sign should have assured her she'd have no problem pulling off the wedding of the decade, even on such short notice. The town boasted a wealth of shops and services, each practically guaranteed to give the bride and groom their special day.

But that was the problem, wasn't it? The shopkeepers in Heart's Landing worked with brides day in and day out. She couldn't shake the feeling that the moment they met her, they'd know she was hiding something. She wasn't an actress. She'd never even tried out for a role in her high school plays. Instead, she'd concentrated on her studies and had left the artistic endeavors to the one who'd been blessed with the beauty and talent in the family, her cousin. But now, Kay's happiness depended on her ability to act the part of a blushing bride well enough to convince everyone in one of America's top wedding destinations that she was getting married.

She groaned. How would she ever face her cousin or her aunt if she failed? Or if some eager reporter caught wind of what she was up to and spread the word? She couldn't stand the thought of having the paparazzi descend on Kay's wedding. Which was exactly what would happen if anyone saw through her ruse. After all Aunt Maggie had done for her, she couldn't—she wouldn't—let the press ruin her cousin's special day.

Willing her rebellious stomach to settle down, she reached into her bag for the thin notebook containing the biographical sketch Karolyn had created for her. On the long plane ride here, she'd committed every detail to memory, but sitting in her car, she whispered her fake fiancé's name, occupation, and age until they rolled off her tongue like butter. When she was as ready as she felt she'd ever be, she tucked the notebook out of sight.

She crossed her fingers. Everything hinged on the next few minutes and, with a steadying breath, she stepped from her car and mounted the three wooden steps to the entrance to the bed and breakfast.

The front door opened onto a sitting area that was far more spacious than she'd expected from the photographs online. Gleaming hardwood floors and white wainscoting gave the entry a welcome feel. Several overstuffed chairs and ottomans dotted the room, making it a great spot to linger at the beginning or the end of the day. A guest book lay atop the antique secretary nestled into a space under the stairs, but no one sat at the desk or in the formal living room beyond where couches offered ample seating for a dozen or so.

"Hello?" she called softly. A nervous rush shimmied through her, and she gave the fake engagement ring on her finger a twist while she squared her shoulders.

"I'll be right there." Distant footsteps grew louder until at last, wiping her hands on a dish towel, a plump woman with tight curls emerged from the bowels of the house. "Welcome to Union Street Bed and Breakfast. I'm Marybeth Williams," she announced, a cheery welcome shining in her dark eyes. "You must be Jenny. We've been expecting you. Did you have any trouble finding us?"

"None at all. I hope I'm not too early." The check-in time posted on the website had said four pm. It was nearly that now.

"Actually, you couldn't have planned it better. Sarah just finished getting your suite ready." Marybeth tapped the old-fashioned guest register. "If you'll sign in, I'll have my husband Matt bring up your bags." The hostess waited a beat before asking, "Will anyone be joining you while you're here?"

"No." Jenny gave her head a firm shake. "My fiancé…" *Oh, phooey.* Her voice trailed off as she blanked on the name of a man who didn't exist. She struggled to hold her smile in place despite the bitter taste that filled her mouth every time she thought of the secrets she'd have to protect for the next two weeks. But she didn't have any choice, did she? Helping to plan Karolyn's wedding seemed like the least she could do to repay her cousin's family. If that meant going incognito as a bride-to-be, so be it.

Besides, she reminded herself, she wasn't going to cheat or steal from anyone. She really was planning a wedding—it just wasn't her own.

"Tom," she said at last, hoping Marybeth hadn't noticed her hesitation. "He, um, he can't get away right now. He's an investment broker on the West Coast, and he's putting in a lot of extra hours so he can take time off for our honeymoon." Though she wanted to add more, she stopped herself.

The more straightforward the story, the easier it'll be to remember, her cousin had advised.

"Someplace wonderfully romantic, I trust." Marybeth's head canted to one side.

Jenny bit her lower lip. "I'm sure it will be," she said with far more assurance than she felt. Kay had left those plans up to Chad. Taking a page out of their book, she blurted, "My fiancé is, um, handling that end of things."

"Oh, isn't that nice." An odd expression passed over Marybeth's face but, like a fleeting shadow, it quickly disappeared. "Are you parked out front, dear?" When Jenny nodded, the hostess motioned toward the rear of the building. "You're welcome to leave your vehicle on the street, but there's also a private lot around back, on the other side of the garden."

"Sounds good," Jenny agreed, relieved now that the conversation had moved away from her fake fiancé. "I'll park there when I get back from dinner." She'd narrowed the choices for the rehearsal dinner down to three restaurants and had reservations at the first of them this evening.

Together, the two women made quick work of the business end of things before Marybeth led the way up a flight of stairs to a two-room suite at the back of the house. "It'll be quiet here. The rooms facing the street tend to get a little more noise," she explained, opening the door on a generously-appointed bedroom. "Will this do while you're staying with us?"

A warm feeling started in the pit of her stomach and spread upward as Jenny took her first peek at the place she'd call home for the next two weeks. "It's lovely," she said, trailing her fingers over the footboard of a canopy bed covered in plush linens. From eyelet curtains at the windows to a thick Oriental carpet at her feet, the room gave off a cheery, peaceful air. She crossed to the connecting room. Here, the windows overlooked a garden where flowers bloomed in riotous colors. A conveniently placed desk and chair made the perfect spot for organizing her notes each day. A small sofa and footstool made an inviting spot to curl up with a good book whenever she had a free moment. There was even a fireplace, though she doubted she'd use it, considering the spring-like temperatures.

"So, when's the wedding?" Marybeth asked from her spot near the doorway.

Jenny whirled. She'd been so entranced by the room that she'd practically forgotten her hostess. "In four weeks and two days." Her plans to get an earlier start had dissolved when Kay had needed some serious hand-holding through the talk-show appearances. Throwing her cousin's engagement party had delayed her even more. She'd left for the airport right after the lavish affair.

"Why, that's right around the corner. I guess you'll be busy finalizing things while you're here." Marybeth clucked sympathetically.

"Actually, I'm just starting. Tom and I had planned to wait until next spring," she said, sticking to the story she and Karolyn had agreed on. "When I heard of a cancellation at the Captain's Cottage, we rearranged our schedule. I've always wanted a Heart's Landing wedding." That was the absolute truth. "But it'll be a simple wedding, so I'm hoping to handle everything over the next two weeks." After that, she'd fly back to California and oversee the last-minute details from there. Smiling, wrapped a loose strand of hair around her finger and gave it a good-luck tug.

"If you haven't chosen your baker yet, be sure to stop by I Do Cakes on Bridal Carriage. Nick is a good friend of ours, and he makes the best cakes." Marybeth paused. "A month, though. That's not much lead time." She gave her chin a thoughtful tap. "I probably shouldn't have suggested that particular bakery. Nick usually books up months ahead."

Jenny allowed herself a small smile. One mention of her famous cousin's name would move her to the head of any line.

Except, she couldn't do that, could she?

Her smile faltered. She'd grown so used to dropping Karolyn's name whenever she needed a last-minute reservation that she hadn't stopped to consider how she was supposed to get things done without anyone discovering her connection to the movie star.

Suddenly, planning her cousin's wedding didn't sound as easy as she'd expected it to be. Though she'd lined up a series of appointments before she'd left L.A., she had no guarantees that the vendors could fit Kay's wedding into their schedules.

She checked her watch. There was no time to waste. If she left right now, she could stop by the bakery for an impromptu taste testing before her dinner reservation.

Nick touched one finger to the bottom of one of the four dozen cupcakes he'd pulled from the oven an hour earlier. It had cooled enough to decorate, which meant the others had, too. He surveyed the collection of ingredients he'd gathered on the counter. Tomorrow's special would feature a salted caramel base covered in his famed buttercream frosting. Topped with a light sprinkling of crushed toffee and a drizzle of chocolate ganache, the customer favorite would sell out by mid-morning.

Unease rippled through him. He pressed a fist to his chest. A slight frown bent his brows inward. He gave the assembled equipment a second glance. Everything he needed sat ready and waiting, so why was he on edge?

Jimmy.

The urge to treat himself to a serious facepalm rippled through him when he hit on the reason for the extra tension in his shoulders. Though he'd been working with the young baker for some time now, today Jimmy was making his first solo delivery. Not that there was anything to worry about. He and his apprentice had delivered cakes throughout the area these past few weeks. On every occasion, the young man had proven up to the task. Jimmy followed orders without complaint and, the few times he'd slipped up, he'd learned from his mistakes. Take the delivery they'd made to the Cottage, for example. After brushing the curb that one time, Jimmy had steered clear of anything that might jar the precious cargo in the back of the van.

Nick gave the strings of his apron an extra tug. Jimmy's training had been going well. So well, in fact, he'd started watching for a chance to let the boy handle things on his own. Not a wedding, of course. Though he'd be the first to sing the young man's praises, an apprentice baker with Jimmy's level of experience wasn't ready for that kind of pressure. But weddings weren't the only events the bakery handled.

When Mrs. Halperteen had called to ask if Nick could put her son's birthday party onto the schedule, he'd found the perfect opportunity and had promptly handed the job to Jimmy. Though he'd kept a close eye on each step of the process, his young protégé had handled every aspect—from sitting down with the mother of the birthday boy to designing and executing a swim party-themed cake. He'd even followed the bakery's tradition of going one step beyond by decorating a dozen matching cupcakes to use as party favors.

Nick smiled. He really had nothing to worry about. Jimmy was a talented young baker with a good head on his shoulders. He'd been right to let the boy handle this customer on his own.

Content that he'd identified the source of his concern and dealt with it, Nick returned to work. He'd carefully spooned a helping of icing into the decorating bag and had just dipped up a second one when his cell phone buzzed. Tempted to let the caller go to voicemail, he glanced at the screen. His stomach clenched.

"Oh, boy," he whispered. So much for nothing to worry about. He set his decorating equipment aside. Mustering a tone far calmer than he felt, he managed, "Hey, what's up?"

"Um, I'm so sorry, Mr. Bell. I don't know what happened. I just—"

"Take a breath, Jimmy," Nick said while images of car

crashes and ambulances filled his thoughts. “Did anyone get hurt? Are you all right?”

“What? No, it’s nothing like that.”

Nick followed his own advice and took a breath, a relieved one at that. “Well, that’s good. I’m glad to hear it. So, what’s up?” There had to be a reason for the call and, judging from the note of panic in Jimmy’s voice, he’d bet it was a serious one.

“I’m at the Halperteen residence. I delivered the cake, just like you showed me. Mrs. Halperteen, she wants me to stick around and serve it in a little bit, and I don’t mind. The kids are so cute. You should see the Halperteen boy. He’s wearing these water wings that are bigger than he is.”

“Cut to the chase, Jimmy,” Nick interrupted while his heart race slowed to near-normal.

“Oh, right. I, um, I forgot the cupcakes. I thought they were in the van, honest I did. But I must have left them behind. Can you see them anywhere?”

Searching for anything out of place, Nick scoured the roomy kitchen. At Jimmy’s end of the counter, a brown box bearing the bakery’s logo stood out like a sore thumb. For the second time in less than sixty minutes, Nick fought down an urge to slap his head. The cardboard contrasted so sharply with the white marble countertop, he should have spotted it the moment he’d stepped through the kitchen’s swinging doors. How had he missed it? No matter. He’d found it. That was the important thing. “They’re here.” He squelched a tiny urge to scold the boy and shouldered the blame. “This is just as much my fault as it is yours. I should have double-checked that you had everything you needed. Want me to run them out to you?” The Halperteens lived a short drive from downtown. If he left right now, he could make it there and back well before the party broke up.

"Would you?" A relief so palpable Nick could almost touch it flooded through his ear piece. "I'd come and get it myself, but I've got to cut the cake in a few minutes."

"Nah, it's okay, kiddo." He'd made his own share of mistakes when he'd started out. Back then, his dad had stood by him, backing him up with an unruffled attitude that had helped him stay calm and cool, even when those around him had been in a panic. Determined to do the same for Jimmy, he finished with an effortless, "See you in a few."

Surveying his workstation, he decided everything could stay right where it was until he got back. Everything except for the frosting. The blend of cream cheese, butter, and powdered sugar tended to separate when warmed. So, despite a thermostat set to a cool seventy-two, the bowl went into the fridge, along with the half-filled decorating bag. Hanging his apron on a nearby hook, Nick grabbed the box of cupcakes and headed for the front of the store.

"Hey, Denise," he called, passing through the swinging doors into the customer area. "I need to make a quick delivery. You're okay on your own for a few minutes, aren't you?" He shot an appraising glance at the young woman who'd been working the lunch shift and the slower afternoons for the last six months.

"Sure thing, Mr. Bell." Denise marked her place with her finger and hastily closed a book.

"Whatcha reading?" Nick gave the tidy counter area a cursory look. A half-dozen cupcakes dotted the shelves in the display case that had overflowed with an assortment of baked goods this morning. At one of the corner tables, a couple of regulars chatted over coffee in the otherwise quiet shop.

The college sophomore pulled a long face. "Economics. I need to get a B in the class to keep my scholarship."

"Better get back to your studies, then." Glad he could do his part in helping one of Heart's Landing's own get her degree, he nodded. "I won't be long. I'll call if I'm delayed for any reason."

"Yes, sir."

Intent on making the delivery as quickly as possible so he could finish decorating his cupcakes before it got too late, Nick stepped smartly toward the front door. A passing horse-drawn carriage drowned out the merry jingling of the bell that signaled the arrival and departure of the shop's customers. Out of the corner of one eye, Nick spotted the slim figure of a woman who'd stopped mid-stride, her lips slightly parted, stars in a pair of dark eyes she'd trained on the carriage that turned the corner at a sedate pace.

Another bride. The town was chock full of them.

He shrugged and hoped she didn't have her heart set on a wedding cake from his bakery. So many orders already crowded his calendar that, even with Jimmy's help, he'd have to put in extra hours to fill them all. He checked the woman on the sidewalk again. When she remained rooted to the spot, he picked up his own pace, eager complete his errand and get back on schedule.

Chapter Four

Fifteen minutes after she signed the registry at the Union Street Bed and Breakfast, Jenny parked her rental in a public lot near the center of town. She headed in the direction of I Do Cakes, which, according to the map, was a five-minute walk. The light at the first cross-street turned red just before she reached it. Stepping to the curb, she cocked her head as a peppy rendition of "Ode to Joy" played from speakers mounted on the sign post. She tapped her toes in time to the music while she waited for the Don't Walk sign to change. When the light blinked at last, the music switched to "The Wedding March." Chuckling to herself, she hurried across the street.

A white sign with bright pink lettering swung beneath a chocolate-colored awning in the middle of the next block. Closing in on I Do Cakes, she picked up her pace. She was only a few feet from the door when the sound of jangling harnesses and the clop-clop of horses' hooves filled the air. The sound drew her as effectively as the soft chiming of her cell phone. She spun toward the noise in time to see a high-stepping team turn the corner. She couldn't help but stop and stare when, light glinting off its shiny metal trim, a spotless carriage followed the horses around the bend. Sitting high on the front seat, the driver wore a morning coat. He doffed his tall top hat to shoppers and pedestrians who stopped in mid-stride to watch. A smattering of applause broke out when the bride, resplendent in white lace, rode past a group of bystanders.

"That," Jenny whispered, her eyes locked on the carriage. "Yes, that."

A split-second later, an empty spot opened in the center of her chest. She shook her head and brushed an unexpected dampness from her eyes. Who was she kidding? It didn't matter that she'd had her heart set on a Heart's Landing wedding ever since she was a little girl. Or that she'd filled a notebook with samples and drawings of exactly what she wanted on her special day. Her plan to ride in a horse-drawn carriage to wed the man of her dreams might never come true. And even if it did, would it still be in Heart's Landing, now that her very own cousin had chosen to get married here?

Not that she blamed Kay for stealing her idea. It wasn't like they routinely compared notes on their ideal weddings over their morning coffee. Kay hadn't known how much getting married here had meant to her.

But it was one thing for her brain to acknowledge that her dream wedding wasn't in the cards she'd been dealt. It was quite another for her heart to accept it. A fresh longing for something out of her reach filled her. Unable to take her eyes off the lucky bride, Jenny stared after the carriage until it veered onto Procession Avenue. Only when it had disappeared around the corner did she blink slowly like someone waking after a hundred-year nap. The cheerful jingling of the harnesses faded into the distance.

A gradual awareness of her surroundings sank in. Standing stock-still in the middle of the sidewalk, she darted a look around. Their heads bent together, their hands entwined, a couple across the street studied posters of honeymoon destinations on display in the window of a travel agency. The sparse traffic in the center of town ebbed and flowed in time to the traffic lights. Elsewhere, people went about their business while she alone stood frozen in place.

What was that all about? She didn't have time to stand on the sidewalk and gawk. She had work to do. She'd been tasked with making all the arrangements for her cousin's wedding. With just four weeks to accomplish the monumental task, she needed to get moving. Shaking off the spell she'd been under, she spun. Her head down, she hurried onward.

"Whoa! Watch out!"

Jenny sucked in a breath as a tall figure barreled out of the bakery straight at her. Trying her best to move out of his path, she stumbled to one side. She almost made it past him, probably would have avoided a collision altogether, but her left foot tangled with her right one and both refused to budge. In a blur of motion, the figure in blue plowed into her. Something stiff crumpled at her waist. A cloud of sugary sweetness surrounded her while she flailed her arms, tried to regain her balance, and failed. She had the vaguest impression of muscular arms reaching for her. She slipped out of their grasp just as her legs gave out beneath her.

Down she went.

An instant later, she landed with a soft "Ooof" on the unforgiving sidewalk. As a final insult, something soft plopped into her lap.

"Oh, gosh. Are you hurt?" Deep and masculine, a voice to match the broad shoulders of the man who'd collided with her cut through her confused fog.

"What just happened?" Trying to figure out how she'd ended up sitting on the ground and covered in sticky goo, Jenny whipped her head from side to side. She flexed her arms and legs and felt a wash of relief when nothing sent up a twinge or a sharp, painful protest. The hand she brushed over her jacket left trails of blue and green streaks. With nothing more than a little hurt pride and stains to show for her fall, she followed faded denim upward past a blue shirt to a pair of piercing eyes the color of a stormy afternoon sky.

"You ran into me," she said, still trying to fit the pieces together. "I was walking into the bakery, and you barged out like you were headed to a fire somewhere. What in heaven's name was so important?"

"Cupcakes." A shock of dark hair fell forward on to his forehead as the man leaned down over her.

"Cupcakes," she echoed. As if that explained anything.

The stranger's gaze sharpened. "Are you okay? Nothing's broken? You didn't bang your head?"

"I didn't land on my head." The sharp retort rolled off her tongue before she had a chance to stop it. She clamped a hand over her mouth and immediately regretted it when the sticky goo on her hands stuck to her face. "Don't mind me. I'm not usually so snippy. It's just that, well…" She ran out of steam. Figuring the fall must have taken the wind out of her sails, she straightened her shoulders and schooled her attitude. It was about time for her to get up off the ground, wasn't it? "What *is* all this?" She held her fingers up while she stared down at a kaleidoscope of color.

"You're wearing my cupcakes." The stranger's lips thinned. "Or what's left of them." The gray in his eyes hardened into silver as his gaze shifted to the mess that covered her. A muscle ticked along one side of his jaw.

That explained why she smelled like she'd been drenched in butter and sugar. As though her tongue had a will of its own, she licked her lips. Flavor burst in her mouth, setting her taste buds alight and leaving her hungry for more. She swallowed, and the sweetness spread into her throat. She eyed the man who stared down at her with a mix of concern and irritation. No wonder he seemed upset. The icing was the best she'd ever tasted.

"Here," he said, reaching down with an outstretched hand. "Let me help you up."

"What? No, I can—" Her protest faltered in mid-sentence. Before she could point out that she was perfectly capable of getting herself off the sidewalk, strong hands wrapped around her wrists. In one fluid motion, the stranger pulled her to her feet. Refusing to let her go, he hung on a second or two longer than it took her to regain her balance. Heat crawled up her neck when the backs of her hands warmed beneath his touch.

Her focus dropped from the firm grip that held her in place and landed on the icing and bits of cake that dripped from her clothes. A rather large blue dollop chose that particular moment to separate itself from her jacket. It splattered to the sidewalk with a wince-inducing plop. Jenny heaved a heavy sigh at the waste of something so yummy.

"No scrapes, no broken bones, no twisted ankles?"

She looked up in time to see concern replace the silver in the bluish-gray eyes that swept over her. "I'm fine," she murmured. To prove it, she slid from his grasp. "My clothes are another matter." Suddenly aware of how closely she resembled an artist's palette, she darted a glance over his shoulder at the bakery. "I don't suppose there'd be any place inside where I could clean up?"

"The ladies' room," he suggested. At her curt nod, he held the door for her. "In the back, on the left. I'll see if I can't scour up something else for you to put on."

Jenny rejected the offer with an abrupt, "I think you've done enough already. I'll take it from here." The last thing she needed was an absolute stranger asking the owner of the bakery for a favor. Not when she already needed to beg him to make Karolyn's cake on such short notice.

Trailing crumbs and sticky blotches, she moved away from the man with the intriguing eyes as fast as her legs would carry her. In the bathroom, she brushed the worst of the mess into the trash can. Then, gripping the sink, she stared into the mirror. A little soap and water erased the icing that stubbornly clung to her cheeks, but only widened the speckles of blue and green on her slacks, blouse, and jacket. Her lips pursed. The mess served her right for not sticking to her original plan. If she'd gone straight from the B&B to dinner, right now she'd be deciding which appetizers to serve Karolyn's guests. Instead, she was wearing a stained shirt and a jacket that smelled like something from the dessert cart. Now she'd have to change before she went to the restaurant. Which meant she'd be late for her reservation.

At that unhappy thought, her empty stomach gurgled a protest.

"Sorry," she whispered. But she couldn't very well show up at a four-star restaurant looking like a child's watercolor picture. Even if it wasn't her fault.

Or was it?

As much a jumbled mess as the rest of her, her thoughts swirled. Sure, the man had plowed into her, but he'd done everything he could to make things right. And what had he gotten for his troubles? Ruined cupcakes and a waspish retort.

Honestly, what had gotten into her? It wasn't like her to be so rude. Certainly not to someone she'd barely met, no matter what the circumstances. Besides, she shared at least a little bit of the blame. If she'd been watching where she was going instead of dreaming about a horse-drawn carriage ride she'd never take, they could have avoided the collision altogether.

A long, shuddery sigh worked its way through her chest. She really was as sorry as she could be about the stranger's ruined cupcakes. She probably ought to offer to replace them.

No time like the present.

With a last check to make sure she'd wiped the last of the icing from her face, she squared her shoulders. She needed to make things right.

Outside the ladies' room, her stomach shimmied at the thought of staring into that intense pair of blue-gray eyes again. She sucked in a breath of air for strength. The move nearly proved her undoing when tantalizing smells filled her nose. Her stomach rumbled again, this time issuing an earnest reminder that far too many hours had passed since the flight attendant had pressed a tiny bag of chips into her hand. Promising herself she'd eat soon, she searched the bakery for the stranger so she could apologize and move on.

The cozy seating area, where framed paintings of pink and white flowers hung above striped wainscoting on fawn-colored walls, sat empty. No one waited in the larger, upholstered chairs clustered around low tasting tables or stood in front of the display cases on the other side of the room, either.

Ignoring a twinge of disappointment, Jenny told herself it was just as well that the man hadn't stuck around. Tall, ruggedly handsome strangers with sharply chiseled jaws definitely weren't on her agenda. She had a wedding to plan.

But thinking of Kay's wedding reminded her why she'd come to the bakery in the first place. She headed for the cash register. Before she reached it, the bell over the door jingled merrily. A burst of traffic noise filled the storefront. The sound quickly died as the door swung shut behind a willowy young woman carrying a broom and dustpan.

Warmth flooded Jenny's face and spread down her neck when she spotted the I Do Cakes logo on the girl's apron. "I'm so, so sorry for the mess outside." She shook her head, embarrassed.

A mix of compassion and concern swirled onto the young woman's heart-shaped face. "Don't even think about it," she said with a welcome smile. She walked as she spoke, crossing the room to a set of swinging doors behind the counter. "I'll be just a sec," she promised and ducked out of sight.

For the next minute or so, muffled sounds echoed through the empty bakery. By the time a trash can lid clanged, Jenny had spotted several large baskets filled with cellophane-wrapped muffins near the display case. She was sorting through a mouth-watering selection of flavors when the clerk returned to the front of the store.

"There, that's all taken care of," the girl said, brushing one last crumb from her apron on her way to the sales counter. "Welcome to I Do Cakes. I'm Denise. Can I get you anything? A cup of coffee? Tea? Mr. Bell said you can take your pick." With a wave of her hand, she indicated the mammoth glass-fronted cases that stretched out on either side of the checkout counter.

"Mr. Bell." Jenny nodded, glad to have a name to put with the stranger's face. "I'm Jenny Longley. When you see him again, please tell him he doesn't owe me a thing. I was just as much at fault as he was. Were you able to refill his order? I want to pay for it, if I can." If she couldn't apologize, at least she could do that much. Reaching for her wallet, she eyed the smattering of cookies and sweet rolls on display.

"That's so nice of you, but it's already taken care of. Now, what can I get you?"

Jenny shifted uneasily. Marybeth's recommendation had been enough to separate I Do Cakes from the other bakeries in town. A single taste of rich buttercream icing had finalized her decision—this was the baker she wanted to hire. "I was actually on my way here to order my wedding cake before"—grinning, she brushed one hand over her stained clothes—"this happened."

"Thank goodness no one was hurt." Denise nodded. A moment later, her eyes widened as the importance of Jenny's announcement sank in. "You're getting married? Congratulations. You must be so excited." She held out her hand expectantly. "Let me see the ring."

A sudden guilt ran through Jenny like one of Southern California's flash floods after a heavy rainstorm. She hated pretending to be a real bride when she wasn't even dating someone, much less engaged. But she'd given Kay her word, and it was too late to back out now. Gritting her teeth, she plastered a smile over her misgivings and flashed the dazzling piece of jewelry borrowed from the studio's costume department. She held her breath as Denise bent over her fingers. Her cousin had worn the flashy rock in a blockbuster hit and had insisted only a jeweler with a loupe could tell the difference between it and the real thing. Still, she knew she'd breathe easier once the ring passed its first test.

"Whew," Denise whistled softly. "That's gorgeous. Your fiancé must be a bazillionaire or something."

"Not really." Jenny slipped her fingers from Denise's

grasp. Maybe she should have insisted on a smaller stone, one that wouldn't raise questions she'd rather not answer. Hoping to distract the clerk, she sighed. "But Bob's simply wonderful. He didn't even bat an eye when I insisted on a Heart's Landing wedding. I've always wanted to get married here."

As if by magic, an order pad and pen appeared in Denise's hands. "Jenny Longley," she scribbled in one blank. "And Bob?"

"Bob Chase." *Wait. That's not right, is it?*

When Denise dutifully recorded the name, Jenny fought the urge to give herself a swift kick. *Tom* was such a simple name. Too simple to remember, apparently. She should have insisted on calling her fake fiancé something that would stick in her head. Malcolm or Heathcliff. Those were names no one ever forgot.

A gentle throat clearing broke the silence that had filled the bakery. "So, where's the wedding? What's your headcount? When can we schedule a taste testing?"

Jenny gave her head a little shake. "The veranda of the Captain's Cottage. Only fifty guests—an intimate gathering of our immediate families and our closest friends," she recited. One corner of her mouth lifted. Did Denise have an immediate opening? "How about now?"

"Hmmm." The clerk tapped the pen on her pad. "We'd need at least twenty-four hours' notice. Could you come back on Wednesday at, say, two o'clock?"

It would have to do.

At her nod, Denise pulled a glossy flyer from under the counter. "These are our basic prices and a list of our most popular flavors. You'd need to discuss any special requests with the owner." She leaned closer. "Everything here is wonderful, but what's your favorite? I'll make sure we have it for you."

Her mouth watering, Jenny ran one finger down a long list of options. The single lick of buttercream icing had been so good, she'd be happy to have it slathered over a plain white cake. But this wasn't her wedding, any more than she was a real bride. Dutifully, she recited Kay's preference for a cake to match her color scheme. "Pink champagne, definitely. Let's try the pecan praline, too," she added, recalling a dessert they'd swooned over when Kay had been on location in New Orleans.

"Excellent choices." Denise nodded her approval. "I like a girl who isn't afraid to ask for something more than the standard almond flavor. You should try our chocolate, too. It's so rich, you'll swear your mouth died and went to heaven."

"I could go for that." She swallowed, wishing she had some right now to fill her empty stomach.

"Could you?" A mischievous glint sparkled in Denise's brown eyes. "I'm pretty sure there's a fudge cupcake left over from the morning rush. Let me get it for you? Maybe with a cup of coffee or tea?"

Jenny bit her lower lip. She should turn down Denise's offer, rush to the B&B for a change of clothes and at least try to make it to Bow Tie Pasta in time for her reservation. That was what she should do, what she'd planned to do. She tugged on a loose strand of hair. The long day of travel had exhausted her, but it wasn't nearly over. A veritable mountain of decisions about the wedding waited for her at the B&B. With everything she had left to do, she'd be lucky if she drew the covers up to her chin in her suite's comfy-looking bed before midnight tonight. When she factored in an embarrassing fall, didn't she deserve a little break?

Deciding she did indeed, she nodded. "I think I'll take you up on that, Denise. And coffee, if it's not too much trouble." Chocolate and caffeine. Two of her favorite vices. Her only two vices, to be perfectly honest. Together, they'd power her through the work that lay ahead.

A few minutes later, the scent of rich chocolate rose from the plate she carried to a nearby table. Staring down at dark swirls sprinkled with sea salt, she licked her lips. Though Denise hadn't asked for her wedding date, she wasn't going to let it bother her. Any more than she'd worry that she'd given the wrong answer when asked about her fiancé's name. Not with a delectable confection staring up at her, begging to be eaten. With that, she forked a bite of the decadent cupcake into her mouth…and moaned.

A second batch of cupcakes securely strapped into the seat beside him, Nick tapped his fingers on the steering wheel while the car idled at the corner of Bridal Carriage and Champagne. Though he did his best to temper his impatience, he revved the engine a bit when the light finally changed. He was pretty sure the situation demanded it. After all, it wasn't every day he had to dash across town to get his assistant out of a jam. Or lost an entire order in a freakish accident. And he'd never—ever—mowed down a bride before.

He ran a hand through his hair. That little error in judgment had both thrown him off schedule and dinged his pocket. Once the shock had worn off and he'd assured himself the bride was unharmed, he'd come face-to-face with the fact that the reason he'd been going out the front door in the first place now lay smashed to smithereens on the sidewalk. He'd had no choice but to cobble together twelve replacements by borrowing from the batch he'd meant for tomorrow's daily special. As a result, he was running woefully behind making the Halperteen delivery, and he'd have a dozen fewer cupcakes to sell in the morning.

All thanks to a bride who hadn't been watching where she was going.

Though, when he gave her a second thought, he had to admit he liked her style. Some of the women who came here to get married would have landed in a puddle of tears after the fall she'd taken. Not only had this one kept on going with barely a hitch in her stride, she'd done so without resorting to a single bridezilla tactic. In his ten years at the helm of I Do Cakes, he'd seen plenty. From teary pleas that wormed an extra ten grand for the florist from their daddy's pockets to angry outbursts that kept a platoon of bridesmaids marching in lock-step on the wedding day, some brides wore a sense of entitlement like a cloak around their shoulders.

Not this one. This one had only licked her lips, dusted herself off, and insisted she was perfectly fine, thank you very much. She was a feisty thing, he'd give her that.

Chuckling to himself, he turned onto Champagne Ave. His laughter died the moment he spotted Jimmy anxiously pacing the sidewalk outside a stately two-story home. The tension that had dissipated on the short drive from the bakery settled once more across Nick's shoulders. He braked sharply at the curb. "Everything all right? The party hasn't broken up, has it?"

"Yes—er, no, boss. Everything'll be fine as soon as I get the cupcakes inside. You did bring them, didn't you?"

Nick hit the button releasing the locks on the car doors. "Right beside me."

Jimmy grabbed the box. He peered through the cellophane window. "Hey, these aren't the ones I made." His face fell. "Did I do something wrong?"

"No," Nick answered in his most soothing voice. "Yours were fine. Great, even," he said, recalling the way a certain bride-to-be's face had lit up at one taste of the icing. "There was a small accident." He brushed aside Jimmy's questions with a wave of one hand. "I'll save the long story for when we have more time. The short version is, I had to decorate a new batch."

Jimmy's forehead creased. Tiny lines formed around his eyes as his lips shifted into a teasing smile. "Must be a woman involved. Who is she, and what did you do?"

"Sorry to disappoint." He stopped to reconsider. "All right," he admitted. "There was a woman, but it wasn't like that at all."

"Whatever happened, I want to hear more about it when I get back to the shop."

The sounds of children playing in a pool and a burst of laughter drifted from the back yard.

Jimmy hefted the box. "Gotta run. These kids need more sugar," he said with a huge grin.

Just as well.

If his young assistant was waiting for a juicy piece of gossip, he'd be sorely disappointed. Nick had knocked a woman flat. She'd barely given him the time of day. End of story. Why, he hadn't even gotten her name.

Pushing aside thoughts of the brunette for the moment, Nick focused on the things he needed to accomplish before he shut down the ovens and retreated to his apartment over the bakery tonight. Two assistant bakers handled the day-to-day task of filling the display cases with brownies, cookies, and all manner of tasty treats prepared using I Do Cake's time-honored recipes. A specialist took care of the delicate piping for their most elaborate designs. That freed him and Jimmy to handle the cakes and cupcakes. And with the busy wedding season upon them, cake orders crowded the bakery's calendar through the summer and well into the fall. Some weeks, they'd be so busy that he and the entire staff would pull double-shifts in order to deliver every cake on time.

Which they'd do, no matter what. Both the bakery's and the town's reputation depended on it.

Outside I Do Cakes a few minutes later, Nick scanned the sidewalk and the low hedge beneath the store's window. No matter how closely he examined the area, he couldn't spot a trace of Jimmy's cupcakes. Knowing he owed Denise a big thanks for the cleanup, he cut through the front of the shop. "Hey, Denise. How are things this afternoon?"

For once, the sales associate didn't have her nose in a book. A bottle of spray in one hand, a handful of paper towels in the other, she glanced up from the fingerprints she'd been busy erasing off the display case. "It's been pretty quiet, Mr. Bell. Except for—"

"Hang on a sec." He held up one finger. His dad had made a habit of complimenting employees on a job well done. The practice was one he strove to continue. "You did a great job out front. I appreciate the extra effort." He'd dreaded coming back to a mess.

"Sure, no problem." The girl waved a dismissive hand through the air. "Just doing my part."

"Well, thanks anyway. So, you were saying?"

"Turns out, that woman wanted to order her wedding cake. I know we're busy, but I took her order anyway. I left the paperwork on your desk—Jenny Longley and Bob Chase. They've reserved the Captain's Cottage for the event. It'll be a small affair, just fifty guests, but there's something special about her. You should have seen her eyes sparkle."

Halfway to the kitchen, Nick stopped in his tracks. Slowly, he turned toward Denise. "Are you saying she's a true Heart's Landing bride?" If so, that explained a lot. Starting with why it had been so difficult to shake this Jenny person out of his thoughts.

"Yeah, I think she might be." Denise colored slightly.

"Well, what do you know about that."

Though the town's business owners prided themselves on turning every wedding into a special occasion, every once in a while, an extraordinary bride crossed their path. If anyone asked, Nick would be hard-pressed to put his finger on what set these particular women apart from the others. While they'd dreamed of having their wedding here for years, it took more than that to make a true Heart's Landing Bride. More than just the look that came into their eyes when they described their venue. Or the breathy way they talked about their floral arrangements. Or the hitch in their voices when they described the cake they wanted—whether it was a towering confection for three hundred, or a modest, but just as tasty, dessert for immediate family.

Whatever it was, whenever one of these extra-special brides walked into any of the shops on Bridal Carriage Way, shopkeepers rolled out the proverbial red carpet. From one end of Procession Avenue to the other, store owners greeted her by name. They vied for the privilege of filling her requests. Openings appeared in calendars that had been crammed full of appointments. Seamstresses found extra time in their schedules for alterations. Doors that otherwise might have been closed swung wide. All of which resulted in weddings that were just a tad more wonderful than the rest.

Nick rubbed his hands together. "When's the wedding?" Most brides placed their order six months, or even a year, ahead of time. He hoped it was the former. A wedding during their slow season would give him plenty of time to create a special cake for a special bride.

Denise's face clouded. "I forgot to ask." She brightened almost immediately. "But you can. She's in the dining room."

When Denise motioned toward the small seating area where bridal parties often gathered over coffee and sweet rolls to discuss plans for the day or week ahead, Nick straightened. "She's here?"

"Right around the corner. I served her a cupcake and coffee. On the house, like you said."

"Well, I guess I'd better find out the date for this wedding you've roped me into." He scowled, certain Denise knew he was only joking.

But he did owe someone an apology and, pushing away from the wall, he rounded the corner, intent on delivering it. Halfway to Jenny's table, his footsteps slowed.

She sat, her face angled down, scrolling through messages on her phone. The hair she'd captured in a ponytail curled over one shoulder was thick and dark. An empty plate rested on the table before her. The fork atop it had been licked so clean it shone.

Nick squinted in disbelief. No bride ever ate a cupcake in one sitting. Not one of his, anyway. Most of his customers were so busy starving themselves to fit into their wedding gowns that they swore off sweets altogether.

This Jenny was clearly different from all the others. But was she a true Heart's Landing bride?

He moved closer just as she glanced away from her cell

phone. Recognition broke across her face. Sunshine flooded her features.

"So, hey there. We meet again. I wanted to say—" he began.

"I'm so sorry—" she interrupted.

"—about earlier."

A tender warmth spread through his chest as Jenny finished the thought with him. He grinned. "Now that we've gotten that out of the way, what's this I hear about a wedding cake?"

Her eyes went round. "You're Nick? The baker Nick? The owner of I Do Cakes?"

He held up his hands in mock surrender. "Guilty as charged."

"Oh, if I'd known I'd—"

"Have ordered your cake from someplace else?"

"Well, no." She absently licked her lips. "Marybeth—do you know Marybeth at the Union Street B&B?"

He nodded. The bed and breakfast had been in the Williams family for several generations.

"She told me you were the best. I thought she might have been exaggerating just a little, but this cupcake, that icing." Jenny pointed to her empty plate. "No wonder you're busy. I was beyond thrilled when Denise said you could fit me in for a tasting."

"We make exceptions for certain people."

"Like people you mow down?"

"Not exactly." He chuckled, glad to know the day's events hadn't doused Jenny's feisty spirit. "Denise vouched for you, and that's good enough for me. So, when's the big day?"

Faint lines around her eyes tightened. "In four weeks? On June thirteenth? At three in the afternoon?"

The tentative answers weren't what he'd expect to hear from a true Heart's Landing bride. Determined not to leap to a hasty decision, he gave her one more chance. "Tell me about the ceremony."

"We're holding it in the Captain's Cottage. The roses will be in bloom then. They surround the veranda, climb the trellises, you know." As if she were standing on the porch surrounded by flowers, a faraway look filled her eyes. Her features relaxed. The taut expression on her face melted. "I've heard that the scent is absolutely heavenly."

There it is.

The dreamy expression on Jenny's face was exactly what he'd hoped to see. It made her stand out from the other brides who flooded Heart's Landing during the wedding season.

He nodded. It didn't matter that her wedding was only four weeks away, that she'd already cost him a dozen cupcakes, or that his schedule was so full he'd have to skip a few nights' sleep in order to fill her order. He didn't have a choice. He had to do whatever it took to give this bride the wedding of her dreams. "Have you had a chance to get your bearings yet? I'm free for the next hour or two if you'd like the nickel tour of our little town." He held his breath, not sure why it mattered but suddenly quite certain he wanted to be the one to introduce her to a few key shop owners.

Across the table, Jenny's eyes narrowed. "I appreciate the offer, but—"

"Look, it's no trouble." A sudden anxiousness rippled through him. Would she turn him down? "We only have a little while before most of the stores close for the day. You can meet some of the owners and get a feel for which ones are best suited to help with your wedding plans. Besides..."

He glanced pointedly at blue and green streaks on her jacket. "You owe me."

"Hey!" Jenny's eyebrows slammed together. She brushed a hand over her stained jacket. "I think you've got that backward."

"The chance to make it up to you, I mean," Nick finished, his voice light and teasing.

"Well, there is that." Grinning, she rubbed at a smudge of blue icing. "Is there time for me to run to the bed and breakfast and change into something a little less, um, colorful, first?"

"No problem." Nick nodded. What he had in mind wouldn't take long. They wouldn't need to stop at every store on Bridal Carriage Way. Once he introduced Jenny to one or two of shopkeepers, word of a true Heart's Landing bride would spread throughout town faster than an eager groom could say "I do!"

Chapter Five

On L.A.'s crowded streets, niceties like letting the lady go first were often sacrificed in the name of efficiency. So Jenny was pleasantly surprised when Nick insisted on holding the door for her as they left I Do Cakes. She'd thought chivalry was dead. Apparently, though, the good manners her grade-school teachers had drilled into her hadn't died or faded into nonexistence. They had simply moved to Heart's Landing. She gave the tall baker a grateful smile as she preceded him onto the sidewalk. Her smile deepened when Nick stepped in beside her.

"What do you think about all this?" Guiding them away from the bakery, his expansive wave took in most of the downtown area.

"From the moment I saw a photograph of the Captain's Cottage in a bridal magazine, I've known this was where I wanted to get married. Just being here is a dream come true. But some things are a little different from what I expected." For one thing, she never thought she'd be planning Kay's wedding instead of her own.

Leafy trees along the curb dappled the sidewalks with pools of shadow and light. On a warm spring day, the shade was an unexpected bonus. She inclined her head toward a couple dressed in period costume who entered the restaurant across the street. "There's something else I never expected to see."

"That's Jason Heart and his cousin, Evelyn. Their ancestors founded the town."

"Do they usually dress like that for dinner?" Her gaze dropped from Jason's feathered hat to the white silk stockings and pointed shoes he wore beneath knee-length breeches. Beside him, Evelyn drew a shawl around her shoulders with one hand while, with the other, she lifted the wide skirts that fell from her dress's pinched waist.

"Nah." Nick's chuckle warmed the space between them. "Jason and Evelyn are talented musicians. Singers. They're in big demand for weddings and receptions. They're probably headed to one tonight."

As the duo disappeared into the restaurant, Jenny bit her lower lip. In keeping with Kay's insistence on a wedding with a minimum of fuss, she hadn't really considered lining up entertainment. But she liked the idea of adding a touch of regional history to the reception. She'd make a point to suggest it the next time she spoke with her cousin.

"Here we are."

Nick's voice broke into her train of thought. The first few bars of "Time After Time" chimed when Jenny stepped into Something Old, Something New. She'd barely taken in the glass-front jewelry cases and a rack of vintage gowns before a mousy sneeze erupted from the back of the shop. A second later, a sturdy-looking blonde emerged from the rear of the store.

"Oh, hi, Nick." The woman swiped her nose with a tissue. "Sorry. My allergies are acting up again. Must be the dust."

She gestured toward the curtained-off area. "It's worth it, though. Wait till you see what I picked up today. You won't believe it."

"Sure. But first, Paula, let me introduce you to Jenny Longley. She's new in town and needs our help with her wedding later this month." Nick swiveled as he spoke. "Jenny. This is Paula, the owner of Something Old, Something New."

"Nice to meet you. I'd shake your hand, but…" Paula pressed a tissue against her nose and sniffed. "You'd think someone with allergies would choose a different profession, wouldn't you? But I love what I do, so I just deal." Without waiting for an answer, she beckoned them to follow. "Come on in the back. I can't wait to show you what I have."

Given Paula's excitement, Jenny rubbed her hands together. Had the shop owner stumbled onto a cache of pirate gold? A piece of long-lost artwork? She ducked behind the curtain, eager to see what the fuss was about. Lumps of gray rock covered in loose soil and lichen weren't at all what she'd expected. Her brow furrowed as questions filled her thoughts.

"Isn't it fantastic?" Tears escaped Paula's eyelids and ran down her cheeks. Blotting them, she beamed up at Nick.

"Is that what I think it is?"

At Nick's reverent tone, Jenny had to restrain the urge to scratch her head. What was so special about rocks? Especially ones that looked like they'd just come from someone's backyard? Paula must have noticed her doubtful expression. The shop owner turned toward her.

"In your travels about town, you'll see heart-shaped stones mounted on some of the buildings. They date back to the 1800s and Captain Thaddeus Heart. We know there were thirteen or more originally. Today, there are only a half dozen. Everyone assumed the missing hearts were gone forever, but last week, a gardener up at the Captain's Cottage discovered this one buried under an azalea bush. I was lucky enough to snap it up."

Jenny gave the chunks on the table a second chance. If she squinted just right and someone shoved them together, she could see how the pieces might form a heart. An unexpected excitement rushed through her. It took a second before she recognized it as the same feeling that had enveloped her on her drive down from Providence.

"Sorry for bending your ear. I get carried away sometimes. It's part of being a history buff, I guess." Paula's cheeks turned rosy.

"No need to apologize on my account." Jenny stared at the shards with a new respect for their role in the town's past.

"I shouldn't have rambled on, though. What say I make it up to you and help you find the right pieces to carry down the aisle with you on your wedding day? Unless you already have your something old, new, borrowed, and blue?"

"We don't have much time right now, but I do need a quick word with Paula." This came from Nick, who'd bent down and lightly traced a finger along the curved edge of one of the rocks. "Jenny, if you'd like to take a look around, we won't be long."

"I'd like that," she answered agreeably. She turned away from Nick and the cute blonde. Were they a couple? She hadn't caught so much as a lingering glance between them, but it stood to reason that they'd be interested in one another. They worked next door to each other. Each ran their own business and apparently shared an interest in the history of Heart's Landing. Relationships had been built on a lot less.

Not that she had any intention of asking Nick about it. The handsome baker had taken time out of his busy schedule to show her around town, but whether he was seeing someone or not really wasn't any of her business. Between planning Kay's wedding and pretending to be a bride, she already had enough to occupy herself for the next two weeks.

Speaking of which, a real bride would probably take advantage of the chance to shop, wouldn't she? Nodding to herself, she glanced about. The store was such an eclectic mix of old and new, vintage and modern that she had trouble choosing where to look first. Deciding on the tabletop displays, she scrutinized an array of gold-and-silver pendants. She could spend hours browsing the jewelry alone.

In less time than she'd expected, though, Nick and Paula joined her. Whatever had transpired between them while they were alone in the back, it had filled Paula's eyes with a new vibrancy.

"So, Jenny, Nick tells me your wedding is less than a month away." The shop owner ran her fingers through her hair. "If there's anything I can do to help out—anything at all—ask. I'll be happy to help."

"That's so nice of you." She wished she had time to explore the rest that the store had to offer, but Nick had already headed for the exit. Hating to leave, she promised to return soon and followed the man who'd so generously given up his time to be her guide.

When she caught up with him on the sidewalk, he asked, "Do you have a veil yet?"

She shook her head. Kay hadn't even bought a dress, let alone a veil to go with it. She crossed her fingers and hoped this week's appointment at the bridal salon was a huge success. It needed to be. Time was running short.

"We'll stop in at Chantilly Veils next," he said. "It's just down the block on Honeymoon Avenue. I'm told Ames has the best selection on the East Coast."

"I liked Paula," she ventured when they'd reached the next corner. "Have you known each other long?"

"Since we were kids. She dated my best friend when we were in high school, but they broke up before they left for college."

"You two aren't seeing each other?" Jenny tucked a loose strand of hair behind her ear. So much for her good intentions. She'd sworn she wasn't going to pry, yet here she was, doing exactly that.

"Who? Me and Paula?" Nick chortled. "Nah. We're friends. I've helped her drown her sorrows in a couple of ice cream sodas when she found out a Mr. Potentially Right was sadly lacking in potential. She did the same for me when I discovered the woman I thought might be *the one*"—he made air quotes with his fingers—"wasn't who she pretended to be. But that's as far as it's ever gone between us. Or ever will."

Jenny cut her eyes toward Nick. Did he suspect *she* was only pretending to be a bride? Suddenly, the fake engagement ring on her finger felt like it weighed ten pounds. She hated lying to Nick—and everyone else—about her reason for being in Heart's Landing, but she couldn't let anyone discover she was merely a stand-in for the real bride. Not with her cousin's happiness on the line.

"It's really none of my business," she said. "I guess I just want everyone to be as happy as I am." She twisted the ring on her finger and held out her hand like she was showing it off a little. The faux diamond sparkled in the afternoon sun, and she firmed her steps, determined to do a better job of impersonating a bride-to-be.

In no time at all, she and Nick arrived at Chantilly Veils.

She'd barely noted the crystal chandeliers, swags of pink fabric at the windows, or the recessed nooks where gauzy wisps hung from padded hangers before a slender man rushed across the showroom to greet them. Wearing a toothy grin beneath carefully styled dark hair, he grasped both her hands and raised her arms.

"My word, Nick!" he gushed while laughter twinkled in pale blue eyes. "How have you kept this gorgeous creature a secret? I didn't know you were seeing someone. Much less serious enough to put a ring on her finger and take her shopping. Now, tell me, who is this lovely woman, and when's the big day?"

"Uh, Ames, it's not…" A flush started above Nick's collar and rose rapidly.

Amusement tugged at Jenny's lips. She hadn't thought Nick capable of embarrassment, but he was clearly unnerved by the shop owner's misunderstanding. "It's nothing like that," she said, leaning forward as if sharing a secret. "Nick and I ran quite literally ran into each other outside I Do Cakes this afternoon. I ended up covered in smashed cupcakes. To make it up to me, he's taking me on a little tour and introducing me to some of his favorite shop owners."

Ames's eyebrows rose until they hid behind dark bangs that gave Jenny a slight case of hair envy. "Really?" When she nodded, he relinquished his hold on her. He perched one hand at the waist of a pair of white linen trousers. "How'd you get him to do that?"

Nick's deep voice intervened. "It's not every day I knock a true Heart's Landing bride onto the sidewalk."

"Are you serious?" His eyes wide, Ames's gaze bounced between Nick and Jenny.

"Serious." Nick paused to clear his throat. "Jenny was

such a good sport about it, the least I could do was introduce her to a few of my friends. This is Ames, by the way. In case you haven't already figured it out. Jenny's planning her own wedding in a month."

"A month?" Ames clapped a hand over his mouth. "I couldn't possibly custom-make a veil for you by then." He seemed to catch himself. "But I have some lovely ready-made ones." He sidled toward a mannequin on top of a table draped in white. His fingers fluffed the nearly translucent creation pinned to its head. "This one would be beautiful on you."

"It's lovely." Jenny moved closer to the gossamer number. The discreet price tag displayed on the stand made her shudder, but Ames certainly knew his merchandise. Everything about the veil was sheer perfection, from the comb adorned with freshwater pearls to the pencil-thin satin edging. Even the length was exactly right for her. The veil was out of her price range, but she'd choose it in a heartbeat. Not that she had any say in the matter. She wasn't the one who'd be walking down the aisle at the Captain's Cottage. Nor was it her responsibility to pick out the accessories her movie-star cousin would wear. Kay would do that for herself at Madame Eleanor's. She summoned a smile for Ames. "I'm not quite ready to shop today. Maybe some other time?"

"Anytime," came the ready assurance. As if by magic, a business card appeared in between Ames's fingers. He pressed it into her hand. "If you need anything, day or night, call me. You hear?"

While she doubted she'd have a veil emergency so urgent it justified waking the shop owner in the middle of the night, Jenny nonetheless tucked Ames's card in her wallet. They said their goodbyes, and Nick guided them toward their next stop.

They hadn't gone far before he inclined his head to hers. "You nearly turned green when you looked at that price tag. Too rich for your tastes?"

Jenny gulped. For a second there, she'd forgotten she was supposed to be marrying a man with very deep pockets. "Sometimes, I forget I'm not still in college and eating ramen noodles every night because that's all I can afford."

Nick's laugh, deep and throaty, rose from his chest. "I hear you. While I worked my way up the ladder from apprentice to assistant to head *pâtissier* in Paris, I lived in an actual garret. It wasn't nearly as romantic as the novelists make it out to be."

Picturing Nick's tall form stooped beneath the rafters of a tiny attic apartment, Jenny smiled. It was nice to know that neither of them came from wealthy backgrounds. It gave them something in common. Besides a dozen smashed cupcakes, that was.

A couple of doors down, a young woman twisted the key in the lock outside a store called The Memory Box.

"Closing up for the night, Helen?" Nick's footsteps slowed to a stop.

"Yes. It's about that t-time." The fashionably dressed brunette hesitated. "Did you want s-something?"

"Nothing special. I was just showing Jenny around town a bit and thought we'd drop by for a minute or two."

"S-sorry, Nick. I'd open back up, but it's my mom's birthday. I don't want to be late." Turning, Helen pocketed the key.

"That's okay." Nick smiled agreeably. "Helen, meet Jenny Longley. She's getting married at the Captain's Cottage in *true* Heart's Landing tradition later this month. Jenny, this is Helen Berger, co-owner of The Memory Box."

"Pleased to meet you," Jenny said, her hand outstretched. She glanced over Helen's shoulder at the intricately carved boxes on display in the front window. Even through the thick glass, the detail was stunning, and she longed for a closer look.

For several beats, Helen stood as though rooted to the sidewalk while her delicate nose crinkled with indecision. "Would you like to go inside and l-look around?" she asked, giving Jenny's hand a quick shake.

Touched by the offer, Jenny shook her head. "I wouldn't dream of making you late on such an important night. But I'm intrigued. I'll have to stop by again while I'm in town."

"You do that." Helen's voice and her features smoothed. "You won't find anything quite like our boxes anywhere else. I'd be happy to help you pick out something really special to hold your wedding memorabilia." She straightened the strap on her shoulder bag and gave Nick a brisk nod. "S-sorry, but I have to run."

As Helen hurried off, bells chimed the hour from the steeple on the church at the end of the block. Jenny surveyed the rapidly emptying sidewalks. Up and down Honeymoon Avenue, store lights had been turned off, and signs in windows had been flipped from Open to Closed. Taking their cue, she aimed a grateful smile toward her host for the afternoon. It was time to go.

"I appreciate your showing me around, Nick. I hope I haven't kept you away from the bakery too long."

"Not at all." His deep voice rumbled in his chest. A mischievous sparkle ignited in his dark eyes. "So, are we even now? Have I repaid my debt?"

"I suppose. As long as you promise not to smash into anyone else."

"And waste another batch of cupcakes?" Nick shuddered. "Got it. No more plowing into unsuspecting brides. At least, not for the rest of the week."

Standing there, seeing the mirth dance in his eyes, she wished for an instant she could tell him she'd only come to Heart's Landing as a favor for her cousin. She even thought about asking him to join her for dinner.

She quickly slammed the lid over that idea. The run-in with the baker notwithstanding, her stay in town had gotten off on the right foot. Not one person had questioned her claim that she was a harried bride-to-be, here to plan a last-minute wedding. In fact, everyone she'd met had gone out of their way to be helpful. Nick especially.

But sooner or later, someone would see through her act if she wandered too far from the script. And that was something she definitely needed to avoid.

Chapter Six

The sun had barely risen the next morning when Jenny pushed the covers aside in the bed that had been every bit as comfortable to sleep in as it had looked. Eager to get an early start, she shut off the alarm before it had a chance to ring. A tour of the grounds at the Captain's Cottage, appointments with florists, photographers, and DJs crowded her schedule. With any luck, she'd cross the biggest items for Karolyn's wedding off her To-Do list this week, leaving her plenty of time to handle the rest of the not-so-minor details, like arranging transportation to and from the airport for the happy couple, before she returned to California.

As she showered and dressed, she couldn't stop thinking how well things had gone so far. Everyone she'd met in Heart's Landing had been more than helpful. Granted, the accident outside I Do Cakes yesterday hadn't been her finest moment, and when the same man she'd run into had rounded the corner of the bakery a little while later and introduced himself as the owner, she'd thought her heart would stop beating altogether.

Though Nick would have been well within his rights to blame her for his ruined cupcakes, he'd gone out of his way to assure her he didn't hold a grudge. When he'd agreed to bake Karolyn's wedding cake, she'd nearly swooned. She loved how he'd taken her under his wing, so to speak, and introduced her to some of the nearby shop owners. It had been a long time since she'd met anyone like him. Certainly not since she moved to L.A. There, wannabe actors were so focused on taking advantage of every opportunity to get their big break that people often forgot about being just plain nice to each other.

Yes, Nick was different, all right. She wouldn't mind a second—or even a third—glimpse of his gray-blue eyes. As if that wasn't reason enough see him again, one thought of his amazing buttercream frosting made her hungry. She licked her lips. There was nothing for it, she supposed. She'd simply have to find the time to stop by the bakery later today and treat herself to another of his luscious cupcakes. No matter what it cost.

With that to look forward to, she slipped into a favorite sleeveless floral dress. Paired with a light jacket and low heels, the outfit was one of her favorites and perfect for the busy day ahead. By the time she grabbed her purse, the inviting smells of freshly brewed coffee and sweet rolls straight from the oven wafted in the air. She sniffed appreciatively and followed her nose to the dining room, where domed lids covered two different breakfast casseroles and enough baked goods to fuel a small army. While she ate, she exchanged snatches of conversation with Marybeth, who bustled about refilling coffee urns and replenishing dishes as her guests came and went. A little before nine, Jenny tucked her portfolio under one arm, adjusted the strap of her purse at her shoulder, and ventured out the door.

A short ride took her to the Captain's Cottage. From the

circular drive, she stared up the mansion that far surpassed its name.

Her breath caught in her throat. How long had she been dreaming of coming here? She'd probably been ten or twelve the first time she'd seen pictures of Heart's Landing in a bridal magazine her aunt had brought home from a beauty salon. While Kay had oohed and aahed over the hairstyles and insisted on trying out every makeup tip in the Features section, she'd instantly fallen in love with the house and the gardens described as "the perfect destination for a summer wedding."

At the time, she'd agreed. But seeing the cottage up close and personal, she was even more impressed. From the widow's walk atop the mansard roof to the tall black shutters at the windows, right down to the thick green hedges surrounding the white masonry walls, the house countless brides had chosen to marry in was even better than she'd imagined it. Better than in the photograph she'd tucked under her pillow each night until the glossy paper had literally disintegrated.

A whisper of regret stirred in her chest. Now that Kay would get married here first, it rubbed a little bit of the shine off her own dream of a Heart's Landing wedding. It wasn't quite as bad as asking Santa for a pony for Christmas and finding a stuffed animal under the tree, but just the same, it hurt.

She doused her misgivings by drinking in the scents of freshly cut grass and the flowers that grew in thick clumps beside the path. She'd still find her Prince Charming one day. She'd still have her own wonderful wedding, maybe even at the Captain's Cottage.

When she was ready, she headed up the curving sidewalk that led to the main entrance. As if reminding her that she'd come to the Captain's Cottage to make all the arrangements for her cousin's wedding instead of her own, her heels clicked hollowly on the brick pavers. The portfolio filled with plans for Kay's wedding, not hers, hung limply from her shoulder. She straightened the strap.

At the main entrance, she stepped from warmth and sunshine into the cool recesses of a house that had been well-loved throughout its long history. At the entry to the dining room, where she and Alicia had agreed to meet, she paused to soak in the ambience. A long, gleaming cherry table stretched practically the length of the room. Though it had once provided ample seating for Captain Thaddeus Heart, his wife, and their children, the family had most likely followed the custom of the times and relegated the younger children to the nursery for meals.

Jenny smoothed one hand over her dress. Had the Captain's wife felt lonely, sitting alone at her end of the table while her husband sat so far away? She gave her head a little shake, glad that dining customs had changed over the years. Under an immense painting of a sailing ship, coffee urns stood atop the sideboard. She helped herself, then settled in at one of the four smaller tables that filled each corner of the room. She'd barely pulled the plans for Karolyn's wedding from her portfolio when a soft throat clearing drew her attention to a woman in a black suit.

"Jennifer Longley?"

"That's me," Jenny answered, though her response wasn't necessary.

Assured and cheery, Alicia Thorn strode toward her table. "It's so nice to meet you. Did you have a good trip? When did you get in?"

"I flew into Providence yesterday afternoon and drove down." Jenny's smile deepened as she recounted details of her trip. "I hadn't ever been in this part of the country before, so I followed the scenic route along the coast." Rather than bore Alicia with a lengthy description, she stuck to a straightforward, "It was beautiful."

"I like that drive, too." Alicia smiled dreamily. "I haven't done that in a while—my job here keeps me too busy. But it's definitely on my bucket list once I retire." Her eyes crinkled. "What good is life if we don't enjoy it, right?" She flipped one strand of well-salted dark hair over her shoulder. "So, tell me a little bit about yourself, Jenny. What do you and your fiancé do when you're not hip-deep in wedding plans?"

"I'm the assistant to the president of a corporation on the West Coast," Jenny said, bending the truth only the tiniest bit by failing to mention that, in addition to sitting at the helm of several companies, Karolyn was at the top of Hollywood's A-List. "I keep track of my boss's schedule, do whatever I can to make her life run smoothly and efficiently." She paused. "Some of what I do is probably similar to your job here. The events I plan run the gamut from birthday parties to fundraisers." She enjoyed that part of her job so much that she'd often thought of opening her own event planning business one day.

Alicia's smile deepened. "It sounds like we have some things in common, then. There are so many moving parts to a big celebration. I always hold my breath a little until everything finally comes together on the big day."

"That's the part I like the most," Jenny agreed. She shifted in her seat. She could probably learn a lot from Alicia.

"And your fiancé? What does he do?"

She gave herself a little shake. This wasn't the time or the place to dream about her future. She had to stay focused. Taking a breath, she repeated the story she and Kay had crafted.

This time, though, she used the same name she'd given at the bakery the day before. "Bob is in investments. He wanted to be more involved in this"—her gesture took in the plans she'd pulled from her portfolio and spread on the table—"but he's tied up in a merger right now. He'll fly in the day before the wedding."

Alicia nodded, as if Bob wasn't the first groom to opt out of the wedding preparations. "Are you all settled in? You're staying at the Union Street B&B, aren't you? Are Marybeth and Matt treating you well?"

The interest in her well-being was yet another difference between her hectic life on the West Coast and the unhurried pace of Heart's Landing. Jenny met Alicia's probing gaze and smiled warmly in return. "They couldn't be nicer. And it's so calm and peaceful there, the perfect home-away-from-home."

"Are you enjoying this weather? It's a little different from what you're used to in California, isn't it?"

Jenny's focus drifted to the window. On the other side of thick, wavy glass, the leaves on a pear tree rippled in the breeze. "The humidity is taking some getting used to, but I like how it makes everything so green. And the flowers," she gushed. "I've never seen so many beautiful flowers."

"We're a little spoiled with all the greenery. Especially here at the Captain's Cottage. Except for the dead of winter, something's always in bloom. Right now, our roses are just beginning to open."

"I've seen pictures. They're spectacular." She closed her eyes for a minute, imagining herself in a white dress, surrounded by red blossoms.

"How many guests did you say?" Alicia glanced up from a map of the cottage. "Oh, fifty—that's right. Have you thought about holding the ceremony on the veranda?"

Had Alicia read her mind? Jenny tipped her head. "That would be perfect."

"The roses should be at their peak in another four weeks. That spot will make a stunning location for your wedding."

My wedding.

As if a cloud had passed over the sun, some of the light went out of the day. She and Alicia weren't thinking along the same lines at all. A heaviness pressed down on her. She hated the pretense, cringed at the thought of keeping secrets from the woman who'd shown such an interest in her welfare, but she didn't have a choice. She'd promised to keep her cousin's famous name out of the wedding plans. Breaking away from Alicia's probing look, she referred to her notes. "I was hoping you'd suggest exactly that." She smiled past her ache in her heart. "With one of the smaller rooms as a backup plan. Just in case it rains."

"Either the library or our smallest ballroom would make a wonderful site for your reception. If your guest list is a bit larger, I can suggest any number of other locations."

"No, that'll work. We're expecting fifty guests, max."

"That's perfect for the library, although…" Alicia's voice trailed off.

Jenny frowned into the other woman's face. "Yes?"

"It's just that, well, for a guest list that size, it wasn't necessary for you reserve the *entire* cottage."

Jenny took a sip of coffee to buy herself time to think of a good response. She liked Alicia and didn't want the event planner to think of her as the kind of person who threw her weight around, someone who'd rent out an entire restaurant simply so she could enjoy her meal in peace and quiet. An expense that she, personally, could never, ever justify. Kay's priorities, though, were different. From getting a facial to going out on a date, keeping the paparazzi at bay factored hugely in everything the star did. Still, Jenny couldn't very well explain that to Alicia. Not without confessing the bride's real identity. She took another sip as her answer became clearer. "It was my fiancé's idea," she said, shifting the blame to a man who didn't exist. "He's a very private person."

"Men." Laughing, Alicia shook her head. "Once, I dealt with a groom who went on and on about the cost of the wedding. Then, he wanted peacocks roaming the grounds during the reception. Peacocks!"

Alicia's laughter warmed the empty spaces in Jenny's heart. Her smile spread until it tugged at her eyes. "If I left it up to my fiancé, we'd be exchanging our vows on an island in Tahiti—just the two of us and the minister. But sharing our special day with family and close friends is as important to me as getting married in Heart's Landing." She took a breath. "I know we only snagged this reservation because you had a cancellation, but truthfully, I've dreamed of getting married here for so long that I'd be happy if we held the ceremony in the hallway." She hesitated the slightest bit to make sure she got the name right. "Bob agreed, as long as we had the place to ourselves."

"I think we can do much better than a hallway." Alicia's features softened. Her brown eyes grew serious. "Let's take a tour of the grounds before you make your final decision. Then, we'll walk through the house. You might find something you like even more than the veranda."

With Alicia pointing out the plusses and minuses of each location, they spent the next hour or so driving around in a sporty little golf cart. Jenny had to agree with her host—the weeping willow trees by a small creek made the perfect spot for stunning photographs. A wind-swept spot overlooking the ocean was even more amazing, and she imagined standing on the rocky crag in a flowing gown, her veil swirling around her in the breeze. She eyed the immense tents workers were erecting in an open field where, according to Alicia, up to four hundred guests would dance beneath the stars at an upcoming wedding. She gaped at the space that was as perfect a place to get married as she'd ever seen.

"Well, what do you think?" Alicia asked.

Pressing her hands over her heart, Jenny tamped down her enthusiasm. Even on her wedding day—okay, *especially* on her wedding day—a mega-star like Karolyn had to look perfect. She'd never risk having the sun, wind, or even rain spoil her hair and makeup. More than a little disappointed that they couldn't use any of the spectacular sites Alicia had shown her, Jenny motioned toward the house. "If you don't mind, I'd like to see everything before I decide."

"We have so many lovely spots in the cottage itself. I'm sure we can find the right one for you." Alicia beckoned her back to the golf cart. "Wait till you see some of the rooms. You'll love them."

Abandoning the cart near the rear entrance to the mansion, they spent another hour climbing up and down staircases and peeking into rooms that ranged from a ballroom for three hundred to one of several elegant suites reserved especially for brides and grooms. At the entrance to the library, Jenny lingered on the threshold. No matter what gown her cousin chose, the room's dim lighting and dark paneling would make the perfect backdrop. Without a second's hesitation, she chose it for the reception.

With the locations settled, Alicia stood at the base of the stairwell. "Normally, I'd say we've made enough decisions for one day. But since we're working with such a tight schedule, and especially since you've had experience planning big events in your job, what say we tackle the table settings next? Are you up to it?"

At Jenny's nod, Alicia steered them down the hall to a room she called the linen closet.

"This was once the butler's pantry," she explained, opening the door to a roomy space where floor-to-ceiling shelves lined the walls. "The family used to store linens and cutlery in the shelves and pull-outs. Now, we house our samples here. What colors have you chosen?"

"Rose-gold and gray."

"I think we can work with that." Alicia pulled table linens in a half-dozen shades from the drawers. "See anything you like?"

"Each one is prettier than the last," Jenny answered, though she had a tough time tearing her gaze away from a mauve-and-blue floral print she spied in one of the other drawers. At length, she selected a pinkish fabric she thought Karolyn would adore. A pale gray napkin and matching drape complemented the metallic threads in the table covering, which Alicia expertly arranged on a stand in the center of the room. From there, they moved on to silver, china and crystal.

"Have you decided on a menu?" Her back turned, Alicia pulled several items from a built-in cabinet.

The question sent a shiver of apprehension through Jenny's chest. Getting an appointment with a caterer had proved more difficult than she'd expected. She'd spent hours flipping from one website to another without finding one that could meet her timeline, much less provide the stellar food Karolyn would expect. She looked up from the glass stem she'd been twisting. From across the small room, Alicia stared at her with a quizzical expression.

"I haven't exactly found a caterer," she confessed.

"Why didn't you say so? Hang on a sec." Alicia held up one finger and whipped out her phone. "I know it's last minute, Janet," she said a moment later, "but I have a Heart's Landing bride here who needs your help." After the briefest of pauses, she smiled. "Yes, a small wedding. Fifty or so guests. Four weeks from Saturday. You can?" She lowered the phone from her face. "Are you available for an appointment this afternoon?"

"I'll have to shift some things around, but yes, definitely." The thick knot in Jenny's stomach unfurled.

Alicia struck a thumbs up sign and resumed her phone call. "That'll work. I'll send her by this afternoon." Once she'd disconnected, the event planner explained. "Janet is the executive chef at Food Fit For A Queen. They're the best in town." She scribbled an address on the back of a business card and handed it across.

A bit awed by how easily Alicia had averted a major wedding crisis, Jenny tucked the paper in her pocket while the coordinator continued sorting stemware as if nothing out of the ordinary had just happened. "Narrow or wide? Tapered or straight?" she asked, holding up a selection of glasses.

"Narrow," Jenny answered based on Kay's preferences. "That one will be perfect." She pointed to an elegant crystal flute quite unlike one she'd choose for herself.

For the next little while, she forced herself to ignore the uncomplicated patterns she preferred in favor of the intricately designed glassware and utensils that would appeal most to her cousin. As she made each choice, Alicia built the place setting piece-by-piece so that, by the time Jenny picked a gold-rimmed plate over one with a floral design, the entire arrangement was on display. Jenny had just snapped a few pictures for Kay when the event coordinator declared they'd done enough for one day.

"I can't thank you enough for all your help," Jenny said as they returned to the dining room. "My head is so full of information and we've made so many decisions, I think I might explode."

Alicia chuckled. "It's easier if you can spread the planning out over several months. We don't have that option in your case, though." She stood, her hands on her ample hips at the door. "So, what's on the agenda for this afternoon? A little downtime?"

As nice as that sounded, Jenny shook her head. "My schedule is jam-packed. From here, I go to Forget Me Knot Flowers. After that, Ideal Image said they could fit me in. If there's time before I meet with Janet, I'll swing by Moving Pictures to see if they can handle the videography."

"Hmmm." Alicia tapped her fingers on the door jamb. "JoJo and Roy at Ideal Image will do both video and stills, if you ask them."

"Gosh, Alicia. I had no idea." She'd scoured Ideal's website without picking up that tidy tidbit of information.

"Tell them I sent you. I'm sure they'll do their best for your wedding." Concern tightened the corners of Alicia's ever-present smile. "But don't overdo. You don't want to get too stressed out before your big day."

"If the rest of the time goes like this morning, the next couple of weeks will be a breeze." Alicia's suggestions had doused the pesky heartburn that had plagued her last night. And learning she only had to hire one photography studio would save at least an hour this afternoon. She tugged on the end of her ponytail. She might have time to stop at the bakery after all.

She waved goodbye to the event coordinator, who already had her phone pressed to her ear, talking, no doubt, with another bride. Though she understood that part of Alicia's job depended on her ability to soothe jittery nerves, Jenny thought they'd hit it off pretty well. She admired the other woman's bubbling personality and drive. Plus, Alicia had helped her in totally unexpected ways. Under different circumstances, she'd like to think they could become good friends.

She stopped herself. Unfortunately, any friendship based on a lie was bound to fall apart as soon as the truth came out. And people would learn the truth about the wedding the moment Karolyn and Chad stepped from their limo.

With that sobering thought, she slid behind the wheel of her rental car and headed for her next appointment. Traffic, which had been practically nonexistent earlier, had grown so heavy that, by the time she reached one of the town's few signals, three cars waited for the light to change. Accustomed to driving at a snail's pace on L.A.'s busy streets, she stifled a laugh when an impatient driver tapped his horn behind her. When the light finally did change, she moved through the intersection while she kept her eye out for a parking space.

Unlike her foray into town the day before, though, cars lined the streets and filled the public lot. She had nearly decided she'd have to leave her car at the B&B and walk when she spied a lone empty spot right in front of Forget Me Knot Flowers. Hardly believing her luck, Jenny pulled to the curb, gathered her portfolio and purse, and stepped from the car.

The moment her door swung open, a woman who'd been tending to racks of fresh-cut blossoms outside the florist shop lowered her watering can. She turned toward Jenny, her lively blue eyes following her every move. The smile lines bracketing her mouth deepened. A dark green smock shifted over a well-padded figure as the woman glided forward with an easy grace, her hand extended.

"Hi! Welcome to Forget Me Knot. I'm Mildred Morrey, the owner. You must be Jenny Longley. How can I help you?"

Jenny barely had time to wonder why Mildred had been waiting outside for her before the owner took her hand. Work-toughened palms met her own as she explained, "I'm here to choose the arrangements for my wedding."

"Of course, you are," Mildred grinned. "Now, don't you worry about a thing. We'll take excellent care of you here at Forget Me Knot. Why don't you come inside where it's cooler? Can I get you a cup of coffee or a glass of tea?"

"I'm fine, thanks," she said, waving the offer aside. She'd downed a bottle of water during her tour of the Captain's Cottage, in addition to her morning coffee. Any more, and she'd start to feel like a camel.

"So, tell me about your venue. Give me a sense of your vision for the wedding." Mildred steered her toward the back of the shop.

"Well, it's a small wedding. I was thinking we'd keep the flowers down to a minimum."

"No towering floral displays, then? I do love those so." Breathless, Mildred clasped her hands together.

"You and me both, but in this case I think they'd be too much." She hesitated when the shop owner's forlorn expression tempted her to add one or two. But she had a plan and, resolved to stick to it, she explained, "We're holding the ceremony on the veranda of the Captain's Cottage. With the roses as a backdrop, I'll need an arch at one end, floral swags on each row and, of course, boutonnieres and the bouquet."

At each item, Mildred's expression brightened. "And your reception?"

"It'll be across the hall. In the library. There'll be six tables, plus a head table. Everything should be understated and intimate—more like a dinner party for close friends than a formal wedding reception."

"That sounds absolutely lovely," Mildred said, her eyes brimming. "I'm sure we can come up with the perfect arrangements." She cleared her throat. "Let's go in back and see if there's anything in particular you like."

The brush of Mildred's fingers at her forearm brought a smile to Jenny's lips as she followed the shop owner down an aisle crowded with waxy green plants. An intoxicating blend of floral scents intensified when Mildred pushed open a set of swinging doors behind the sales counter. Stepping into the room, Jenny gasped. She'd visited numerous florists in L.A., but nothing there had prepared her for the sight and smell of so many different varieties of flowers crowding the two walls of glass-fronted coolers. Colors popped from arrangements in various stages of assembly on several long wooden work tables. Baskets overflowed with spools of green wire, clippers, ribbons, and bows, ranging from the deepest black to the palest of pastels. Vases in a multitude of shapes, hues, and sizes stood on shelves along the back wall.

"This," Mildred said with a flick of her wrist, "is where the magic happens. You won't need to worry about a thing. We'll handle the delivery and setup so you can concentrate on more important things, like enjoying your special day with friends and family." She smiled.

"This is quite impressive." Jenny caught a fresh wave of

her favorite scent when one of Mildred's assistants hefted a large tub of white roses from one of the glass cases.

"She's putting together the arrangements for a wedding tomorrow morning," Mildred said with a nod toward the woman who'd pulled a handful of stems from the bucket. "Speaking of which, what did you have in mind for the ceremony?"

"Hmmm. My favorite color is…" Jenny clamped her lips shut before *red* rolled off her tongue. "Rose gold," she finished. Pulling several sample swatches from her portfolio, she held them out. "Alicia helped me choose these table coverings and napkins for the reception. I'd like to use flowers that complement those colors."

"Any particular kind?"

"White hydrangeas and pink roses, I think." The flowers were two of Kay's favorites.

Mildred snapped her fingers. "I think I have just the thing." From the back wall, she selected a shallow golden vase, which she then filled with dense round blooms and a selection of pale buds. In seconds, she held up a stunning arrangement. "Something like this?"

Jenny eyed the elegant centerpiece. How Mildred had fashioned it with so little effort was beyond her, but the woman clearly had a gift. "That's perfect," she breathed.

"We'll cover the arch with them, too. We'd be happy to move it into the reception area for photographs after the ceremony."

Confident that her cousin's wedding was in good hands, Jenny warmed to the task of ordering flowers for the rest of the wedding. An hour flew by as she and the shop owner discussed the merits of carrying a cascade, rather than a hand-tied bouquet. In the end, Jenny chose a stunning posy for the bride and a similar nosegay for Karolyn's attendants. Once those decisions were made, the boutonnieres, wreaths for the aisles, and centerpieces for the tables quickly fell into place.

Happy with the results, Jenny tucked a hank of hair behind one ear. "Well, if that's everything, I'm off to my next appointment." She eyed Mildred as the shop owner ran one finger down the list of arrangements she'd ordered. Had they forgotten anything?

"This looks wonderful." Mildred laid her pen on the table. Her blue eyes shining, she stared at Jenny. "You're going to have the most beautiful wedding. The hydrangeas and roses are stunning together."

"But simple," Jenny cautioned. "Nothing too dramatic."

"Don't you worry." Mildred gave her head an agreeable shake. "Everything will be exactly as you requested. Nothing but the best for our Heart's Landing brides." She straightened, smoothing the smock she wore over black slacks. "Where are you headed next?"

Jenny checked her watch. "I have a half hour before my appointment at Ideal Images." She swallowed a frown. She could use a break, but thirty minutes wasn't enough time to stop at the bakery for coffee and a cupcake.

"I'd be happy to call the photographer for you. I saw JoJo this morning. She was planning to handle some office jobs today. She'd probably be glad to talk to you instead."

"Would you? Alicia was kind enough to get me an appointment with the caterer this afternoon, but that wasn't on my schedule, so I'm in a bit of a rush."

"Oh?" Mildred's eyebrows rose. "Who did she recommend?"

"I'm supposed to see Janet at Food Fit For A Queen. I don't know what I was thinking. In all the excitement of moving up the wedding date so we could get married here, I actually forgot about food for the reception. Alicia sorted it out with one phone call. That was pretty amazing."

"That's what we do." Mildred cupped her jaw in one hand. "We go the extra mile for our brides."

"I'm sure you hear this every day, but everyone—and I mean it, everyone—has been so kind and so helpful since I got here. I've always heard about the town's marvelous reputation for creating perfect weddings, but honestly, I wasn't sure I believed it until I saw it for myself."

And how was she repaying the help she'd been given? By lying to everyone she met. The fresh realization sent tears to her eyes. She brushed them away with her fingertips.

From out of nowhere, a tissue appeared in Mildred's hand. "There, there, now. Dry your eyes. You won't be the first bride who's been a little overwhelmed by the pressure and the planning. I'm sure you won't be the last. But you can count on us." She handed over the tissue while she sent a meaningful glance down the street. "All of us. We'll help give you the wedding of your dreams, 'cause that's what we do here in Heart's Landing."

Stepping out into the sunlight of the early afternoon a few minutes later, Jenny blinked. Mildred had meant well, but her pledge to provide the wedding of Jenny's dreams only made her feel worse for hiding the truth from the very people who were being so helpful. She drew herself straighter while she swore that everything would turn out okay. Once the shop owners realized whose wedding she'd really been planning, they'd forgive her for lying to them. She hoped. Her fingers crossed, she headed to the photography studio.

The bell over the door in the front part of the bakery jangled. Lost in the task of stirring the final drops of vanilla into the icing for tomorrow's special, Nick barely registered the sound.

"Denise? Nick? Is anyone here?"

The vaguely familiar voice reminded him that Denise had left early to take one of her last semester exams. Until Jimmy returned from a late afternoon delivery, Nick was holding down the fort alone. He gave the frosting another stir. "Just a sec," he called. Setting the bowl aside, he dusted his hands.

A cloud of confectioners' sugar rose from his fingers. The fine particles drifted down. In seconds, they coated his apron like a snowy blanket.

Clucking his tongue, Nick grabbed the damp towel he kept at hand for cases just like this. He ran it over the fabric, his lips thinning. He should never have let that salesman talk him into buying dark aprons for the shop. No matter how much his clients loved I Do Cake's chocolate-and-pink decor, the next time he gave the shop a makeover, something lighter and brighter and better suited to camouflaging an ever-present coating of sugar and flour was definitely in order.

"No problem. Take your time."

Nick stopped dead in his tracks at the sound of the voice he recognized from the day before. His pulse rate jumped the tiniest bit. The standard grin he reserved for customers widened just a tad. Afraid Jenny might leave before he had a chance to ask what had brought her to I Do Cakes, he got his feet moving again. Two seconds later, the swinging doors swished quietly behind him as he stepped into the front part of the shop. "Sorry about the wait," he said, hurrying to the counter. "I was busy in the back."

"Nothing's going to burn, is it? 'Cause that would be a real shame." She glanced over the door toward the kitchen.

"You like my cupcakes, then, I guess." Her concern rocked him back on his heels. Most customers simply wanted reassurances that he could fill their order and deliver it on time.

"They're the best I've ever tasted."

She looked so earnest, standing there in her summer dress, her wavy, dark hair framing her face. But then, he'd noticed something different about Jenny the moment he'd met her. She wasn't the typical bride who stopped in to order their wedding cake. For one thing, most of the others had a doting fiancé at their elbow. Quite often, an entire troupe of attendants surrounded the bride as she moved from tastings to fittings to days at the spa. Barring that, they had a relative on hand to provide advice, though whether they followed it or not was another matter.

But Jenny had come to Heart's Landing all by herself. A bride flying solo was such a rare thing, it stirred his curiosity. Where were the people who should be helping her plan one of the most important days of her life?

"What brings you by? Your tasting isn't until tomorrow, right?" He spared a glance at the alcove reserved for prospective brides and grooms.

"Oh, yes. I mean, no. I mean…" On the other side of the counter, Jenny adjusted the portfolio that hung from her shoulder on a strap. "Yes, my tasting is scheduled for tomorrow. I just wondered if"—she scanned the display case, hope fading from her dark eyes—"if I could buy a cupcake. But it looks like I'm too late. You've sold out?"

"Tuesday's special is salted caramel. We always sell out." Especially on days like today, when he'd started out a dozen cupcakes short.

"You don't have any? Not even one?" She frowned when he shook his head. Bending at the waist, she peered into the display case in case one had been overlooked somehow. "Were there any left over from yesterday?"

"I'm sorry. No." He gave another rueful shake of his head.

With many of the shops in town closed for the day, Mondays were usually slow. But Tuesdays made up for that with brisk sales. As a result, only a few shelf-worn cookies remained in the trays that had been filled to overflowing when he'd turned on the lights this morning.

"I guess you're right," Jenny said in a small voice. She straightened. "I'll have to come earlier next time."

Her crestfallen expression stirred every sympathetic bone in his body, but he firmed his chin. Jenny couldn't possibly know that behind the swinging doors, dozens of unfrosted cupcakes sat on cooling trays. And he couldn't tell her. It was against I Do Cake's policy to sell the next day's special. He'd established the ironclad rule himself to prevent customers from buying up their favorites ahead of time and leaving him with empty display cases.

He could make an exception for this one bride, couldn't he? He wavered on the fine edge of making a decision and finally shrugged. What good was it to be the owner if he didn't bend the rules from time to time? "Now that you mention it…"

"Yes?" Jenny stared at him, her expression hopeful.

"I was just getting ready to frost tomorrow's special, a mocha chocolate cupcake with vanilla icing. And sprinkles," he added with a smile. "If that sounds good to you—"

"Chocolate?" A dreamy expression crossed Jenny's face. The tip of her tongue swept over her lips.

Nick swallowed to make up for the fact that his mouth had gone oddly dry. He wrenched his focus off the bride who stood on the other side of his counter. Beckoning Jenny to follow, he realized he still gripped the damp rag in his hand. He tossed it under the counter while he retraced his steps to the kitchen.

Startled by his attraction to a woman he had no business having any kind of feelings toward at all, he held the swinging door open and told himself it was the gentlemanly thing to do. Jenny's burnished curls and ready smile had nothing to do with it. He felt sorry for her, that was all. She was alone in a new town, struggling to put together a wedding in less time than most brides spent choosing the flavors of their cake. And not just any wedding, but her own. To a man she'd soon promise to love and honor for the rest of her life.

A fact he'd better not forget.

With that in mind, he made sure to stand to the side as she walked past him. He could have saved himself the trouble. His arms weren't long enough to keep Jenny's light floral scent from tickling his nose. He couldn't avoid hearing her soft gasp when she spied the long lines of cupcakes arrayed on the counter.

"You'll sell all these in one day?"

"Probably before lunch." He straightened his shoulders and schooled his attitude. Jenny was simply a customer, nothing more.

"Have you always wanted to be a baker?"

Motioning her toward a nearby stool, he scooped frosting into a decorating bag while he considered the question. Though he never discussed his personal life with customers, he ached to tell her about himself. Especially if she'd return the favor. "My family moved here and opened I Do Cakes before I started grade school. I grew up in this kitchen." He pointed toward large storage bins filled with different types of flours and sugars. "My mom taught me how to read by tracing the letters in flour. I learned my numbers playing with measuring cups and spoons."

"What a wonderful childhood." Fabric rustled as Jenny slid onto the tall stool.

"It was. After high school, I went to culinary school and traveled, working as a bakery chef to beef up my resume."

He stopped to clear his throat. The rest was personal. A stranger wouldn't understand how much he loved Heart's Landing, that he wouldn't dream of living anywhere else. He felt fulfilled and happy here like he never had in New York or Rome. True, his prospects of finding someone special to share his life with were slim in a town where everyone came to get married, but he had his friends, his work, and an occasional date. None of which was any of Jenny's business.

"So, how are those wedding plans going?" he asked, not sure whether he was asking for his own benefit or just to fill the awkward silence.

"Good. Great, actually. I met with Alicia Thorn first thing this morning. We toured the grounds of the Captain's Cottage, chose the locations for the ceremony and reception, and picked out everything for the tables. When she found out I hadn't lined up a caterer, she got me an appointment with the folks at Food Fit For A Queen."

"You can't go wrong with Janet. She's fantastic." Nick chose a cupcake at random and concentrated on piping perfect circles around its top.

"That's what everyone tells me." Jenny patted a flat stomach. "It's a wonder I'm still hungry after the tasting she arranged. Every dish was better than the last one."

"Did you try the mini lobster rolls? Those are always a hit."

"They were fabulous. But so was everything else. It was too hard to choose, so I told her to serve whatever she wanted."

Nick's brow creased. For a woman with an obvious sweet tooth, Jenny's attitude toward the food for her reception was far more casual than he'd expected. Why was that? "You really did get a lot done," he said while he shook sprinkles over the swirls. To finish off the cupcake, he arranged a miniature chocolate bar on top at a jaunty angle.

"Mm-hmm. Everyone makes it so easy. I'd almost swear Alicia could read my mind. Mildred understood exactly what I wanted. And JoJo at Ideal Images was a dream to work with. She handed me a nifty little checklist and told me to choose the poses I wanted. And just like that, I crossed another item off my To Do list."

Knowing they'd be thrilled to receive a compliment from a true Heart's Landing bride, Nick made special note of the people Jenny had mentioned. When he was sure the cupcake was perfect, he slid it onto a plate, added a fork and napkin, and gently placed it on the workbench in front of her. "Your special, Madame," he said with a flourish.

Jenny stared down at the plate, her lips parted. "Oh," she breathed. "That's amazing." As if it was the hardest task she'd faced today, she wrenched her gaze from the cupcake to his and whispered her thanks.

"You're welcome." The warm spot in his chest expanded. He'd been right to bring Jenny back here and fix a cupcake just for her. The delight and wonder in her eyes rivaled the expressions he'd seen on his niece and nephew's faces on Christmas morning.

With a soft sigh, she broke off a tiny portion of the frosting. "Mmmmm. I've been waiting for this all day."

The soft sound that Jenny made sent awareness racing up and down Nick's spine. He turned aside, determined to focus on the task in front of him and not the bride in his kitchen.

He grabbed the next cupcake and slathered frosting over the top of it. Reaching for a safe topic, he asked, "So, is your fiancé leaving everything up to you?"

"Bob. Bob," she repeated as if she needed to practice saying the man's name. "He's very interested. I'm sending him pictures of everything, but his job keeps him far too busy to drill down on the details."

His brow furrowing, Nick glanced at Jenny. He would have sworn her expression soured when he mentioned her fiancé, but that had to be his imagination, didn't it? He watched as she slowly chewed another bite. He couldn't deny that she'd shown far more interest in her cupcake than the man she was going to marry.

What is going on?

The question came from out of nowhere, but once it was in his head, a troublesome thought stuck there. He considered probing deeper, trying to learn more about her relationship with the man she was about to marry. Slowly, he shook his head. The best thing for him to do was to completely avoid the subject.

Jenny was, after all, a bride-to-be. And not just any bride, but a true Heart's Landing bride. Whatever was going on between her and her fiancé, it was none of his business.

And with that, he went to work while the bride-to-be took one dainty bite after another, making her cupcake last as long as possible without any awareness of how much her presence in his bakery troubled him.

Chapter Seven

Seated at the desk in the sitting room of her well-appointed suite, Jenny ran one finger down the long list of tasks she'd needed to accomplish during her two-week stay at the bed and breakfast on Union Street. Her eyes narrowed in disbelief. She started at the top and went down the page a second time. The results didn't change.

Except for a few items she could easily knock off with a phone call or two, she'd finalized every detail of her cousin's wedding in record time. The flowers had been chosen, the venue decided, the order for a three-tiered cake placed. She'd lined up a stringed quartet to provide music for the bride as she walked down the aisle. A classic rock band would play during the reception. She'd even made reservations for the rehearsal dinner. Over her meal at Bow Tie Pasta tonight, she would finalize the menu.

Lifting her phone, she couldn't help but smile as she scrolled through photographs of the flower arrangements and the venue, the cake tasting, the band rehearsal. She'd sent so many of them to Kay's uber-private inbox that, by now, the account had to be bursting at the seams.

Oddly, though, her cousin hadn't responded to a single

email or to any of the many texts she'd sent. Concern shivered through her. Determined not to let it overwhelm her, she reassured herself that Kay was probably doing what most newly engaged women did—spending every possible second with her fiancé. Besides, Jenny had nothing to worry about. She'd followed her cousin's instructions to the letter. The result was simple, yet elegant, perfect for the understated wedding of one of Hollywood's biggest stars.

Not bad for a week's work.

She tapped her pencil on the table. Now that she'd crossed most of the items off her To Do list, she probably ought to go back to California. She should call the airlines and book a flight for the first thing in the morning. That would be the smart thing to do. She could easily arrange the rest of the details from there. If need be, she could return a week or so before the wedding to smooth out any last-minute glitches. When she got right down to it, she couldn't think of one good reason why she should stay in Heart's Landing a minute longer.

Except.

There was so much she still wanted to see and do while she was here. She hadn't stopped by The Memory Box to look at those pretty storage boxes. She'd promised to find out the significance of the statue she'd spotted in the little park at the end of Champagne Avenue—she hadn't done that yet. She hadn't taken a walk along the cliffs overlooking the ocean. Or had her fill of Nick Bell and his luscious cupcakes.

Yeah, especially that last part.

She clamped one hand over her mouth, cutting off a breathy sigh. She'd fallen into the habit of dropping by the bakery each afternoon this week. As soon as the bell rang, announcing her arrival in the bakery, Nick would emerge from the back with one of the day's specials, a cupcake he'd set aside just for her. Though she was certain he had other, more pressing business to attend to, he'd pull up a chair and keep her company while she sipped coffee and savored every bite. The caring baker seemed to understand that by the time she reached I Do Cakes, she was done, done, done with making choices for the day. Instead, they talked. About nothing, really. One day, they might swap childhood memories. On another, they'd talk about school and college. No matter what the topic, she enjoyed their time together.

Lifting her phone, she scrolled through countless pictures until her finger hovered over one of Nick at the cake tasting on Wednesday. He'd looked so impressive in his chef's whites and toque, his dark hair barely brushing his collar. She'd been hard-pressed to hide how drawn she was to him. When he'd hovered over her, seeing to her every need, she'd had to constantly remind herself that he probably did the same thing for every bride. Even then, she could barely wrench her gaze from his hands while he prepared slivers of cake for her to taste. She'd grown so thirsty that she'd gulped icy cold water between each bite.

She might as well admit it—she liked Nick more than she should. A lot more. Visiting with him in the bakery had become the highlight of her day, and it was getting harder and harder not to let her feelings for him show. But she couldn't very well confess her growing attraction to him, admit that she wanted to get to know him better. Not while she was pretending to be engaged to someone else. Or planning her wedding to the mythical Bob.

What kind of bride would do such a thing? And what kind of man would take advantage of the situation if she did? Certainly not Nick. From what she'd learned about the baker during their conversations, Nick was far too honorable to show any interest in someone else's fiancé.

If only she could tell him the truth, she'd at least find out if he felt the same way about her.

But she couldn't. She was sworn to secrecy.

She buried her head in her hands. For now, she was trapped in Karolyn's ruse, and there wasn't a single thing she could do about it. Her only hope was that one day—after the wedding, after the truth came out—maybe then, she and Nick could start over.

Except, that wasn't going to work.

Once Karolyn and Chad said their "I Do's", her sojourn in Heart's Landing would come to an abrupt end. The morning after the wedding, she'd be on a plane back to L.A. She'd probably never even see Nick again, since he lived on one coast while her job was clear across the country on the other one. She might as well face it—her friendship with him wasn't going anywhere. She'd never even have the chance to learn whether her attraction was all one-sided.

Her elbows on the table, she pressed her fingers against her eyelids and sighed. Though the decision weighed heavily on her, she picked up her phone and punched her airline's app. Now that her work here was done, heading home was the best thing she could do for herself.

Her finger hovered over the Buy Ticket button when her phone buzzed.

"Saved by the bell," she whispered, exiting the app while her cousin's image swam into focus on the screen. Jenny pressed the phone to her ear. "Hey! I've been waiting to hear from you. How's everything in Beverly Hills?"

"Good, now that I'm back." Kay gave a long-suffering

groan. "I spent the last three days filming on location in the Mojave."

Jenny's eyebrows hiked. The entire crew of Kay's latest film had spent a week on location south of Death Valley this spring. "I thought you already shot those scenes."

"We did. And the dailies looked great. But you know Guzman—he's such a perfectionist. He wanted retakes. So, there I was, stuck in the middle of the desert for three whole days. It was brutal."

"How awful for you." Jenny made the expected, sympathetic noises even though, for someone of Karolyn's stature, spending time on location wasn't exactly a hardship. Her cousin's fully stocked and air-conditioned trailer was the size of a Greyhound bus. Plus, onsite caterers provided everything from PB&J's to prime rib with all the fixings around the clock.

"Now that I'm home, I finally had a chance to study those pictures you sent. You've been, um, busy."

That was it? Busy? No gushing over the floral arrangements? No swooning over the delectable cakes? Jenny stiffened. "But?"

"But don't you think they're a little—hmmm. What's the word? Plain?"

Jenny pressed her lips together while she slowly counted to ten. Her cousin was having last-minute doubts, that was all. And no wonder. Kay didn't have her perspective. Kay hadn't walked the streets of Heart's Landing or seen other brides finalizing their wedding plans. She didn't know how much effort the thoughtful and caring shop owners had put into her last-minute wedding. Her cousin could see the photographs, sure, but no picture taken with an iPhone could possibly do justice to the intricately carved mantle in the library or the metallic threads woven into the table linens. A picture didn't carry the lingering scent of roses; it didn't convey the sweetness of the frosting or fill her mouth with the bright taste of pink champagne.

"It'll be all right," she finally soothed. "You'll see, once you get here. You'll be amazed."

"My wedding has to be special. It needs more pop and sizzle. Some pizzazz," Kay whined.

Jenny sucked in a breath and prayed for patience. "You asked for a minimum of fuss. You were quite insistent on it, in fact." She reached for the notebook that contained Kay's very specific requirements.

"I thought you'd understand that things had changed when we expanded the guest list."

Jenny's hand, like her heart, stilled. "What do you mean?"

"The guest list. We added to it."

Jenny started to shake her head but stopped, realizing she was wasting the effort on someone who couldn't see the motion. "I don't know what you're talking about."

"You didn't get my message? I sent you a text."

"No," she said, drawing out the word while she swiped over to her messages and scrolled through them. Nothing. She hadn't received a single email or text message from Kay since her arrival in Heart's Landing.

"Whatev."

Jenny didn't need to see her cousin's face to know that Kay's frustration was showing. She heard it in the exasperated tone that grated on her nerves.

"Once word of our engagement spread, Chad and I realized we hadn't given our plans enough thought. Our agents will have to be there, of course. And my Aunt Gertrude. I left her off the list before, but it wouldn't be right to exclude her now."

Jenny grabbed a pen and started jotting notes. Agents, his and hers. They'd probably bring dates, so that made four more. Kay's aging aunt on her father's side never ventured far from home without a companion. That meant another two. Since Chad had probably overlooked a couple of relatives, as well, she doubled that figure and studied the result. She'd have to add another row of chairs on the veranda, one or two more tables in the library. That wasn't so bad. Certainly not anything to cause this much drama.

She tugged on a loose strand of hair. Was this another example of Kay simply being Kay? Her cousin's flair for the dramatic was part of what made her one of Hollywood's leading ladies, but she did tend to get excited over the smallest things. The over-the-top personality could wear a little thin at times.

"Directors. Producers. The studio big shots." Kay rambled on from the other side of the country. "Altogether, it comes to just over two hundred. Better make that two-fifty in case we have to add anyone at the last minute. This *is* Hollywood," she said as if Jenny needed the reminder. "We can't afford to slight anybody."

"Two—?" Jenny's mouth dropped open. Did she dare argue with Kay? No one said no to one of Hollywood's biggest stars. Doing so was a sure-fire way to get fired. But she wasn't one of Kay's usual crowd of yes-men. She and Kay were practically sisters, and, as such, she'd always been able to tell her cousin exactly what she thought. Something she needed to do right now, before things got out of hand. She swallowed.

"Karolyn, that's impossible. You asked me to plan a small wedding for fifty guests. Intimate friends and immediate family. We can't possibly cram more than two hundred people onto the veranda. It can't be done."

"You're forgetting I rented the entire estate for the weekend," came her cousin's dry response. "I'm sure they handle weddings this large all the time." "Not on a month's notice. No." She stopped to catch her breath. "Make that three weeks' notice. Besides, everything's been arranged. I've put down deposits on the catering, the flowers, the wedding flavors. Just like you wanted. What you're asking is impossible. To say nothing of how much it will cost to change things this late in the game." Thinking of the enormous expense, she rubbed her forehead. "You need to stick to the original plan."

"It's too late for that. The invitations have already gone out."

"How? What?" Jenny stammered. She eyed the addressed envelopes stacked on one corner of her desk. The ones she'd slaved over for hours, writing out names and addresses in her finest penmanship. With a fountain pen, no less. To protect her cousin's privacy, she'd scheduled a courier service to hand-deliver each of the fifty invitations next week.

"Chad's assistant says it's practically criminal to use paper when it's so easy to do everything online. He designed a beautiful e-vite for our guests and sent them out days ago. The RSVP's are pouring in. No one wants to miss the wedding of the decade."

A hollow, tapping sound echoed in the ear Jenny had pressed against the phone. Recognizing the signal that her cousin had grown weary of the conversation and had begun drumming her nails on the closest hard surface, she massaged her temples. Tension tightened its grip on her head with every drum roll.

"So you see, the arrangements you've made simply won't do. Be a doll and fix things, won't you?"

Why should I?

Jenny pressed one hand over a stomach that had turned positively mutinous. She hadn't created this mess. She'd planned perfectly wonderful, simple wedding, exactly what her cousin had asked her to do. It wasn't her fault Karolyn and Chad had changed everything at the last minute. She didn't have to go along with their plans. She could walk out right now and go…

Her thoughts skidded to a halt. Where could she go?

Not back to L.A. If she didn't deliver on her promise to throw the wedding of Kay's dreams—cousin or not—she could forget about her job as the personal assistant to one of the top names in Hollywood. She wouldn't land another job like it, either. Her reputation as a top-notch assistant would be shot once word got around that she'd quit in the middle of the planning stages of Kay's wedding. And word would get around. In L.A., it always did. After that, no one else would hire her.

Then, there was the problem of where she'd live. She couldn't expect to keep her room in Kay's stately Beverly Hills mansion. Though she had savings to fall back on, her money wouldn't last long in L.A.'s high-rent district. Which meant she'd have no choice but to return to her aunt's farm in Pennsylvania to lick her wounds while she hunted for a new job, a new career.

But no. That wouldn't work. Not once her cousin heaped the blame for the wrecked wedding on her shoulders, it wouldn't. Of course, Kay would conveniently fail to mention her own part in the disaster, or how she'd quadrupled the guest list less than a month before the ceremony. As much as her aunt loved her, Jenny doubted she'd even have the chance to tell her side of things before Aunt Maggie shut the door in her face. After all her aunt had done for her—taking her in after her parents had died, making sure she got a college education and a thousand other things—was that how she wanted things to end up between them?

Jenny inhaled. Air shuddered through her. Kay hadn't left her much choice. She had to do what her cousin wanted. No matter how much she hated the thought of starting over from scratch—of becoming another of the dreaded yes-men—she had to give Kay the wedding she wanted.

Her lips pursed as she considered the problem from every angle. Her breathing eased when she realized there was one upside to the new plan. Now that the invitations were in the mail, it'd be impossible to keep the bride's identity a secret anymore. Shop and business owners throughout Heart's Landing were bound to be upset by the adjustments she'd have to make to the wedding plans. But their resistance would melt away like butter once they found out who was really tying the knot at The Captain's Cottage. Everyone wanted to be associated with a superstar like Karolyn Karter.

Best of all, she wouldn't have to tell any more lies.

Her heart beat a little faster at the thought of telling Nick the truth. Would the tall, handsome baker be relieved to learn she wasn't engaged after all?

As if she was reading her mind, Kay's voice whispered into her ear. "No one knows it's my wedding you're planning, right?"

"No," she mumbled, though by now, word had most certainly leaked to the tabloids.

"Good. Mum's the word. Remember, you promised. I'm sure everyone's talking about where we're holding the ceremony and making guesses, but Chad and I are still keeping things under wraps."

"How is that even possible?" Her hand clenched until her nails bit into her palms. Deliberately, she flexed her fingers. "You sent out invitations."

"Chad thought of that. He's chartered a jet. No one will know where we're headed until we're in the air. Wasn't that smart?"

"Smart," Jenny whispered. Unlike her, who had to be the dumbest person in the world for letting her cousin trap her into planning the wedding of the decade for the second time around.

When Kay didn't respond, she lowered the phone from her ear. The screen had gone dark, her cousin undoubtedly on to other things. She reached for her purse and the stash of Tylenol she kept on hand for the times when Kay's shenanigans got the best of her. This was one of those times.

She should have known better than to believe her cousin would go through with an understated, but elegant, wedding for family and a few close friends. Kay had always been the flamboyant one, the one who thrived on attention. Even when they'd been kids. Like a lot of children, they'd put on plays in the backyard on summer afternoons. But unlike their friends, Kay had lugged wooden pallets home from the nearby lumber yard and assembled them into a sturdy stage. She'd created elaborate costumes using jewelry from the discount store and clothes she'd salvaged from the ragbag. And she had always, always, been the star of the show. So, no. Nothing about Hollywood's darling of the screen had ever been simple. Nothing at all.

Why had she ever thought Kay's wedding would be any different?

Nick gave a firm tug on the handle on the rear door of I Do Cake's delivery van. Hinges in need of a good oiling complained bitterly. He resisted the urge to head to the nearest car repair shop. Instead, he ran a smoothing hand over the plaid shirt he'd changed into because someone had once told him it brought out the blue in his eyes. His shirttail had worked loose. He tucked it into the waist of his best jeans.

He frowned down at himself. Why was he so on edge? The delivery van received regular service. He usually didn't give his clothes much more than a passing thought. Clean and reasonably wrinkle-free, and he was good to go. But tonight—what made tonight different?

He wasn't trying to impress anyone. Leastways, not anyone at the Union Street B&B. Just because he'd volunteered to take their usual Wednesday delivery off Jimmy's hands, that didn't mean he expected to run into any particular bride-to-be. Not him. Why, he probably wouldn't even see Jenny this evening. She was most likely out on the town, doing whatever engaged women did on one of a dwindling number of nights before they said "I do."

If, on the off chance, he did spot her at the bed and breakfast, he'd simply greet her like he would any casual friend and be on his way. Because friendship was all he felt for her.

All he could ever feel for another man's bride.

Even if, other than the rock on the third finger of her left hand, she showed none of the normal signs of someone in love. No long, lingering looks at her fiancé's picture. No constant flow of texts during her initial consultation about her wedding cake. No whispered phone calls and emails to interrupt the tasting. Not so much as a single reference to the love of her life unless she was asked a direct question about the man.

Not that it mattered to him any more than a dash of vanilla. No, siree. Whatever was going on—or not going on—between Jenny and her fiancé, it was absolutely none of his business. More to the point, it had to stay that way. She was a bride-to-be, something it would do well for him to keep in mind. As much as he enjoyed her sassy wit, as much as he liked seeing her face light up whenever she took her first taste of one of his cupcakes, Jenny was engaged to someone else.

And he needed to keep his distance.

Satisfied that he'd reached the only possible decision, he hefted the two heavy trays destined for the kitchen in the Union Street Bed and Breakfast and headed up the sidewalk to the rear entrance.

The sound of sniffles reached him before he made it to the first of the steps leading to the back porch. Instantly, the hairs on the back of his neck sprang to attention. Had someone fallen and hurt themselves? Did they need his help?

Listening intently, he stilled his breathing. No. Those weren't cries of pain. At least, not physical pain. He was nearly certain a woman huddled in the shadowy recesses of the porch. From the sound of things, she'd had her heart broken.

Torn between the urge to run as far away as he could get from crying women and an insistent desire to rush forward, he hesitated. The weeping continued. It twisted his gut until he couldn't take it anymore. He had to help. Or at least try.

He mounted the stairs two a time. Quietly, he lowered the trays of baked goods to one of the tables that dotted the wide back porch. He approached the corner on soundless feet. As he neared the rattan couch protected by a screen of climbing ivy, his heart lurched.

Jenny sat, her head buried in the crook of one arm, her dark ponytail draped over her shoulder. With her feet tucked under her, she looked so small and forlorn, he couldn't help being drawn to the petite brunette. Unable to stop himself, he took another step closer.

"Jenny," he whispered, his voice low and steady, "what's wrong?"

"Oh. I—" Her head popped up out of her arms.

Nick studied the wet cheeks she blotted with a balled-up tissue. Had her fiancé been in an accident? Had he called off the wedding? Whatever had happened, it had to be bad. Jenny was one of the most spirited women he'd ever met. After all, she'd planned an entire wedding by herself in a matter of days. "Did something happen to Bob?"

"Who?" She swiped her nose. "Oh." She blew gently. "No. Bob's fine. Everything's fine."

That couldn't be true. If everything was hunky dory, she wouldn't be sitting alone in the dark, bawling her eyes out. He grabbed a handful of tissues from a nearby box and handed them across. "You might need these."

"Thanks." She pressed the thin sheets to her face.

Wanting to give her a minute to pull herself together, he motioned toward the trays. "Let me drop those off in the kitchen. I'll be right back, and we can talk about what upset you. Can I get you something? A cup of tea? A glass of water?"

"Coffee would be nice. It's going to be a long night," she said on a heavy sigh.

His heart clenched at the brokenness in her voice. The longing to help solve her problem—whatever it was—intensified.

In the kitchen, he slid the trays onto the shelf reserved

for baked goods, then hurriedly sloshed coffee from a carafe into two heavy mugs. He'd watched Jenny fix her own coffee in the bakery often enough that he knew she took hers milky sweet. He hesitated only a second before stirring two spoons of sugar and a large dollop of cream into one of the mugs while he left his black. Carrying both, he returned to the porch.

By the time the screened door slapped shut behind him, Jenny sat upright in her corner of the couch. When she gripped the mug he handed her, her fingers were steady enough. She'd banished her tears, though she hadn't been able to erase the puffiness around her eyes. Relieved to see her doing better, he lowered himself onto the other cushion on the couch.

"So, what happened? Did you and Bob have a fight or something?" he asked over the rim of his coffee cup.

"No. Nothing like that." She stared down. "It's nothing, really. There's some stuff I have to do, and I let it get the best of me for a minute there. I was feeling sorry for myself, I guess." She blew across her coffee. "Pity—party of one," she called, sounding exactly like a restaurant hostess.

Though her answer extinguished the tiny flame of hope that she and her fiancé had called off the wedding, he had to smile at her ability to poke fun at herself. "Considering everything you've accomplished in the past few days, I'd say you deserved a good cry. You certainly wouldn't be the first bride to have a little meltdown." Though he longed to pat her on the shoulder, the light glinting off the ring on her finger helped him resist the urge.

"I know. And I shouldn't complain. It's just…"

"It's just what?" he prompted.

She stood. Abandoning her cup to the coffee table, she

moved to the porch railing. "I need to make some changes to the wedding plans, and I'm afraid it's going to upset everyone in town. They've been so nice."

Is that all? He went to stand beside her. "I'll let you in on a little secret—brides change their minds. It happens so often around here, we're kind of used to it. Everyone just wants you to have a perfect wedding—a Heart's Landing wedding. We kind of pride ourselves on that."

"Yeah, I get that." She swayed, her bare shoulder brushing against his shirt.

The slight touch sent his pulse racing. He stilled. This couldn't happen. He couldn't be attracted to her. Swallowing hard, he stared into the darkness beyond the porch. A warm breeze fanned his face. It carried the salty tang of the ocean, mixed with the light scent of Jenny's perfume. Or maybe the smell came from flowers from the B&B's garden. He wasn't sure it mattered. "These changes, you need to make them?"

"Yes. But—"

"No buts. If you need to adjust the plans, just do it." He managed to angle his body away from hers, a move that backfired when he ended up facing her. Staring down at Jenny's pert features, he cleared his throat. "Why waste the energy fighting it? If you know it's something you're going to end up doing anyway, you'll save yourself a lot of time and heartache if you just tackle it head on."

Jenny's dark eyes brightened. "That's exactly what I needed to hear. Thanks, Nick."

"Now, how can I help?"

She reached out. Her fingers barely made contact with his arm, but her touch sent tingles of awareness coursing through him. He tried telling himself that his was nothing more than the usual reaction of a man in the presence of a pretty woman, but he knew there was more to it than that. He was dangerously close to crossing a line with Jenny, something he absolutely wouldn't do. Not even if she wanted him to.

"Well." Jenny tilted her head and issued a challenge. "I need a bigger cake."

"No problem." He could easily add another layer to her wedding cake, maybe even two. But something in Jenny's expression triggered a flicker of doubt. Had he just committed to more than he could deliver? Not exactly sure he was going to like her answer, he ventured a tentative, "How much bigger?"

Her gaze cut to one side. "Enough to serve two hundred and fifty guests."

"Whooo." Air whistled through his teeth. That was a *lot* more cake.

"I've been having second thoughts about the flavor, too."

"Okay," he said bracing himself. He'd known about Jenny's soft spot for chocolate since the day they met. But to craft a cake in her favorite flavor for that many people would require extra work. He'd need to dowels to support each layer of the dense, heavy…

"Almond," she said firmly.

Not chocolate? He frowned, recalling how her nose had scrunched up during the tasting. She didn't even like almond.

"And it needs more, uh."

"More what?" he asked, growing more perplexed by the moment.

"It needs more pizzazz."

He took a breath. Of all the brides he'd worked with over the years, he would have sworn Jenny was the least likely to want a lavishly decorated cake. But maybe he didn't know her as well as he thought he did. "I could pipe the icing to match the pattern of your dress," he suggested, certain she'd consider the idea too ornate. "And add a cascade of rose-gold flowers down one side."

A happy smile teased Jenny's lips. "Yes. That's it. Exactly."

Nick folded his arms across his chest. They said no good deed went unpunished. He should have known offering advice to a bride-to-be would come back to haunt him. This larger, fancier cake would take the better part of a week to create. Worse, just when he'd sworn he'd keep his distance from Jenny, he'd have to work closely with her on a whole new design. "I'll get on it first thing in the morning," he promised on his way to the stairs.

"I'll stop by in the afternoon so we can go over the particulars. Save me a cupcake?"

Though he automatically agreed, he shook his head as he headed for the van. His determination to keep his distance from Jenny had lasted less than two minutes before she'd melted it, just like she'd melted his heart.

Chapter Eight

Jenny trudged down Bridal Carriage Way. A couple traveling in the opposite direction neared her on the shaded sidewalk. Arm-in-arm, they laughed at some private joke. The man brushed an airy kiss through the woman's hair and snugged her the tiniest bit closer to his side.

Jenny mustered a weary smile. Someday, she wanted a love like that. Someday. But not in Heart's Landing. And not today.

Today, she needed to fix a wedding that had grown more complicated than she'd ever imagined. Nick's reaction to the expanded guest list had been so blasé, so matter-of-fact, that she'd been sure everyone else in town would take the news in stride as well. She'd been wrong about that. But for very different reasons than she'd expected.

Jenny had never been good at lying. But with as much practice as she'd had since her arrival in her favorite wedding destination, she'd gotten better at it. Too much better. She hated how, at their meeting this morning, Alicia hadn't so much as lifted a doubtful eyebrow when she heard Jenny's convoluted tale of how she'd been pressured into adding to the guest list by her future mother-in-law. She was certain

Alicia had only had her best interests at heart when she'd advised Jenny to stick to her guns and plan the wedding of her dreams, not anyone else's. The tears that had shimmered in Alicia's eyes when Jenny explained that the invitations had already been mailed nearly caused her to blurt out the truth. The whole truth. She hadn't, though. And in the end, they'd agreed to serve cocktails and hors d'oeuvres on the veranda, but hold the ceremony and reception in the grand ballroom.

Her heart heavy with the weight of everything she had to do to protect Kay's secret, Jenny had headed to Forget Me Knot next. There, Mildred had been visibly shaken by the news of the larger wedding. When she couldn't locate enough hydrangeas to top an additional twenty-five tables and suggested using white freesia and large garden roses as substitutes, the florist had actually trembled like a leaf in a storm. Though Jenny thought the new combination was sheer perfection, she'd spent the better part of an hour reassuring Mildred that she trusted the woman's judgment.

Wasn't that supposed to work the other way around?

Jenny ran her fingers through her hair. She had just reached the crosswalk when a horse and buggy trotted past, carrying another lucky bride to the church at the end of the street. Unable to wrench her eyes from the passing vehicle, she tapped her foot in time with the horse's hooves.

"One day," she whispered. One day, she'd take her own carriage ride through the center of town. She pinched her lower lip between two fingers. She'd set her heart on a Heart's Landing wedding, and now she was in the middle of planning one. Only it was for someone else.

A passerby cleared his throat. The noise startled her. She blinked slowly and took a breath. Around her, people went about their business. Shoppers ducked in and out of stores.

Couples meandered down the sidewalks hand in hand. She glanced toward the end of the street. The space in front of the church stood vacant, the ringing sound of hooves against the pavement long since faded. She shook herself. She had no business standing here mooning after some other bride's carriage ride when she still had so much left to do.

Straightening, she waited for the opening bars of "The Wedding March." When they played, she crossed the street. A few minutes later, she stepped into Favors Galore, ready to face her next task in finalizing the plans for her cousin's big day.

The instant she crossed the store's threshold, the smell of rich chocolate engulfed her. Pausing to get her bearings, she drank in the candy-scented air. The wonderful aroma drew her, and she made her way down the wide aisle that cut through the center of the shop. Shelves on the left housed party favors that ran the gamut from matchbooks to cookie tins. An extensive wine collection lined wooden shelves on the right. At the back of the store, tray after tray of hand-crafted chocolates filled a low display case.

"Hi, Jenny!" One of a matching set of willowy, raven-haired twins looked up from the marble slab balanced in one of her hands. Arrayed in circles, hand-crafted candies dotted the stone platter.

"Hey…" Uncertain whether she was talking to Alexis or Ashley, Jenny halted.

"Are you here to check on your order? I think Alexis said we received the last of it this morning."

Thankful for the hint, Jenny nodded. "That, and I need to add to it, Ashley."

"More guests?" The fine sprinkling of freckles across the twin's nose crinkled, and a teasing grin lifted the corners of her mouth. "Did you find out your cousin-once-removed decided to bring a plus-one to your wedding? They always do. Don't worry. We'll take care of it. But first, you have to try one of these." She held out the tray. "It's a brand-new flavor. A pistachio cream dipped in white chocolate with a sprinkling of toasted coconut."

"That sounds divine." This was a lot more than a plus-one situation, but she couldn't ignore how the sights and smells made her mouth water. Taking one of the candies, Jenny bit into the creamy confection. The flavors melted on her tongue. "Heavenly," she pronounced.

"That's just the reaction I was hoping for. Let me put the rest of these away, and we'll get you taken care of." Using tongs, Ashley placed the last of the candies on a plain white tray, slid it forward in the display case, and closed the glass door.

Jenny shifted her weight from one foot to another. Unlike the other shop owners she'd dealt with today, Ashley didn't seem a bit perturbed by her news. Maybe changing her order wasn't going to be as big a deal as she'd feared. She took a calming breath while the store's co-owner moved to the cash register.

Taking an iPad out from underneath the counter, Ashley swiped through several forms until she reached the one she wanted. "Okay. It says here you ordered fifty bottles of the Saba Palm Napa Valley Chardonnay, fifty four-piece boxes filled with pink truffles wrapped in gold foil, along with gray tissue and rose-toned gift bags. So, how many more do you need? Ten? Twenty?"

Jenny gulped. She'd been wrong to let her guard down. Word of her expanded guest list apparently hadn't spread this far. "I, um, need another two hundred."

"Wow!" Ashley's hazel eyes widened. "That's a whole lot more. How did that happen?"

"Turns out…" Jenny's mouth went so dry her tongue stuck to the roof. She grimaced. So much for the idea that the more she repeated the story she'd concocted to explain Kay's change of plans, the easier it'd get to tell. Signaling that she needed a sec, she swigged water from the bottle she carried in her purse and took a steadying breath. "Sorry about that," she said when she was able to speak again. For once, she was glad she hadn't worn her hair up today. Thick and long, it hid the heat that burned the back of her neck. "Turns out, my future mother-in-law has invited everyone in her family to our wedding. Without saying a word about it to me or my fiancé. I'd probably still be in the dark if one of his relatives hadn't asked where we were registered."

"So, you need another two hundred?" Ashley's voice thinned. She held up a finger. "I'll be right back." Leaving her iPad on the counter, she race-walked to the end of the counter and disappeared through the door that led to the back of the shop. She emerged seconds later with an equally flustered twin at her side.

Jenny's gaze shifted between the tall women who wore matching pink smocks over identical pairs of black jeans. With their long, straight hair worn in the same blunt cut, she doubted their own mother could tell them apart. How was she supposed to know which twin was which?

"Ashley tells me you need to increase your order?"

Imagining the tricks the pair had pulled on teachers and friends when they were younger, Jenny nodded. "Yes. I'll need two hundred more of, well, everything."

In tandem, concerned frowns bowed two pairs of heart-shaped lips.

Jenny focused on the woman who'd spoken last. "Is that a problem, Alexis?"

"Sadly, yes." A sheaf of jet black fell forward onto Alexis's face. She brushed it back with a shaky hand. "I don't want to say we can't fill your order, but we don't have that much of the Sabal Palm in stock. I'll need to call our distributor to see if he can get it to us in time."

"The pink chocolate is a special-order item. I don't have enough of that to fill another two hundred boxes, and I *know* I can't get it in time for your wedding." Ashley pressed her fingers to her eyes. "I'm so sorry."

Jenny took in the twins' mournful expressions. Squaring her shoulders, she summoned a can-do attitude. "What if you"—she pointed to Alexis—"call your distributor and check out the wine situation while Ashley and I come up with different candies for the boxes? Sound good?"

Their mouths open, the twins stared at each other for a long minute. Slowly, they turned to face her.

"You'd do that?" Alexis started.

"And you're not upset?" Ashley added.

Jenny grinned. "A good friend recently reminded me that I'd be better off trying to find a solution than wasting my time and energy crying over a problem." She tapped her finger on the glass countertop. If one more store owner melted down over Kay's wedding, she might just cross-stitch Nick's advice on pillow cases and hand them to shopkeepers throughout the town. "So, what do you say? Can we do this?" She pointed to the phone Alexis held.

While one twin tucked herself into a corner to make the call, Jenny aimed a pointed look at the other. "So, what can you make in time for the wedding?"

"Truffles are still the best bet. You can have them dipped

in either white or dark chocolate. Or some of each." Grabbing an empty tray, Ashley filled it as she worked her way down the display case. "This chocolate cardamom is to die for. So's the mascarpone. Customers rave about our white cranberry cashew. And this new pistachio." When she finished, she presented her eight favorites.

Jenny didn't have to taste the raspberry cream with pink sprinkles. She chose it to go in the box simply because it matched Kay's color scheme. After sampling the others, she chose the three she liked the best to round out the selection. "I think that'll do it," she said, happy with the choices. Not that she could have chosen wrong. Mouth-watering goodness filled each hand-crafted chocolate in Favors Galore.

She turned expectantly when Alexis stepped away from the wall where she'd huddled with the phone pressed against her ear. One glimpse of the girl's blotchy face told Jenny things with the supplier hadn't gone well. "Whatever it is, we'll deal with it," she said, forcing a confident air into her tone.

"He can't get the 2016 Chardonnay. If we had another month, maybe," she announced in the hushed tone suitable for a funeral.

"But we don't," Jenny reminded her. Kay's wedding was less than three weeks away. That, at least, hadn't changed.

"He faxed this list." Alexis handed across a single sheet of paper. "It's everything he can get in the quantities you need."

Alexis looked so sad that Jenny had to work hard at resisting the urge to pat the young woman's arm. Doubling down on her own determination to make light of the situation, she pushed an extra measure of self-confidence into her voice. "We're going to make this work. I'm sure we can find something just as good." She traced a finger down the list until she reached a particularly fruity moscato. "This." She pointed to a wine that had been served at a recent cocktail party. It had tasted like summer in a bottle. "This one right here will be fine."

"Really?"

"I'm positive." Pricey enough to impress their guests, it would pair well with the chocolates.

Relief flooded Alexis' face. "Okay. Where should we deliver all this?"

Jenny's forehead scrunched. "To the bed and breakfast on Union Street, I guess. I want to assemble the gift bags myself."

Well, not exactly. But the labels she planned to put on the bottles had been engraved with the names of the happy couple. She couldn't let anyone see them before the wedding.

"Whoa!" Ashley or Alexis—she'd lost track again—held up a hand. "Do you know how much space you'll need?"

Jenny slowly blinked. Assembling the gift bags hadn't seemed like such a big deal when there were only fifty guests. But now there were more. A lot more. She ran the numbers. Twenty cases of wine would fill her suite from the floor to the ceiling. "I guess that won't work, huh?"

The twins shook their heads in unison. "Then there's the not-so-little problem of moving the bags when you're finished with them. How are you going to get them to the Captain's Cottage?"

She closed her eyes. The odds were against her having enough time between now and the wedding to center a label on each bottle, place it in a gift bag along with a box of chocolates, and finish it off with tissue and ribbon. Plus, she'd still have to run up and down the stairs of the B&B like a madwoman, ferrying the completed favors to the trunk of her car. She'd need a truck to do the job right.

She nibbled her lower lip while she considered possible solutions to the problem. Settling on one, she texted Alicia. When the event planner not only agreed but seemed delighted with the opportunity to help out, Jenny gave the twins two thumbs up.

"Have everything delivered to the Captain's Cottage," she said at last. The supplies could remain there until right before the wedding. After the rehearsal dinner, she'd press Kay and her bridal party into an assembly line. Working together, they'd finish the job in no time. She stifled a laugh at the thought of Karolyn and Chad applying labels and stuffing tissue into bags. But, seriously, it was the least the two of them could do for their own wedding.

The very least.

Walking out of Favors Galore a few minutes later, Jenny patted herself on the back. Things in the gift shop hadn't gone as smoothly as she'd hoped, but she'd been able to put Nick's advice to good use. As a result, no one had broken down in tears or fainted dead away at the thought of adding another two hundred guests. From where she stood, that was progress.

But thinking of Nick sent her gaze straight toward I Do Cakes. After the chocolates she'd sampled at Flavors Galore, she'd more than met her sugar quota for the day. Still, the bakery drew her like a magnet, and she couldn't quite explain why.

Not true, she corrected as images of a certain dark-haired baker flashed before her.

Her face warmed. She'd been thinking about Nick a lot. Certainly more than she should, considering the short time they'd known each other, and how everything he thought he knew about her was a lie. When he'd stopped by the bed and breakfast last night, she'd had the strangest desire to confide in him. To tell him the real reason for her presence in Heart's Landing.

She couldn't, of course. Not until after the wedding. Once the truth was out and everyone understood why the identity of the real bride and groom had been such a closely guarded secret, maybe then she and Nick could be friends. Maybe even more than that. But not now. For the next three weeks, no one could find out she was only pretending to be a bride-to-be. Not even Nick.

Nick eyed the ingredients arrayed on the wooden counter in the kitchen of I Do Cakes. Bins of dark cocoa, flour, and sugar lined up behind a box of baking soda on his left. On his right, a carafe of bitter coffee joined a bowl of cracked eggs and a tin of oil. In between lay the rest of the equipment and flavorings he required for the chocolate-and-peanut-butter cupcakes that were his second biggest seller. Would Jenny enjoy this cupcake as much as she had his others? He hoped so. Satisfied that everything he needed was within reach, he measured flour into the hand-cranked sifter he'd inherited from his grandmother and turned the handle. He nodded his approval at the white shower that drifted down into the mixing bowl.

The bakery's back door swung open and shut. Hurried footsteps announced the arrival of his assistant well before Jimmy burst into the room. The freckles across his pale face nearly popping with excitement, the young man snagged an unfrosted cookie from a cooling tray. "Have you heard the news?"

Nick smiled. Jimmy loved gossip almost as much as he loved baking. "I've been buried in work all day. How'd the delivery to Food Fit For A Queen go?" He'd received their urgent request for hundreds of miniature pie crusts this morning.

"Fine." Jimmy shrugged, as if the entire staff hadn't spent the day on the project. "But you should have been there. It was pandemonium. One of Janet's clients hired her to cater a dinner for fifty. Only, this morning, she sprang the news that the guest list had jumped to two hundred fifty. That's why they needed the mini-crusts. For the hors d'oeuvres. To serve that many, they'll make them up ahead and stick 'em in the freezer."

Nick gulped. Guilt burned in his stomach and moved up until he was reasonably sure it tinted his face. It stood to reason that Jenny's larger guest list would impact most of the other shop owners in town. The moment she'd told him about needing a bigger cake, he should have made some phone calls.

"She's going to make it, though, isn't she?" Janet and her staff had built a sterling reputation for meeting the needs of every bride. For special brides like Jenny, they tried even harder.

"Yeah, I guess." Jimmy helped himself to another cookie. "Just makes you wonder why a bride would do that, doesn't it?"

"Add last-minute guests?" Nick sifted cocoa powder into the mix. He'd asked that question a time or two himself.

"Mm-hmm."

"I guess there could be any number of reasons. Pressure

from parents who've attended the weddings of their friends' children and want them to share their own kid's happy day." Somehow that didn't sound right for Jenny, though. "A fiancé who insists on inviting his business associates." He hoped that wasn't the case.

"All I know is when I get married, I'm gonna have a big party at the Captain's Cottage and invite every one of my friends. We'll have us the best seafood boil you ever saw. Five years later, people will still be saying, 'Remember when Jimmy got married?'"

"You have everything planned out, do you?" Nick suspected the boy's fiancée would have a thing or two to say about his ideas, and none of it good. He hadn't met a single bride yet who said, *Oh, yes! Let's cover my beautiful gown with a huge bib adorned with a bright red lobster.*

Jimmy nodded. "I know what I want."

"You run that past your girlfriend, did you?"

"Nah. I don't have anyone special yet. But when I do, she'll want what I want."

"I hope you're right about that." That was every man's wish, wasn't it? That the girl of his dreams would share his likes and dislikes.

"What do you want for your wedding, boss? You've thought about it, haven't you?"

Living in Heart's Landing, how could he not? He took his time, measuring the baking soda into the mixture while he considered his answer. Roses or orchids? A seated meal or a buffet line? Dashing through a hailstorm of dried rice or a cloud of bubbles? There were pros and cons to each. In the ten years he'd been in charge of I Do Cakes, he'd seen what worked and what didn't at scores of weddings. When all was said and done, the good ones shared one thing in common—

a man and a woman so deeply in love that they wanted to spend the rest of their lives together. The rest was just icing on the cake.

"As long as we love each other, nothing else matters," he said, giving the eggs an extra stir.

"That, and the cake," Jimmy nodded.

"It wouldn't be much of a wedding without cake," he acknowledged with a grin that faded as quickly as it appeared. Thoughts of wedding cakes had led to thoughts of brides, and suddenly, he'd come full circle back to Jenny. He dumped the last of the ingredients into the mix and shook his head as he stirred. Why she'd chosen almond for her wedding when her eyes practically glazed over every time she bit into one of his chocolate cupcakes was beyond him. But then again, he didn't understand much of what made Jenny tick. She was different from every other bride he'd ever met. As different as almond was from chocolate. And, heaven help him, that only made him want to get to know her better.

Chapter Nine

At the end of another long week of meetings and appointments, Jenny kicked her shoes off as she walked into her suite in the B&B. She took a fortifying sip of the coffee she'd picked up at her last stop, dropped into the comfortable Queen Anne chair by the window, and scanned the ever-changing To Do list. Though it had taken a full week of hand-holding and commiserating, and though there'd been compromises at nearly every turn, she'd gotten everything back on track for Kay's wedding. The venue was set, the flowers on order, the favors arranged. Janet at Food Fit For A Queen had sworn she and her staff were up to the challenge of feeding the additional guests on her list. The elaborately tiered cake Nick had designed for the reception was guaranteed to garner nearly as many oohs and aahs as the bride herself.

Jenny sighed in relief. Once she checked off this final item on her To Do list, she'd treat herself to a nice, long soak and a couple of chapters in the romance novel she'd wanted to read. Tomorrow, she'd spend her final day seeing the sights in Heart's Landing before she jetted back to the West Coast. Lifting her phone, she speed-dialed her cousin.

On the other side of the country, Kay answered with a cheery, "Oh, Jenny, thank goodness it's you. I was just getting ready to call you."

"Oh?" Kay rarely called unless she needed something. Instinctively, Jenny braced for bad news.

In the breathy voice Kay used on camera, she whispered, "I need you to make a teensy-weensy change in the plans for the wedding."

Jenny checked the calendar she'd referred to so often, it might as well be imprinted on her brain. With two weeks left before the big day, even the simplest of changes could have serious repercussions. "What now?" she asked, struggling to keep her voice low and even.

"You know how careful I am about my appearance. Especially in public."

"Yes." Kay took hours to dress and put on makeup for something as uncomplicated as a trip to the store for a carton of milk. Not that she drank milk. Or even knew where the nearest grocery store was located.

"Well, Chad absolutely refuses to wear light gray. He says it washes out his skin tone. Even though I tried to explain that it was too late to change the color of his tux, he went with charcoal. So, I need you to swap out the linens for a darker shade to match. I'm texting you the color right now."

Jenny's hand dropped. She stared up at the ceiling, half expecting it to crash down on her. This latest change of plans had "disaster" written all over it. From the tuxes to the floral displays, from the place settings to the bridal bouquet, she had carefully color-coordinated everything according to Kay's wishes. This *teensy-weensy* change would ripple through the entire wedding.

"Are you there? Jenny?"

When the ceiling remained firmly in place, she sighed and pressed the phone to her ear. "Anything else?"

"Funny you should ask," Kay said with a humorless laugh. "I've been reading a few bridal magazines."

Now? Now that she had done everything Kay had asked her to do?

"Pink is so last year. Peach is much fresher and brighter. It'd look better against the dark gray, too. What do you think?"

"It would, but…" Jenny's voice sputtered to a halt. What she thought wasn't fit for words. She needed a moment to regroup.

"But what, sweetie? Don't you want my wedding to be perfect?"

"Yes, of course, but—"

"Well, that settles it, then."

"It's. Not. That. Easy." Jenny bit off the words. She'd just spent an entire week convincing shop owners and vendors from one end of town to the other to accommodate Karolyn's extra guests. How was she supposed to go back to those same people now and tell them to change the entire color scheme?

Kay's tone turned petulant. "I thought Heart's Landing promised a perfect wedding for every bride."

"It does," Jenny said, trying her best to make her cousin listen to reason. "But there comes a point where even the most willing supplier has had enough." Over the past two weeks, she'd worked so closely with the local shopkeepers that she considered them her friends. She valued those relationships, but these new changes would put them to the test.

"Are you telling me I can't have the wedding of my dreams there?"

"I—hmm, no." Jenny back-pedaled. She'd seen what

happened when others had failed to give the star what she wanted, when she wanted it. It wasn't pretty. One push, one whisper of disagreement, and Kay might post a thoughtless comment about Heart's Landing on social media.

She wouldn't set out to deliberately cause any harm. That wasn't the kind of person Kay was. Before the awards and accolades had started pouring in, her cousin had been one of the most selfless people Jenny had ever known. Why, Kay hadn't once complained about having to share her room when Jenny had moved in with her new family. Throughout their teen years, the two of them had been closer than sisters. They'd shared everything from clothes and make-up to shoes and school supplies.

But then, Kay had won back-to-back Oscars, and her popularity had skyrocketed. Despite that, she had no concept of how much clout she wielded. For someone with a half million followers on Twitter alone, one negative tweet was all it would take to damage the town's reputation.

Jenny straightened. She couldn't let that happen. Everyone from the sales clerks behind the counters to the shop owners themselves had gone out of their way to help her put this wedding together. She couldn't let their hard work and effort go to waste. "No. That's not what I'm saying," she said, pulling out all the stops and using the soothing tone that had always calmed Kay in the past. "I'm saying, let's be sure this is what you want this time. Charcoal and peach. You're one-hundred-percent positive."

"Yes, absolutely."

"And two hundred fifty guests. No more? No less?" She held her breath.

"No, that's it."

"All right. I'll stay here and straighten everything out." So much for heading back to California anytime soon. It would take days—and lots of sweet-talking—to make the changes Kay wanted. She checked her watch. She might be able to reach Mildred this evening, but getting in touch with Alicia at the Captain's Cottage would have to wait until tomorrow. She crossed her fingers and prayed Ashley and Alexis hadn't placed their order for the gift bags and tissue yet.

"Are we done now?" A quiet tap-tap signaled Kay's waning interest.

"There's one more thing," Jenny rushed. "The baker suggested piping the icing on your cake in the same pattern as the lace on your gown. How about snapping a picture and texting it to me?"

"I'll be sure to get one while we're at Madame Eleanor's tomorrow."

"Oh? Do you have a fitting?" Jenny leaned forward. Last year, Kay had spent hours discussing the pros and cons of which dress to wear to the Academy Awards, but her cousin hadn't so much as mentioned her wedding gown in any of the recent texts that had flown back and forth between them. Suddenly, she wanted to hear every detail. "What did you choose—a ball gown or a mermaid? What kind of fabric? Who's the designer?"

"You're so sweet to ask, but we're just getting started. I had Mom move the appointment while I was shooting in the Mojave."

"So, you haven't started looking yet?" Her stomach sank. Kay had only one thing to do for her wedding and, with the date only two weeks away, she hadn't done it.

"You worry too much," Kay said, her laugh disarming. "Don't. I'm sure Mom and I will find the perfect dress tomorrow."

Jenny propped her chin in her hand. She hoped her cousin was right. But based on how things had gone so far, she didn't like the odds.

Nick whistled a jaunty tune on his way down the stairs from his apartment over the bakery. Today was going to be fantastic. And why shouldn't it be? He got such joy out of helping brides plan their wedding cakes, and there were three new tastings on the today's schedule. Before the first of them, he'd kick the morning off by whipping up a batch of lemon cream cupcakes that would make the whole bakery smell like sunshine. Then, this afternoon, he'd get started on the cake for Jenny's wedding.

At the bottom of the stairs, he stepped into the still-darkened bakery. A lingering trace of vinegar tickled his nose, reassurance that the cleaning crew had worked their magic overnight. As if to confirm it, a ray of light from one of the streetlamps bounced off spotlessly clean counters and floors. He unlocked the back door and left it ajar for the morning crew who would soon trickle in. Crossing to the massive built-in ovens, he twisted dials and smiled at the hiss of gas followed by a soft whoosh as the ovens began heating for the day's bake. Coffee was next on the agenda, and he stepped through the swinging doors into the storefront.

The first streaks of sunlight turned low-hanging clouds pink and gold on the other side of the bakery's picture windows. One by one, the old-fashioned street lights along Bridal Carriage Way winked out. Above the sidewalks, birds stirred in the trees. As the first of them flew off in search of breakfast, his smile deepened. The peaceful quiet of an early morning in the bakery was the best time of all. Not that he didn't enjoy the hustle and bustle of customers and staff.

Speaking of which, when the doors did open, people would want their coffee. At the brewing station, he'd just dumped the first pre-measured packet of grounds into the waiting basket when something rapped on the window behind him.

"Pesky bird," he muttered with a grin. It wasn't unusual for one or more of them to attack their own reflection in the glass. Ignoring the noise for the moment, he added water to the brewing chamber. Once coffee began to trickle into the carafe, he turned, intending to shoo the bird away before it hurt itself.

But the bird, if it had been there in the first place, had flown off. In its place stood Mildred Morrey.

His grin twisted into a wry grimace. No matter how he wracked his brain, he couldn't think of a single good reason for the florist to show up on his doorstep before dawn. His footsteps growing heavy, he cut across the room. Before he reached the entrance, at least a half-dozen other figures emerged out of the darkness to stand beside Mildred. Nick's misgivings deepened as he held the door open for his unexpected guests.

"Nick." Mildred's gray curls bobbed as she moved past him with a curt nod.

Alicia, Janet, Alexis, and Ashley filed past next. Marybeth and Matt joined the others. Next came Paula and Ames. His cousin JoJo and her videographer Roy brought up the rear. Nick's heart sank when the group spread out on chairs in the dining area. Whatever problem had brought them to the bakery this early in the morning, they planned on staying until the situation was resolved.

"Coffee, anyone?"

When a chorus of, "No, thanks," rose in answer, he poured a fortifying cup for himself and carried it into the dining area.

Propping one shoulder against the wall, he faced the group. "What's going on?"

Every eye in the room focused on Mildred. From a nearby chair, Janet nodded encouragement. The soft-spoken florist cleared her throat. "This Jennifer Longley person is out of control."

Jenny?

Nodding, the others murmured their agreement.

Nick swigged coffee. His regret was instantaneous when the scalding-hot brew burned his mouth. He swallowed. Heat traveled down his throat to his stomach.

"Don't get me wrong. She's a sweetheart. We all love her to death, but..." Mildred took a breath. "She said she was planning a small wedding. Fifty people, she said. With only four weeks' notice, that was hard enough, but we did it. Everything was settled, including some of the prettiest floral arrangements I've ever designed. Hydrangeas and roses. It would have been lovely." Mildred gave her head a sad shake.

"Then, with no warning, her guest list jumped to two-fifty," Alicia put in. "I could hardly object, since she'd rented the entire cottage for the weekend. But honestly, who does that?"

JoJo jumped in before Alicia finished. "We couldn't let a true Heart's Landing bride down, so we did our best. But there were problems, added expenses. I had to bring in an extra photographer."

Mildred picked up the thread of conversation. "I called

every florist within three states. There just aren't enough hydrangeas available this time of year."

Alexis frowned. "My distributor didn't have that much wine in stock."

"My pastry and sous chefs are pulling their hair out," Janet added quietly.

"I understand." He'd had his share of difficulties with Jenny's order, too. "A cake for fifty on short notice is bad enough, but two-fifty? I'll be piping the icing right up to the start of the ceremony." Uncertain whether the coffee or the thought of Jenny walking down the aisle caused his throat to tighten, he rubbed his neck.

"To her credit, she's one of the nicest people I've ever met," Ashley pointed out.

"And she's willing to compromise," Alexis chimed in.

"Freesia and garden roses instead of hydrangeas." Mildred's displeasure showed in a glum nod.

"When we couldn't get enough chardonnay, she chose a nice moscato," Alexis said. "Instead of plated service, we'll set things up buffet-style. That'll save both time and money."

"Well, that's good, isn't it?" Not sure where his friends were going with this conversation, Nick blew on his coffee and waited.

"She's almost *too* accommodating," Alexis pointed out. "Most brides at least quibble over substitutions."

Ashley recited a few of the more memorable moments. "Some do a lot more than that. We've all dealt with bridal tears after a well-meaning father poured the wrong champagne for the first toast, or the butterflies released after the reception had a different shade of blue wings than she expected."

Around the room, heads bobbed.

Nick took a careful sip. He'd had a similar experience when Jenny had stopped by to review his ideas for her larger wedding cake. His first design had been a tower. The second, a multi-tiered layout. The difference was so great, he'd expected her to object. When she'd only shrugged aside his concerns, her reaction had left him scratching his head. "At least everything's resolved now."

"You'd think so." Mildred glanced up from the hands she'd folded in her lap. "But she called me at home last night. Now she wants to change the entire color scheme. Two weeks before the wedding."

"She what?" Nick pushed himself away from the wall. "I just saw her yesterday afternoon. She didn't say a thing." His gaze circled the room. The stricken faces of his friends and coworkers stared back at him.

"None of the flowers I've ordered will work now." Mildred's voice shook.

"I'll have to get new table linens." Alicia's frown deepened.

Ashley leaned forward, her elbows on the table. "We had to cancel our orders for gift bags and tissue and get replacements."

Mildred cleared her throat. "Never in the history of Heart's Landing have we failed to come through for one of our brides. Some have stretched us to our limits, but none as far as this one. I'm telling you, Nick, this is the last straw. We'll do what we can to accommodate this new color scheme, but nothing more. She can't make another change. Not one."

In a tone he'd never heard JoJo use before, his cousin said, "You've got to take her in hand."

"Me?" Coffee sloshed over the rim of his cup. He pressed his back against the wall. "Why me?"

"You found her," Janet pointed out. The others in the

room murmured their agreement. "You're the one who identified her as a true Heart's Landing Bride. She's your responsibility."

"We can't afford to mess this up, Nick. We promise a perfect wedding for every bride who comes here. That goes double for someone like Jenny. Only, she has to do her part. You've got to make sure she does."

The need to defend Jenny coursed through him as he mopped the floor with a napkin he grabbed from a table dispenser. "You know it's not entirely her fault." He pitched the damp paper into a nearby trash can. "Her fiancé's mother invited those extra people to the wedding. The groom is the one who insists that nothing but the best will do." From what he knew of Jenny, none of the pomp and extravagance were her idea.

"Then, she needs to stiffen her spine and tell them to back off," insisted Alicia. "What kind of marriage will the girl have if she constantly gives in to everyone else's demands?"

What kind indeed?

"Look, Nick, you're the only one here who has some sway with her. We need you to take her under your wing, so to speak. Talk her out of making any new changes before her big day."

"If you don't," Janet warned, "we'll end up disappointing her. Then, whether her demands were unrealistic or not, it won't matter. Word will spread. I don't have to tell you what it'll do to us if our image gets tarnished."

One way or another, the livelihood of every person in Heart's Landing depended on the town's A+ reputation. He had to do his part to protect it.

Nick lowered his coffee cup to the table and pulled himself erect. "I'll do the best I can," he promised.

Roy lingered behind when the others filed through the door. "You got a sec?" the videographer asked.

"Just about that long," Nick answered. He'd already had a hectic schedule before his friends had dropped this new responsibility in his lap.

"Well, I was thinking about when my sister got married last year. The closer we got to the big day, the more harried she was. I don't know if she'd have made it, except my brother-in-law made her get away from it all for a day or two. They took a break from the wedding stuff and spent the weekend in Newport."

Nick's eyebrows rose. A wry grimace twisted his lips. "You aren't seriously suggesting I whisk Jenny off on a weekend getaway, are you?" His friends and fellow business owners already held him accountable for their wayward bride. They'd run him out of town on a rail if he ran off with her.

"Nah. Nothing like that." Roy punched Nick's arm. "But you could take her sight-seeing. There are plenty of historic places around here."

Nick rubbed his chin. Roy's suggestion was worth considering. "I'll come up with something," he said, wondering how he'd gotten himself into this mess and, better still, how he'd get out of it.

Just exactly how was he supposed to keep his distance from Jenny when he'd promised to take the wishy-washy bride-to-be under his wing?

Chapter Ten

People moved through the hallway outside Jenny's door, their footsteps clattering on the hardwood floors. Laughter punctuated the low murmur of conversation that drifted up the stairs from the lobby where guests gathered for an early evening wedding. Late arrivals added to the volume until, finally, doors opened and closed. Gravel crunched beneath shoes and high heels as the party moved around the house to the parking lot. Standing at her window, Jenny caught snatches of banter while the departing group piled into waiting cars. Another round of doors slammed. Engines revved. And then they were gone, off to the wedding that had been the main subject of conversation around the breakfast table this morning.

Her stomach issued a low grumble. Not that the hunger surprised her. Nervous about having to break the distressing news of Kay's latest round of changes to her friends in town, she'd only downed a couple of cups of coffee before heading out this morning. Lunchtime had come and gone before she'd visited half the shops, where her excuse for switching colors sounded thin, even to her. With no other option, she'd kept at it. By the time she'd convinced the last store owner to adjust their order, Open signs were being flipped to Closed, and doors were being locked from one end of Bridal Carriage to the other.

Her shoulders slumped, she'd picked her slow way along the emptying sidewalks to her temporary home. Her spirits had plummeted lower still when she reached the bed and breakfast and spotted the group gathering in the lobby. Unable to think about anyone's wedding—and certainly not the one she was planning—she'd rushed upstairs. No sooner had she reached her room, though, when her stomach sent up a protest.

Too late, she realized she'd spent the entire day rushing from one place to another without a single break. She hadn't even stopped by I Do Cakes to see Nick and have her daily cupcake.

Nick.

What would he think of her when he found out the real reason she'd come to Heart's Landing? Would he understand her need for subterfuge? Would everyone else? For what had to be the hundredth time, she sighed. She'd told herself over and over that once everyone learned Karolyn Karter was the real bride, they'd be so excited they'd forgive her for misleading them. She crossed her fingers and hoped she was right about that.

However the future played out, though, food was her immediate priority. She needed to make some plans for dinner. Unfortunately, dining anywhere within a five-mile radius was out of the question. The odds were too high that she'd run into Mildred or Alicia or any of the dozen other shop owners whose paths she'd crossed today. She supposed she could drive to a nearby town and grab a bite, but that idea didn't hold much appeal, either. She liked it here. She wanted to stay here.

She really did, didn't she?

Startled by the sudden realization of how much Heart's Landing had come to feel like home in such a short time, she rubbed her eyes. But her thoughts didn't change. The idea that if it was up to her, she'd stay here forever, wrapped around her like a warm shawl.

She glanced out the window at garden behind the bed and breakfast. Slowly, she shook her head. Moving here wasn't in the cards. She'd need a job, and her cousin's indecisiveness had tainted her. Thanks to Kay's insistence on changing everything from the size of the wedding to the color of the napkins, she doubted anyone in town believed she could make a decision and stick to it. Who would hire someone that weak?

Besides, she didn't have much of a resume. She'd had one job—as Kay's personal assistant—since college. She doubted many people here needed one of those. As for her dream of opening her own event planning business, that was only a pipe dream. Without the cachet of Kay's name to back her up, how was she supposed to strike out on her own?

She brushed a sudden dampness from her eyes. She needed to forget the idea of moving to Heart's Landing. Her life, her job was in L.A.

Which still left the matter of her empty stomach. Resigned to ordering in a pizza, she thumbed through a phone directory she'd found in the nightstand. Number in hand, she reached for her phone. She'd barely picked it up when a soft chime signaled an incoming call. Her hand froze.

Was it Kay again with more *suggestions* that sounded more like marching orders?

Her heart thudded. She couldn't, simply couldn't, alter

the plans for the wedding one more time. Not only would shop owners all over town revolt, but disaster—which had held off so far—was sure to strike if anything else changed. Holding her breath, barely daring to breathe, she refused to budge until the phone stopped bleating.

When the last chime finally faded, her chest expanded. The welcome feeling of relief didn't last long. Before she had a chance to place her order for a veggie pizza, the phone shimmied to the beat of an incoming text. Her lips pursed. She squeezed her eyes shut.

When she opened them, the I Do Cakes icon on her screen put her worries on a temporary hold. Nick was in the lobby. He wondered if she could meet him downstairs. Suddenly, the need to fill her empty stomach didn't seem quite so pressing.

Be right down, she texted back, doing her best to deny the shiver of anticipation that danced across her midsection.

She brushed a hand over her wrinkled pencil skirt and frowned. The idea of appearing rumpled and worn out when Nick saw her held as much appeal as a cup of lukewarm coffee. As quickly as she could, she stepped into slim-fitting jeans and tugged her favorite T-shirt over her head. She ran a brush through her hair, then captured the unruly mess into a ponytail and checked her reflection in the full-length mirror. She still looked like someone who'd spent the day putting out fires, but she'd managed to hide some of her defeat behind a bit of blush and a dab of lip gloss. For now, it would have to do. Seconds later, her sandals made slapping noises on the treads as she hustled down the stairs to the spot where Nick stood talking with Marybeth.

"Hey," he said, his smile widening as he noticed her approach

"Hey, yourself. I didn't know you were stopping by. Did I forget we were meeting tonight?" Even as she said the words, she knew she hadn't. She might have trouble remembering every detail of her fake fiancé's bio, but she'd never forget a date with Nick, no matter how impromptu. Being around him made her feel warm and fuzzy inside, a feeling she liked a lot more than she had any right to.

But why was that?

Sure, he'd been blessed with movie-star good looks—dark, wavy hair that ended just below a chiseled jaw, deep-set eyes and broad shoulders. But, living in Hollywood, she'd grown used to seeing handsome men wherever she went. No, her attraction to him went more than skin deep. He made her feel good about herself. Not only that, but he'd offered her his friendship, and, at the rate problems were mounting around Kay's wedding, she needed all the friends she could get.

"You didn't come by the bakery this afternoon, so I thought I'd bring you a treat." He held out a dome-shaped container.

Her stomach gurgled happily. "You don't know how much I need this. Thanks."

"Can't have you wasting away before your big day, can we?"

At Nick's innocent reminder of the impending nuptials—and the secrets she'd been keeping since she'd arrived in town—her temporary good mood plummeted. "I guess not," she murmured. It was bad enough that she had to hide the truth from everyone else. Keeping it from him was killing her.

"Heart's Landing is lucky to have you, Nick," Marybeth interrupted. "You take such good care of our guests. Here"—

she held out her hand for the box—"let me dish that up for you. How about some coffee or tea to go with it?"

"Thanks. That'd be nice. Tea for me, if you don't mind." Hoping she didn't come across as desperate for company as she felt, Jenny raised her eyes to meet Nick's. "Can you stay for a bit?"

"Why not?" A lock of dark hair fell onto Nick's forehead. He brushed it back. "If you don't mind, Marybeth, I'll take a cup of tea, too."

Without another word, Marybeth darted into the kitchen.

Alone with Nick, Jenny shifted her weight from one foot to the other. At last, she led them to a pair of matching overstuffed chairs by the fireplace. As she crossed the room that had been so crowded earlier she said, "You should have been here twenty minutes ago. It was standing room only in here."

"The Smith wedding." Nick dropped down on a chair across from her.

Her brow furrowed. "You didn't have to be there?" From what he'd told her during their tasting, he usually handled I Do Cake's deliveries and stayed through the reception.

"Not this time. They didn't want a cake."

"No?" Jenny tucked her feet under her. "Who does that?"

"It takes all kinds." Nick crossed his ankles. "Some people just don't like it."

"They obviously haven't had yours," she interjected.

"There is that," Nick agreed with a slow smile. "It doesn't happen often, but some brides serve a traditional dessert or pie instead. At one reception, the family constructed a wall covered with pegs. No one could figure out what it was for until one of the groomsmen showed up with boxes and boxes of donuts. He hung three or four from every post and let the guests grab them as they walked by."

"Oh, no, they didn't." At the thought of guests simply helping themselves, Jenny gave her head a firm shake. "I won't be doing that at my wedding."

Or Karolyn's, either.

"Too many sticky fingers for me." Nick gave an exaggerated shudder.

She laughed, finally at ease for the first time all day. Nick filled her in on the happenings at the bakery—a tasting that had gone particularly well that morning, a new bread recipe Jimmy planned to try. As if she didn't want to intrude, Marybeth stopped by long enough to settle a tray of tea things on the table between them and left. Jenny filled their cups while Nick finished telling a funny story about his apprentice. While he took his first sip, she eyed the yellow cupcake on her plate. Lemon wasn't her favorite, but with her stomach issuing strict orders to stop being picky and feed it, she forked up a small bite. Like fresh-squeezed citrus on a summer day, flavor burst onto her tongue and dissolved, leaving behind the memory of tart sweetness.

"This is the best," she said, forking up another bite.

Across from her, Nick acknowledged the praise by crossing one leg over the other. "Glad you like it."

All too soon, she stared down at the empty plate and wished for more.

Nick, who'd fallen silent while she ate, cleared his throat. "I heard you stopped by Forget Me Knot this morning. Mildred said something about wanting different flowers for the wedding?"

Despite the slight rise at the end of his sentence, Nick's creased forehead told her he'd already received word of the recent spate of changes to the plans. Her fork rattled against the edge of the plate. She set it aside and folded her hands in her lap. "Yeah. My, um, fiancé changed his mind about wearing a light gray tux. He chose a charcoal one instead. That one choice affected every decision I'd made about the wedding."

"I'm sure no one was happy about that."

Nick's sympathetic tone didn't make her feel one iota less miserable. "No one could have been more upset about it than I was, if that helps any."

One of his eyebrows lifted. "If it bothered you so much, why'd you go along with it?"

"I didn't have much choice, did I?" Suddenly, the pressure of the last few weeks closed in on her. Unable to sit still, she rose and paced the room. "I had a *plan*," she said, emphasizing the word. "It was a good one. This was going to be a small, simple wedding. I should never have gone along with inviting those extra guests. That was my first mistake. After that, things got out of control. Now, the wedding is two weeks away, and everything is a mess. The whole town hates me. Alicia's mad at me. There's so much to do, and I'm running out of time." Her breath hitched, a sure sign she was moments away from falling apart.

At some point during her tirade, Nick must have come to his feet, because he stepped in front of her, his hands out like two stop signs. "Whoa, now. You want to know what I think?"

"What?" She stumbled to a halt in front of him.

"I think you need to get out from under the pressure for a while. Do something to take your mind off the wedding."

Stricken, she pressed a hand over her heart. "I can't. I need to get everything organized. I need a new plan. There's a million other things left to do, too. I haven't even decided on a restaurant for the rehearsal dinner." Though she'd raved about Bow Tie Pasta, Kay had recently expressed a preference for steak and lobster.

Nick dropped his hands. "Things won't get done any faster if you're exhausted. You've been going at this full-steam for weeks. You should take a day off. Refresh and recharge. When you go back to it, you'll be amazed at how much faster everything will fall into place."

So far, every piece of advice Nick had given her had been exactly what she needed. This time, he was right again. She certainly could use a break. The last few days, the weight of Karolyn's wedding had pressed done on her heavier than ever.

Nick lifted one shoulder in a nonchalant shrug. "What do you say? You'll take tomorrow off? Do something fun?"

"Any suggestions?" She was fresh out of ideas.

"Have you done any sightseeing while you've been here? Newport's not too far away. There's lots to do and see there."

As wonderful as that sounded, she couldn't quite justify the hour-long drive to the town famous for summer cottages the size of castles. "Isn't there something a little closer?"

"Lots," Nick said with a confidence she found endearing. "There's a great path along the cliffs. Very scenic. I bet Marybeth would lend you a bike—she has several for the guests' use. How's that sound? Fresh air and sunshine? It's better than being cooped up in your room all day, don't you think?"

"I don't know, Nick." She'd always done the responsible thing. In this case, that meant keeping her nose to the grindstone, though every fiber in her being urged her to try something different. "I have so much work to do." Even as she said the words, she felt her resistance weaken.

Nick stared past her shoulder for a long minute. "In two weeks, over two hundred people are going to show up for your wedding. At least a few of them are going to have some free time on their hands. You should probably look into activities for them, right?"

He had a point there. Chad had arranged for a private jet to ferry friends and family to and from L.A., but the ever-changing wedding plans had kept her so busy that she hadn't given a moment's thought to what Kay's guests were supposed to do while they were in town. They couldn't very well spend the day wandering the halls of the Captain's Cottage. She supposed she really ought to check out the local scenery and leisure activities. But going for a long, solitary bike ride over terrain she wasn't familiar with had the earmarks of an accident waiting to happen. She had a sudden thought and tipped her head to gauge Nick's reaction. "I'll go, but only if you come with me."

"Hmmm. I'll have to think about that for a minute." Nick's gaze dropped to his shoe laces.

Jenny stifled a grin. She hadn't missed the interest that flared in his eyes. "Now who has to adjust the plan?" she prodded.

"Touché," he said, meeting her gaze once more.

At the easy smile that spread across Nick's face, warmth spread from the tips of her toes to her face. "So you'll come?"

He edged the tiniest bit closer. "We'll make a day of it."

"Great," she said, aware of his breath on her cheek. She swallowed slowly. *Get a grip.* Nick was a friend, nothing more. "The B&B has box lunches. I'll ask Marybeth to fix a couple for us."

The moment stretched out between them. She fought a sudden urge to trace one finger along Nick's jaw, but stopped herself before the thought went any further. She had a part to play, one that didn't include falling for a handsome baker, no matter how attracted she was to him. As far Nick knew, she was engaged to be married to another man. Now wasn't the time for him to find out anything else.

A door slammed somewhere in the back of the house. The noise helped stiffen her spine. She shuffled back a step.

Nick glanced out the window; the sky had darkened. "I'd better get going," he said without moving.

"Yeah. Me, too." Aware of how much she needed to put distance between them before she did something she'd regret, she turned toward the stairs. "I'd better go now." She ran halfway up the first flight. There, she paused for a quick glance over her shoulder. When Nick remained exactly where he'd been standing, another dose of warmth spread through her chest.

"I'll see you tomorrow," she called. Then, willing herself not to take a second look, she hurried toward her room while she regretted every step.

Chapter Eleven

By nine thirty the next morning, chocolate smeared the starched white aprons of the two I Do Cakes assistant bakers who divided the duties of rolling, cutting, and decorating dozens of cookies for the display cases. Seated at his own table in a corner of the room, their expert piped ribbons of royal icing onto a nearly finished wedding cake. Meanwhile, at yet another workstation, Jimmy carefully added proofed yeast to the ingredients he'd measured into the gigantic bowl of a commercial mixer.

Nick inhaled the typical smells of the bakery on a busy morning. "Be sure and save me a loaf of that onion bread," he called on his way past Jimmy's station. Baked to golden perfection, the fragrant loaves were a house favorite.

"Will do, boss." Surprise registered on the assistant's face as Jimmy studied Nick's casual clothes. "You going somewhere?"

"Yep." He grinned.

"But what about tomorrow's special?" Jimmy looked around as if afraid he might be on the receiving end of another assignment.

Nick grinned. "All done and in the cooler." He adjusted

the blanket roll he'd slung over one shoulder. He'd set the alarm for three AM and had been hard at work ever since. "I'll have my phone. If anything comes up while I'm gone, call me. Otherwise, I'll see you in the morning."

"You don't say." The young baker dumped the last of the yeast into the enormous bowl. "Been a while since you took a day off. Have a good time."

"I'm looking forward to it."

But he shouldn't be, should he?

The question slowed his exit. The idea of keeping a wayward bride out of trouble hardly qualified as relaxing. Yet, he wanted to spend time with Jenny more than he cared to admit, though he couldn't really put his finger on the reason. She was pretty, he'd give her that much. Hair that was neither black nor brown but an intriguing in-between brushed her shoulders. It fell in soft curls around her face and framed a pair of sparkling brown eyes. The hollows beneath her high cheekbones led to full lips, which frequently widened into a warm smile that made his heart beat faster.

But she wasn't his type. Whereas the women he usually dated tended to be tall and leggy, Jenny packed just the right amount of curves into a compact figure. The top of her head would barely brush his collarbone if he pulled her into an embrace.

Not that he ever intended to get that close to her.

Though his thoughts sometimes drifted in that direction, each time they did, he firmly lassoed them and brought them right back where they belonged. No, he and Jenny had merely struck up a friendship. They were just two ordinary people who enjoyed each other's company. And as long as she planned to walk down the aisle in front of friends and family at the end of the month, there couldn't ever be anything more between them. Lately, he'd been spending extra time with her because the entire town had practically begged him to. That he looked forward to seeing her was just a bonus.

He was still working hard to convince himself he had the best of intentions where Jenny was concerned when he stepped into the alley behind I Do Cakes. There, he stopped to empty his pockets at the bowls he filled before he locked up each night. The faint noise of a handful of treats landing in the metal containers caught the attention of a calico cat that peered at him behind the dumpster. Nick made a friendly clicking noise with his tongue. When the stray only darted out of sight, he shrugged and headed in the opposite direction. Eventually, the young kitty would get used to him.

Striding along Bridal Carriage Way, he spotted an extraordinary amount of activity on the street. Shopkeepers who rarely stepped beyond their front doors during the busy morning rush found excuses to step outside and greet him. He waved to Mildred, who watered the flowers outside Forget Me Knot. The florist returned the gesture with an approving glance. At Food Fit For A Queen, Janet stopped sweeping the sidewalk long enough to wish him well as he passed by.

Aware that word of his plans for the day must have spread, he shoved his hands in his pockets. That was one of the drawbacks of small-town life—everyone knew your business.

Not that he didn't appreciate the good wishes. They served as a reminder that the reputation of Heart's Landing rested on his shoulders. Much as he liked Jenny, much as he'd even begun to suspect that her upcoming marriage to Bob wasn't actually a match made in heaven, he'd agreed to get her through the next couple of weeks with a minimum of fuss. He intended to do just that and nothing else.

Reassured that he was doing the right thing for all the

right reasons, he trotted up the steps to the front entrance of the B&B. The house was quiet, the lobby and living room empty. He passed through the dining area. Freshly brewed coffee, baskets of sweet rolls, and stacks of clean plates sat untouched. Not a surprise. The Smith wedding had lasted into the wee hours. The guests were probably sleeping in. In the kitchen, he spied a large picnic basket. Reading Jenny's name on the tag, he resisted the urge to peek inside while he toted it out the back door to the pair of bikes that stood in the bike rack. He'd just finished strapping the heavy basket on the back of his when Jenny pushed open the screen door.

She rushed down the steps wearing a bright yellow T-shirt above longish shorts. He swallowed at the sight of trim calves that tapered down to slim ankles and forced his gaze down to the pair of sturdy athletic shoes that snugged her feet. Swallowing an appreciative whistle, he thumbed the bell on the bike handle. The clapper struck a cheery note.

"Sorry I'm late," she offered with a grin.

Nick concentrated on checking out the bike chain and brakes. "No hurry. I just got here myself. You ready to go?"

"Ready." Beneath the hair she'd slicked into a ponytail, she'd scrubbed her face clean. Her smile brightened as she gave him the thumbs-up sign. She stuck her ever-present cell phone in a back pocket and mounted the bike with an easy grace he hadn't expected.

Riding single-file, they hugged the side of the road until they were well out of Heart's Landing. Another five minutes took them to the bike path that led north along the rugged coastline. Not sure how far they'd go, he coasted around the corner and headed toward a spot where they could stop for lunch. He glanced over one shoulder at Jenny. Clearly in her element, she zipped along smoothly.

Once they were on the wide path, he motioned her forward until they were riding abreast. "You look like you know what you're doing. You ride much in L.A.?"

"Whenever I can. There are some pretty bike paths throughout the city and up into the foothills. I mostly get out in the winter. Summers are too hot." She expertly steered around a downed branch. "How about yourself?"

"The opposite. Too much snow on the ground in the winter here. I manage to get out once or twice a week from spring through fall. It clears out the cobwebs."

"It does that." She scanned the path ahead. "I can't get over how green everything is. It's so different from the West Coast. Southern California is dry and dusty."

Nick studied the land, trying to view it through the eyes of someone who'd never been here before. On his right, beyond the waves that pounded against the rocky shore, the ocean stretched to the horizon. To his left, tall oaks and maples trees dappled the path with shade. Broken by clumps of wildflowers that bloomed in riotous colors, grass carpeted the ground.

"You're right," he said slowly, thinking about how lucky he was to live in a place where tulips and bulbs burst through the ground each spring. Rhode Island's summers were lush with new life. Its crisp fall days were filled with rich oranges and deep reds. Even the snowy winter had its own stark beauty. "I guess I've taken it for granted." In the distance, a gleaming white house sat on a small hill overlooking the ocean. Nick pedaled slower. "That's the Captain's Cottage up ahead."

Jenny took in the rear of the sprawling, three-story home. "Where we're holding the wedding. I'm not sure I would have recognized it from this angle."

Nick's eyes narrowed. Jenny, unlike most brides, had always referred to *the* wedding rather than *her* wedding. Filing the subtle difference away to discuss at another time, he filled her in on a little bit of the local history. "It's a pretty big house. It had to be. The original owners, Captain Thaddeus Heart and his wife Mary, had a dozen children."

"Whew," Jenny whistled while she gave her head a slow, careful shake. "I've always wanted children, but maybe not quite *that* many."

Nick rubbed one finger over his upper lip. He'd often thought of having kids of his own—children he could pass the tricks of the baking trade down to like his father had with him. Cooing infants who'd wrap him around their little fingers on Day One and never let go. Toddlers to bounce on his knee and play hide-and-seek with. There'd be flag football games on crisp fall afternoons. Dance recitals, science fairs, and spelling bees.

His front wheel struck a pebble. The bike wobbled. He cleared his throat and forced his thoughts back to the present. What had he and Jenny been talking about? Oh yeah, Thaddeus Heart. "There's a statue of him in a small park off Champagne Avenue. Have you seen it?"

"Just a glimpse," Jenny nodded. "I wondered who it was."

"The one and only Captain. He was an eighteenth-century seafarer, the founder of Heart's Landing. We know he plied the seas from Boston to the West Indies. Being a ship's captain was a hard life in those days. There were pirates to battle, bad storms, and weeks when the winds didn't blow. They say his love for Mary was what kept him going. For a dozen years or more, he dropped anchor in Heart's Cove in time for her birthday each year. He'd stay for a few months, long enough to have repairs made to his ship and take on provisions. And make a baby." He laughed, self-conscious. "Rumor has it, every year he brought his wife the same present, a heart he'd chiseled out of stone during the long, lonely nights at sea."

Curiosity colored Jenny's dark eyes. "I've seen one or two on buildings downtown. That's what you're talking about?"

Grinning, Nick nodded. "The very same. Mary and the Captain had them mounted around town. Most of them still exist."

"Paula showed us a broken one the day we visited Something Old, Something New."

"That she did." He nodded as they pedaled past the rear of the mansion. Leaning to one side, he pointed to a white fence atop the mansard roof. "See that railing? That's the widow's walk. They say you could see Mary standing there, day or night, fair weather or foul, watching for her husband's sails for a month before his ship was due. One year, a hurricane struck just before Captain Thaddeus made port. With the winds howling and the storm raging around her, Mary refused to come down. She had the servants lash her to the one of the posts until the storm passed and the good captain made it home. If you're interested, ask Alicia to take you up on the roof. You can still see the path she wore in the slate."

He caught the sidelong glance Jenny shot him. It was clear she wasn't entirely sure about that part of the story. Nick shrugged. He hadn't actually read Mary's diary himself, but children for miles around grew up listening to tales of Mary and Thaddeus's love for one another. And every fall, the town put on a pageant reenacting how the captain had battled the hurricane in order to drop anchor in Heart's Landing in time for Mary's birthday. For the past five years, Jason and his cousin Evelyn had played the lead roles.

In the distance, the land jutted out toward the sea. Nick pointed in that general direction. "The cove where Captain Thaddeus made landing is a mile or so on the other side of that point. We can stop there for lunch, if you're up to it."

"I'm game if you are." With a challenging grin, Jenny stood on her pedals.

"Let's ride, then," Nick called.

As they raced along the bike path, the ground began a slow rise. Crashing onto the rocks, the sea fell away on their right. By the time they reached the top and braked to a stop, the steep cliffs rose high above the ocean.

"Oh, it's beautiful." Jenny peered over her handlebars. Below them, waves rolled smoothly onto the sandy beach of a small harbor. "Can we get down there?"

"Captain Thaddeus had his men cut stairs into the rocks. A few years ago, the town added handrails. The salt spray makes the steps slippery, but it's safe enough if you're careful." The beach was a popular spot on weekends. Today, though, they had it to themselves. "I'll get the picnic basket."

Leaving the bikes behind, they filed down to the snug harbor, where Jenny immediately shucked off her shoes. Scrunching her toes in the sugary sand, she giggled. "I haven't done this in ages."

He ran a hand over his chin. Planning a wedding was a nerve-wracking experience under normal circumstances. Jenny's had tried the patience of everyone in town. After working on the design for her latest wedding cake into the wee hours of the morning, he'd added his own name to the list. But he couldn't deny how good it made him feel to see her enjoying herself for a change. No doubt she was under as much stress as everyone else. Determined to keep the mood light, Nick lifted one eyebrow. "I thought it was all sunshine and surfers in California."

Jenny laughed. "I'm farther inland. A trip to the beach is an all-day affair, and my job keeps me pretty busy. It's hard to find that kind of time. Still, you'd think I'd go more often." She shielded her eyes with her hand. "How's the water?"

"Cold." Nick gave an exaggerated shiver. With the water temperature hovering in the sixties throughout the summer, most swimmers didn't go in without a wetsuit.

"Okay if I check it out?"

"Fine by me. Just be sure to get out before you turn into a popsicle."

He kept one eye on her while he spread the blanket and anchored it down with the basket and their shoes. Just as he expected, her laughter rang out, true and bright, when the first wave washed over her feet. Retreating from the cold water, she walked the water's edge, bending low to pick up the occasional bit here and there.

Eager to catch up with her, he jogged to meet her. "Find anything interesting?"

"Some shells. I'm not sure what kind they are. Do you know?"

"That's a whelk. This one's a mussel," he said retrieving a shell from the damp, gray sand.

"And these?" She opened her hand. Tiny, cone-shaped shells scattered across her palm.

"Careful, that one is somebody's home." He pointed to a tiny pair of crab legs sticking out of the opening.

"Oops." She bent down to whisper to the crab. "Sorry. I didn't mean to disturb you."

She looked so sweet, her face so full of concern as she carefully tucked the shell into the wet sand, that Nick felt his heart lurch. Suddenly, he wished he'd met her earlier. Before she'd fallen in love with someone else. Long before she'd gotten engaged to another man. Certainly before she'd come to Heart's Landing to plan a wedding to someone who wasn't him. He watched as she trotted toward the water's edge, where a piece of driftwood had washed ashore. Silently, he wondered what he'd gotten himself into. Or how he was going to go on with his life without her in it.

Jenny touched the granite at the base of the tall cliff on the far side of the cove and turned to retrace her steps. From behind dark sunglasses, she eyed the semi-circle of beach. Small crabs darted from one strand of dark seaweed to another. Here and there, oddly shaped pieces of driftwood dotted the shore. Sea gulls rode the air currents overhead. The periwinkles Nick had shown her how to find blew bubbles in the gray sand every time a wave receded. She smiled, glad she'd let him talk her into taking a day away from the troubling preparations for her cousin's wedding.

She stole a glimpse of the tall baker at her side. Nick constantly showered her with concern. The cupcake he'd brought her last night was only one of many examples. When she ran into problems she had trouble solving on her own, he never rushed to take over like the few men she'd dated. Instead, he simply offered her advice and left it up to her to take it or leave it. Add in the fact that Nick was more handsome than some movie stars, and the most surprising thing about him was that not one of the single women within a hundred miles had snapped him up already.

They should have. It had certainly taken every ounce of will power she possessed, and then some, to keep her eyes on the bike path and not watch his every move while they rode along the cliffs. As much as she struggled to keep her focus where it belonged, she hadn't been able to keep from stealing quick glances at his muscular calves as he pedaled, or watching how the broad muscles across his back expanded and contracted while they labored up the hill. She stifled a sigh. It really was too bad Nick lived on one coast while she lived on the opposite one.

Or that your entire relationship is built on a tangled web of deceit.

Well, there was that. She rubbed the base of her throat where secrets pressed down like hundred-pound weights. Her closest ally in Heart's Landing thought she was engaged to someone else. Yet, knowing their relationship could go no further, he'd still stuck around. She hated keeping the truth from him because, when it came to potential boyfriends, Nick had definitely raised the bar. Now that she'd met him, whenever someone asked her out in the future, she knew in her heart of hearts she'd always compare them to Nick. She was pretty sure anyone else would fall far short of the standard he'd set.

"Jenny?" Nick tossed a stick into the water.

When the twig rushed back to the shore on an incoming wave, she reeled in her thoughts along with it. "Sorry. What were you saying?"

"You were a million miles away. Penny for your thoughts?" He held out a round, flat shell.

"Oh, no. You're not getting off that easy," she scoffed, unable to confess that her thoughts had been about him.

"No problem." He flung the shell into a calm tidal pool and watched it skip twice before it sank beneath the surface.

"I was saying I wasn't sure I'd ever asked what you do for a living."

"Oh. That." Aware that the conversation had drifted into treacherous waters where one wrong step might lead to disaster, she paused. Kay had concocted a story for her to feed anyone who asked, but her stomach actually hurt when she thought about lying to Nick. He'd been such a good friend that he deserved to hear the truth. At least, as much of it as she could tell without betraying her family. "My cousin leads several companies that are pretty well known in the film industry." That was the truth, though she dismissed Kay's prominence with an airy wave of one hand. "I'm her personal assistant, which sounds far more glamorous than it really is. Basically, I wear a lot of hats. From travel agent to party planner to secretary and sometimes maid, to all-around gofer, I do whatever's necessary to keep her life running smoothly and hiccup-free. I'm pretty much on call 24/7."

Nick make a ticking sound with his mouth. "Sounds like a demanding job. Do you like it?"

"I do. Mostly. The work varies enough to be really interesting. I can be picking up dry cleaning and making dinner reservations one day, taking a meeting with one of the studio heads the next. I've made a lot of connections, met a lot of powerful people." She hesitated. "Lately, though, things have gotten a bit complicated."

"How so?"

"Hmm." She searched for the right words to explain without making Kay sound self-centered. "Growing up, my cousin was as down-to-earth as they come. We played in the mud together. She pulled just as many weeds in my aunt's vegetable garden as I did. But now that she's a *somebody*, she's surrounded by people who cater to her every whim. I try my best not to be one of them, to tell her when I think she's drifting off-track and remind her to exercise some common sense. Recently, though, she's not listening to me as much as she used to. It's like, one day we're on an all-vegan diet, and the next, I'm shopping for steak. It's frustrating. Not only that, it makes it hard to plan."

"And you're all about the plan." Nick nodded to himself.

She dragged her foot through a piece of seaweed. "You've noticed that about me, have you?"

"It's sort of obvious. You never go anywhere without a list of things to do, and you're usually working on it when you're in the bakery. Tell me, do you ever just wing it? Fly by the seat of your pants?"

"Not often," she admitted. She liked the stability of sticking to a plan. It made her feel safe.

"But you came with me today." He plucked a plastic bottle cap from the sand and stuck it in the pocket of his shorts. "That wasn't on your agenda."

"I had set aside some time for sightseeing in my schedule." She sidestepped an incoming wave. "Isn't that what we're doing now?"

"Maybe you should do more of that. Relax a little. Stop letting the plan drive you," he said in answer to her questioning look.

"I don't think so." She folded her arms across her chest. "I'm a lists-and-schedules kind of girl."

"Has that always been important to you?"

"Not always." Her feet stumbled to a halt. Turning, she stared out at the ocean. As a kid, she'd been as carefree and spontaneous as the foam that floated on the waves. But she knew exactly when things had changed—when she'd changed. It wasn't something she talked about with just anyone. Was

Nick someone she could confide in? Would he understand? She took a breath. "My mom fixed the same meals every week when I was a kid. Monday was either beef stew or chicken vegetable soup. Tuesday was taco night. Wednesday, we had hot dogs or hamburgers. Thursday, some kind of roast. Friday nights were family nights. My folks always ordered in pizza. We'd sit at the table, play board games, and eat. It was the best." She plucked at the hem of her shorts. She rarely spoke about what came next.

"That Friday, though," she began again. "That Friday, somebody gave my dad tickets to a play. I remember being upset that we weren't going to have our special night, but Mom promised there'd be other family nights. They left me with a babysitter and took the train into the city for dinner and the show. On the way home, their train derailed. They died in the crash."

She fell silent for a moment, unable to keep from reliving the next morning, when she'd raced to answer a knock on the door and stared into the sad faces of two police officers. Her world had come crashing down around her that day. Though she knew one thing didn't have anything to do with the other, she'd blamed the accident on her parents' departure from the normal routine. Ever since, she'd worked extra hard to have a schedule and stick to it. She supposed that was at least part of the reason why she had such heartburn over Kay's wedding—her cousin was constantly changing the plan.

Nick slipped his hand around hers and squeezed it. "Geez, Jenny. I had no idea. That had to be rough."

Thankful for the warmth of his hand in hers, she shrugged. "It was. It would have been a lot worse if it hadn't been for my Aunt Maggie and my cousin Kay. Aunt Maggie was my mom's sister. She took me in, made sure I knew I'd always be taken care of and loved. Money was tight, but she encouraged me to go to college. I worked my way through school, but I got my degree. By then, Kay had, um, landed a big promotion and needed help keeping her life organized." She awarded herself an imaginary medal for neatly failing to mention that the big promotion was actually the lead role in a major motion picture. "When Aunt Maggie asked if I could help, I couldn't turn her down. It was my chance to pay back all their family had done for me."

She'd grown tired of talking about herself, of walking the tightrope between truth and lie, by the time they reached the blanket Nick had spread over the soft, dry sand. Though she liked how his hand wrapped around hers, she extricated her fingers from his grasp and plopped down next to the picnic basket. Hoping he'd follow her lead, she folded her knees up under her and opened the lid. "Time for lunch?"

"Sounds good. What do we have in there?"

Her hand stilled on one of the plastic boxes when Nick leaned close enough to peer over her shoulder. Aware of his breath in her hair, she steeled herself. "Looks like"—one by one, she pulled out boxes and held them up—"lobster rolls. Potato salad. Coleslaw. Cookies. And, wait." She dug deep and came up with two glass bottles. "Ta-da! Blueberry soda."

"All right!" Nick rubbed his hands together. "That's what I call a lunch! Remind me to thank Marybeth. If I'd packed it, we'd be eating peanut butter sandwiches."

"I wouldn't mind, as long as you brought cupcakes for dessert." Jenny's lips lifted at the corners. When the tips of Nick's ears turned pink, she decided his humility was one more factor in his favor.

Working together, they doled the food out onto paper

plates. Soon they sat cross-legged facing the ocean, their plates balanced on their thighs.

Jenny bit into a soft roll loaded with plenty of fresh-steamed lobster and chopped celery drenched in mayonnaise. It was good—wonderful, in fact—but it still didn't hold a candle to Nick's cupcakes. Not even the lemon one he'd brought her last night. Curious as to how such a talented baker had ended up running a bakery in this particular small town, she swallowed and dabbed at her mouth with a napkin.

"So, Nick," she said, waiting until he'd swigged a gulp of his soda. "Now that you know my story, how about you? What led you to become a baker?"

Nick buried his bottle of pop up to the label in the sand. "My dad worked for a bread company, one of those huge, industrial places where they churned out thousands of identical loaves each day. To hear him tell the story, the job paid the rent but the work wasn't exactly fulfilling. Dad had always talked of starting his own business. When the bread company sold and laid everyone off, he saw his chance. I was four when he moved us here from Virginia. He opened I Do Cakes before I started first grade. I could barely peep over the counter when I began working in the bakery alongside him. Some people might say that flour is in my blood."

She closed her eyes, smiling at the image of a dark-haired little boy stealing bites of dough as, beside him, an older, burlier version of Nick shaped and cut out cookies. "Where is he now, your dad?"

Instead of answering, he tore a piece of bread from his roll and tossed it into the sand. Within seconds, a seagull swept down and scooped it up. After the bird flew off, Nick's words came slowly. "He had his first heart attack eleven years ago. I was in Paris. I'd finally worked my way up to head patissier in a five-star restaurant. But none of that mattered once I got the news. I flew home immediately and took over the bakery while he was in the hospital. At first, I thought it'd only be for a little while. It didn't take long before I realized Dad wasn't coming back to work. So, I stayed on. It's a choice I've never regretted."

Afraid she knew the answer but determined to learn more about the man who'd been so kind to her, she asked, "And your dad?"

"Gone now. About six months after that first heart attack, he had another one. That time, he didn't make it." His chest expanded, stretching his T-shirt. Slowly, his shoulders rounded. "I've always been grateful for the extra time we had together. But, when I get right down to it, it didn't make his passing any easier."

Jenny fell silent. She'd often wished she'd had time to prepare, to say goodbye to her folks. But would it have made any difference in the end? From what Nick had said, it might not have. She cleared her throat. "And your mom?" she asked, her voice barely strong enough to carry above the waves slapping on the shore.

"Florida." Nick took a bite from his sandwich and chewed. "She moved to a retirement community down there. She golfs and plays bingo nearly every day. We talk on the phone Sunday evenings. Twice a year, I either fly down for a visit or she comes up here. My sister has two children—a girl and a boy. They live here in Heart's Landing, too."

They sat in silence for a while, eating and tossing out an occasional scrap to the birds. At last, Nick stretched out his long legs and leaned back on his elbows. With his ankles crossed, he pinned her with a look.

"Yes?" she asked. Uncomfortable beneath his pointed stare, she braced herself.

"You don't talk about your fiancé as much as most brides."

A statement, not a question. She tilted her head at the observation that had seemed to come from nowhere. Not certain what point Nick was trying to make, she tipped her head. "There's not much to tell. Bob's a great guy with a job that keeps him pretty busy."

"That's it—a great guy, huh?" Nick tossed the last bite of a cookie at a flock of gray-colored shorebirds that pecked for tasty tidbits in the sand. "From what you said, you have a demanding job, too. One that requires you to be available around the clock. How's that going to work after you're married? Are you going to quit? Do something else?"

Phooey.

She should have stuck to the story Kay had scripted for her. If she had, she and Nick wouldn't be having this conversation. But it had been her idea to tell him the truth, or as much of it as she'd dared. Thanks to that, though, she'd painted herself into a corner.

She studied the waves washing ashore while she tried to figure a way out. In for a penny, in for a pound, she decided at last. Telling Nick the truth had gotten her into this mess. Telling him more of it might just get her out. "Funny you should ask," she said, laughing at her own mistake. "For someone who's addicted to having a plan, I've been so focused on the wedding that I never thought much beyond it. I'm not sure what'll happen after the honeymoon." That much was true. There were bound to be changes once Karolyn and Chad were married.

"Maybe you should. Think about it, that is. Figure out

what you really want out of life." Nick pitched a shell into the sand.

Jenny leaned back on her palms, her elbows locked. Did she dare tell Nick her grand plan for the future? Realizing how much she wanted to confide in him, how much she trusted him, she took a deep, shuddery breath. "You're right—I'm not sure how much longer I'll be able to work for Kay. Sooner or later, it'll be time to move on. When that happens, I've always thought I'd like to start my own event planning business. That's the one part about my job I really enjoy—pulling together the perfect birthday party, organizing a special anniversary dinner, arranging a surprise celebration."

She'd never mentioned her dream to another soul and felt a nervous shiver run through her. She wouldn't blame Nick for thinking hers was the most ridiculous idea he'd ever heard. After all, everyone in Heart's Landing considered her to be a bride who waffled over every decision. If the word got out that she wanted to plan parties for a living, Mildred and Alicia would think she'd lost her mind. Nick probably did, too.

"I've had lots of practice—working in L.A., there's always something going on," she added, defensive. She forced her shoulders square, refusing to wither beneath Nick's long, studying glance. Seconds ticked by while she waited for his reaction.

Just when she'd grown certain he was trying to figure out a way to let her down easy, he asked, "What's stopping you?"

He'd asked a very good question, one that deserved an honest answer. She reached down deep. "I'm not sure I'd be able to do it on my own," she confessed. "I told you my cousin is a bigwig in the industry." She waited for his nod before she plunged ahead. "Her name has a certain amount of cachet. I'm afraid I'll find out that the success I've had so far has been due to her influence."

"That's not going to happen," Nick said, sounding certain. "Look how well you've planned your wedding. You knew exactly what you wanted and pulled it together in a matter of days."

"Yeah, but then I didn't stick to it," she pointed out.

"All the more reason you should be proud of what you've accomplished. Whatever the reason, you've had to make some pretty significant changes. But there's a lot to be said for persistence. You could have just thrown up your hands and escaped to Bora Bora. You didn't. You stuck with it, sweet-talked the vendors in town, and got them to do what you wanted. Even me." His lips tilted into the crazy smile she liked so much. "And you did it yourself, without any help from your cousin."

Jenny leaned back on her elbows. Nick might be onto something. Maybe she could open her own business. Of course, she'd have to start small, and probably not in L.A., where success depended more on celebrity endorsements than the ability to pull off an event without a hitch.

"There's just one thing." Nick hesitated.

"Yeah?" She glanced sideways at the man sitting on the blanket beside her.

"In order to succeed, you'll have to stiffen your spine a bit."

"Huh?" She cocked her head, not sure she understood what he meant.

"I mean you're going to have to stand up to your clients better than you've stood up for yourself with this wedding." Nick held out one hand and ticked items off on his fingers. "This wedding won't be anything like what it started out to be. You've added to the number of guests, moved the ceremony and the reception from one location to another in the Captain's Cottage. The menu, the flowers, the colors—you've changed them all. Not because you wanted to, but other people insisted on it."

"You must think I'm a nitwit." She hung her head.

"No, never that. You're bright and cheerful, and everyone in town likes you. But I do think you need to decide what you want and then go for it. Don't let anyone push you around."

Her brow puckered. Had Nick discovered the real reason behind what she'd done? "Like who?"

"Well, your fiancé, for one."

"What's he got to do with this?" She canted her head. If she didn't know better, she'd swear Nick sounded a bit put out with a man who didn't exist.

"I thought you said he was the one who added to the guest list."

Her breath hitched when Nick's gaze bore into hers. That was the problem with secrets and lies. One led to another and then another. Pretty soon, it was hard to keep them straight. "Him, but mostly his mother," she corrected. "She invited everyone on both sides of their family."

"Hmm. You'd think…"

"What?" Suddenly, she really wanted to know what Nick thought.

"You'd think Bob would stand up for you, take your side. If I had a fiancée, that's what I'd do. If she wanted a small wedding, I'd insist on it. That's all."

"Yeah." Her soft agreement whispered into the room. "You think it's all Bob's fault."

The mythical, nonexistent Bob.

Nick shrugged. "Who else is there?"

Slowly, Jenny nodded. "Who else, indeed."

Nick folded his legs when the next wave sent water rushing over the sand at his feet. The tide had changed. Within the next hour, the water would rise nearly to the cliff. As sorry as he was to see the day come to an end, it was time for him and Jenny to retrace their steps to the B&B.

While Jenny bagged their trash and stored their empty containers in the picnic basket, he shook sand out of the blanket and rolled it into a tight cylinder. As he worked, he thought hard about Jenny, trying to assemble the pieces of her puzzle. They wouldn't fit.

On the one hand, he admired her strength and determination, her dedication to family and her outlook for the future. She'd had to be strong to survive the deaths of her parents when she'd been so young. He'd known others who hadn't been able to deal with that kind of loss. They'd let their grief overwhelm them. For the rest of their lives, they carried their sorrow with them wherever they went, like the crabs and snails carried shells. As for determination, Jenny had a boatload of that, too. She'd needed it in order to put herself through college. From outward appearances, she was a woman who knew what she wanted and went for it. But given all that, how could someone who was so dedicated to having a schedule and sticking to it get to be so fickle about her own wedding plans?

And then there was her fiancé. Most brides-to-be found one way or another to bring their Mr. Right into every conversation. Not Jenny. She barely mentioned the man she was going to marry in a few days. When pressed for details, the woman who insisted on precisely the right flowers in her wedding bouquet had nothing in particular to say about the man she was going to spend the rest of her life with. To tell the truth, her descriptions of him were so bland, the man sounded more like a cardboard cutout than a husband.

Why was that?

Confusion sent his mouth slanting to one side. He couldn't shake the feeling that there was more to her story. Unfortunately, he had the sneaking suspicion that by the time he figured her out, it'd be too late. In two weeks, she'd walk down the aisle and into the arms of the man she said she loved. He'd whisk her off on their honeymoon, and she'd be out of his life. Probably forever.

All he had to do was let her go. To keep his distance from her in the meantime.

That was the smart thing for him to do. No matter how much he wanted to get to know her better, they should remain nothing more than polite friends. No matter how often he considered pulling her into his arms to see how well she fit, staying as far away as possible from her was the best thing he could do for everyone.

Except he couldn't.

Not only had he promised his friends, his coworkers, that he'd keep a close watch on their fickle bride, he was pretty sure he'd fallen for her. Something about Jenny drew him. He wanted to spend every minute with her. To help her find the strength to stand up to whoever was pushing her around, making her life miserable.

Lost in his thoughts, he led the way back to the B&B in silence. At the porch, Jenny lifted the picnic basket. Their empty bottles rolled around in the bottom, clinking softly.

"Thanks, Nick," she said, her voice low enough that he had to strain to hear it. "I had a really nice time today."

"Yeah, me, too." He scuffed one foot through the grass. "What are you doing tomorrow?"

"Paperwork and bills in the morning. I'll be at Perfectly Flawless most of the afternoon." She shrugged as if self-conscious. "It's sort of a test run—a massage, facial, the works. It was included in the wedding package."

He loved that she felt the need to have an excuse for treating herself to a well-deserved day of pampering. "Sounds nice." It also sounded like she didn't have any intentions of making more changes to the plans for her wedding. Which ought to ease his mind about leaving her on her own while he was at work. Just to be safe, though, he probably should check in on her at least once. The other shopkeepers in town would expect him to do at least that much. "Want to grab a bite to eat tomorrow, after the bakery closes?"

"Um, I actually have a reservation at Bow Tie Pasta."

He held his breath while he waited for her to continue. Would she cancel her plans in order to spend the evening with him?

"But I'd like it if you came with me."

"Hey, a man's gotta eat." Aiming for a laugh, he patted his stomach. But there was nothing funny about how much he wanted to spend time with her, all the while knowing he shouldn't.

Chapter Twelve

Jenny stood at the open closet in her suite at the bed and breakfast on Union Street. Hangers squeaked as she slid them from one end of the bar to the other. One by one, she considered and rejected each outfit. Why couldn't she decide what to wear?

Her hand lingered over the black number she'd worn to dinner at Bow Tie Pasta with Nick. That evening, the glow in his eyes had rivaled the candlelight at their table, but the dress wasn't appropriate for their plans tonight. She flipped past the skirt and jacket she'd had on the day Nick had picked up takeout from a local restaurant and met her in the park for lunch. He'd said he wanted to tell her more about Captain Thaddeus, but she'd gotten the distinct impression that he'd really just wanted to spend time with her. That feeling had intensified when she'd caught his sidelong glances while she was supposed to be studying the statue. She'd caught herself wondering if Nick liked her as much as she liked him. The possibility had sent shivers of awareness down her arms. Later that week, her heart had raced when he'd oh-so casually helped her into her sweater in the chilly diner where they'd met for breakfast one morning.

Tonight, though, they were simply meeting at the bakery for a lesson in how to make cupcakes. Or, rather, how to create them without a recipe. So why couldn't she decide what to wear?

Despite her dilemma, she hummed a happy tune. Most people barely noticed her ever-present list of things to do or how much it bothered her when her schedule fell apart or if someone threw a monkey wrench into her plans. But Nick had, and he hadn't just stopped there. Not content to merely chalk her actions up to a personality quirk, he'd delved deeper, asked questions, and hadn't let up until he understood why winging it without a plan was such a huge problem for her. Then, he'd formulated his own plan to introduce spontaneity into her life. Best of all, he'd insisted on being at her side throughout the whole thing.

She supposed that was why she valued their friendship as much as she did. It wasn't just that Nick was tall, dark and ever-so-handsome. Or that her heart went pit-a-pat every time she gazed into his deep-set blue eyes. She'd felt that zing of physical attraction before with other men, but Nick was the first one who'd ever showered her with care and concern, who hadn't been satisfied with outward appearances, but had insisted on getting to know what really made her tick. Because of that, she felt like she'd known him forever. In the short time since she'd come to Heart's Landing, they'd grown closer than she'd ever thought possible.

Her hand stilled on the next hanger in the closet. Did her feelings for him go deeper than friendship?

She sank onto the edge of her bed at the sudden realization that they did. Nick was everything she'd ever dreamed of—compassionate, warm, funny, caring—and he made her feel complete in a way no one else ever had. Though she hadn't known him long, she'd fallen in love with him. And it nearly broke her heart that she couldn't tell him.

Not now. Probably not ever.

Her chin dropped nearly to her chest. Tears gathered beneath her closed eyelids. She gave her head a rueful shake. As much as she wished things could be different between them, as much as she wanted to drop a not-so-subtle hint that she wouldn't mind a bit if Nick leaned in for a quick kiss, she couldn't. For that to happen, she'd have to tell him the truth, the whole truth. That she was only standing in for the real bride-to-be. That when this Saturday rolled around, she wouldn't walk down the aisle at the Captain's Cottage carrying a bouquet of flowers. Her cousin would. The man standing up front that wouldn't be named Bob, but Chad. And that the real bride and groom had insisted on changing every detail about the upcoming ceremony and reception.

But those were words that could never come out of her mouth.

She'd sworn to protect Kay's identity, and family came first. She wouldn't, couldn't break the promise she'd made her cousin. She couldn't even think of taking such a risk. Not with the wedding only a few days away. No matter how much it hurt to keep the truth from Nick, she had to keep her own feelings under wraps.

She slid another hanger to the front of the closet and reached for the shirt she'd purchased in one of the shops on Procession Drive. Paired with jeans, the outfit would suffice for an evening of baking in I Do Cakes' kitchens. As for her urge to tell Nick the truth, it would remain tucked away beneath the Heart's Landing logo on her T-shirt.

A short time later, she sat at a sidewalk cafe on Bridal Carriage Drive, the remains of her dinner salad in front of her. The town had quieted while she ate. Lugging bags and parcels, the last of the shoppers had loaded their purchases into the trunks of cars and sped off. A few had entered nearby restaurants. Some lined up at the hostess station near the entrance to the cafe she'd chosen. There, they chatted while they waited for reservations and empty tables. One by one, the lights in various shops along the street blinked out. Shadows from the trees and buildings lengthened and then disappeared when the sun sank behind the facade of Forget Me Knot Flowers. The leaves in the trees that edged the sidewalks rustled, and birds twittered as they settled into their nests for the night.

A peaceful feeling spread through her chest as shopkeepers called to one another while they closed and locked their doors for the evening. She leaned back in her chair at a table-for-one while she drank in the atmosphere that was so different from what she was used to in Los Angeles. There, business owners protected their merchandise behind heavy metal gates at night, and cars crowded the freeways until the wee hours of the morning. She closed her eyes, imagining what it'd be like to live in a place like Heart's Landing. The idea held more appeal than she thought it would. While life in the big city made it possible to order a pizza any time, day or night, she was pretty sure she could make do with something from the freezer in exchange for knowing her neighbors by name, sitting in the bleachers to watch a Little League game on the weekend, or joining the local Chamber of Commerce.

She chased a cherry tomato around her nearly empty salad bowl while she considered the For Rent sign she'd spotted on Honeymoon Avenue on her way back from lunch in the park with Nick last week. Located within walking distance of the center of town, the vacant space would make the perfect spot for an event planning business that focused on birthday and retirement parties, anniversaries, and other celebrations. Of course, if she really did move here and set up shop, she'd eventually expand her services to include wedding planning, but that could wait until she'd proved she could handle the job—to herself and everyone else.

She speared the tomato and popped it into her mouth. Immediately, she wished she hadn't. Though nothing tasted better than a great marinara sauce, she didn't really like fresh tomatoes and only ate them because they were supposed to be good for her. Which, when she got right down to it, sounded an awful lot like how she felt about working for her cousin. She'd always known that she'd gone to work for Kay out of obligation rather than any sense of personal fulfillment. At the time, she'd viewed the job as a stepping stone, and in some ways it had been exactly that. She'd certainly learned a lot during the past two years.

But what came next? There weren't any higher rungs to climb on this particular corporate ladder. Nick had been right when he'd suggested that unless she set her own goals, she'd end up planning her cousin's life instead of her own for the next twenty years. She really did need to figure out what she wanted out of her future and where she wanted to go with it.

Right this minute, though, she wanted to be at I Do Cakes. Nick was waiting for her. Signaling the waiter for her bill, she smiled. She, the girl who'd never did anything that wasn't on the agenda, the one who'd never so much as cracked open a box of cake mix, was going to make cupcakes. Without a recipe *or* a plan.

That, at least, sounded like a step in the right direction.

What am I doing?

The question echoed through Nick's head while he gathered the necessary supplies for the evening's baking session with Jenny. He tried telling himself he was merely doing what his friends and neighbors had asked of him, simply helping an uncertain bride-to-be stay the course. Which was true as far as it went. Everyone knew that Jenny's entire wedding had turned into a house of cards. One stiff breeze—or one more change in direction—and the whole thing would collapse.

No one wanted to see that happen. Not even him.

So, when the other shopkeepers in town had asked him to use whatever influence he had to keep Jenny on track, he'd had no choice but to agree. Though he hadn't thought much of the idea at first, he had to admit, their strategy was working. Over the past week, he'd stuck close to her side. One afternoon, they'd admired the azaleas and roses at the Captain's Cottage. On another, they'd counted the carved stone hearts mounted on the facades of businesses throughout Heart's Landing. Through it all, he'd done his best to reinforce the choices Jenny had made for the ceremony that loomed ever closer. And it had worked. A week had passed since she'd made a single change to her wedding plans.

Now, he just had to maintain the status quo for a few more days, and like a long line of dominoes, everything would fall into place. On Saturday, Jenny would walk down the aisle to marry her fiancé. Meanwhile, Mildred was hard at work on the floral arrangements, Janet was making sure everyone would be well fed, Roy and JoJo had mapped out their game plans for videos and pictures, and the twins anticipated the arrival of the last items for the gift bags any day. As long as nothing else changed, in one week everyone would pat themselves on the back for delivering a picture-perfect wedding for yet another Heart's Landing bride. All thanks to his involvement.

So, why, exactly, had he invited Jenny to an impromptu baking session?

He shook his head. He couldn't honestly answer that question. Because, if he were being honest, he'd have to point out that Jenny didn't wear the dreamy-eyed expression of a bride who was deeply in love with her fiancé. If he faced facts, he'd have to say there was something wrong when a man claimed he was too busy to plan his wedding, but countermanded every decision his bride made. If he told the truth, he'd have to admit that his attraction to Jenny went far deeper than the kindness he showed other brides who walked into I Do Cakes.

None of which was something he was prepared to do.

Developing feelings for a bride-to-be wasn't just asking for heartache, it went against his moral code. It warred against the lessons of respect and honor he'd learned from his father. The town had staked its reputation on giving every bride a perfect wedding. He believed in fulfilling that promise, no matter what.

So, he wouldn't comment on Jenny's cool and, yes, often confusing, attitude toward her fiancé. At least, not again. He definitely wouldn't drop a single, solitary hint that he thought she was marrying the wrong man. And he wouldn't admit he liked Jenny far more than he ought to. Or compliment her on her outfit. Or, most especially, wrap his arms around her and brush a kiss through her freshly washed hair.

All of which sounded as easy as whipping up a batch of cookies while he was alone. It was a good bit more challenging when the bride-to-be in question stood at I Do Cakes' back door, looking adorable in a touristy T-shirt and a pair of jeans.

"I hope I'm not too early," she offered, her tentative smile giving her an air of naive vulnerability.

"Not at all. You're right on time." A jolt of unwanted attraction surged through him. He reined in fingers that itched to trace the ponytail that curled over her shoulder. "Grab an apron," he said, his voice uncharacteristically gruff.

He turned abruptly, but not before he caught the puzzled frown that formed on Jenny's face. His spine softened at the hurt in her eyes, and he stifled a groan. It wasn't her fault that he was acting like a jerk, but the more time he spent around her, the more his feelings got the best of him.

Determined to do better, he fought his emotions into submission while he grabbed bowls and measuring cups. He ground his back teeth together as he issued a stern reminder that he was simply giving a cooking lesson to a woman who didn't know her way around a kitchen. Firmly, he clamped a lid over anything that would dilute his focus while Jenny slipped one of I Do Cakes' chocolate-and-pink aprons over her head and deftly tied the strings into a bow. Her footsteps slow, she moved to his side.

"Is everything okay?" she asked, hesitant. "I don't want to be a bother if you have something else to do."

"No, it's not you. It's me. I'm sorry. I don't know what came over me for a minute."

Okay, that last part was a lie, but a necessary one. He couldn't very well admit how he really felt about having her in his kitchen, couldn't say how much he looked forward to spending time with her.

When doubt lingered in Jenny's dark eyes, he summoned the apologetic smile he owed her. Hoping to get things back to normal between them, he offered, "My alarm clock went off a whole lot earlier than I wanted it to."

Which was true. This last week or so, he'd been getting up at three to fill the orders for the bakery and still have time to see Jenny. It was a tough schedule to stick to, but he'd promised the others he'd keep a close eye on her. Though it meant a few less hours of sleep each night, and clamping a heavy lid down over his growing feelings for her, he was a man of his word. Besides, it was only for another few days.

"Oh!" Jenny's lips curved upward. "So, you get grumpy when you need a nap? Don't worry. I'll nudge you if you fall asleep." Her eyes brightening, she prodded his upper arm with her elbow. Her gaze dropped to the array of supplies on the counter. "I guess we'd better get started before you nod off."

Nick cleared his throat. Jenny's light banter had washed away the last of his unwanted tension. Relieved that his momentary lapse hadn't ruined things between them, he tapped a wooden spoon against the side of the bowl he'd prepared before her arrival. "In here, we have flour to bind everything together, sugar to sweeten, a touch of salt, and some baking soda." He pointed to a different bowl. "That one holds butter, milk, and eggs. When we mix the two together, the soda will combine with the liquid and cause tiny bubbles of air. Those are essential. They get trapped in the batter and make the cake rise."

Jenny eyed him solemnly. "You make baking sound like a chemistry experiment. You add the right ingredients in the right proportions, and you get a certain reaction."

"Right," he agreed, pleased that she appreciated the science of baking as much as he did. "In this case, we'll get a soft, tender cupcake instead of something like a scone or a flatbread. Next, you have to decide what flavor you want."

Jenny's lips pursed. "What are my choices?"

He gestured toward a line of containers. Each bore a label in the bakery's signature colors. "Whatever you want."

He shrugged. "Dutch chocolate. Peanut butter. Madagascar vanilla. A wide variety of fruits. What's your favorite?"

Without a moment's hesitation, Jenny reached for the tin of cocoa. "Chocolate, of course."

Nick stifled a grin as she dumped an insane amount of dark powder into the bowl that already contained the flour. To compensate for the extra dry ingredient, he deftly added a bit more butter and an extra splash of milk to the liquids.

"Now what?"

"Next comes the fun part. We mix." Ignoring the oversized industrial unit at the opposite end of the counter, he pulled out a small hand-held mixer he used for the occasional small batch or single cake. His grin widened when Jenny reached for the device. Her awkward grip on the handle told him she'd never used one before. He stated the obvious. "You don't cook much."

"I'll have you know I made a mean mac 'n' cheese when I was in college." In mock indignation, she propped one hand at her waist.

"From a box?" A smile tugged at his mouth.

"Okay, you got me." Her fingers dropped to her side. "But it was still pretty good." As though she owed him an explanation, she continued, "My aunt worked full time and helped my uncle with the family farm. She didn't have time to have us girls underfoot in her kitchen. In college, I lived on fast food and the occasional meal from the cafeteria. After graduation, I went to work for my cousin. She has a full-time housekeeper. These days, toast and coffee are about the extent of my cooking repertoire."

"We're going to add to that tonight," he assured her. "By the time we finish, you'll know how to make your own cupcakes from scratch."

"I won't know how much of each ingredient to use."

"That's the easy part. There are plenty of recipes available. You can find one in practically any cookbook."

Doubt flickered in Jenny's eyes. She lowered the mixer. "But they won't be as good as yours."

"No. They won't be as good as mine," he admitted. His recipes were closely guarded secrets, but even if he shared them with Jenny, hers still wouldn't turn out quite the same. He'd spent many years honing the techniques for the fluffy buttercream frosting that was the mainstay of his business. She wouldn't be able to learn that in a single cooking lesson. "You'll get better with practice. Are you ready?"

She nodded and followed his direction to lower the beaters into the bowl. Like most novice bakers, she held the mixer at an angle. Which was fine, as long as she didn't mind spraying batter over the entire kitchen.

"A little straighter," he coached from just far enough away to avoid getting splattered or, worse, brushing against her shoulder.

When Jenny only tipped the beaters at a steeper angle, he gritted his teeth. So much for keeping his distance. He'd have to demonstrate. Cautiously, he slipped his hand over hers. Trying without much luck to ignore the floral scent that floated atop the sugary-sweet smell of the ingredients, he showed her how to hold the mixer parallel to the counter. With the flick of a switch, the motor purred to life.

Jenny's laughter rose over the noise as the sturdy little machine churned. His heart skipped a beat as two of his favorite sounds echoed through the empty kitchen, and he gave himself another stern reminder that he and Jenny could never be more than friends. Needing an excuse to put some much-needed space between himself and the woman who was engaged to someone else, he relinquished his hold on her to grab a spatula that was just out of reach. "Be sure you scrape the sides of the bowl," he said, handing across the plastic scraper.

Though he stayed one step out of reach, he remained alert, ready to spring into action if the beaters tipped and threatened to splatter them both with batter. Fortunately for both of them, Jenny proved an apt student.

"Good. Good," he encouraged while the ingredients blended.

When she'd thoroughly combined the wet stuff, he grabbed the other bowl. Positioning it between them, he slowly spooned in the dry ingredients while she continued mixing. Despite his efforts to keep space between them, a sudden awareness flooded him. To compensate, he kept his head bent, his eyes on the task at hand while he did his best to concentrate on not spilling any of the mixture.

He'd barely sifted a cupful into the bowl when Jenny's soft gasp rattled his focus. Worried that she'd somehow caught a finger in the beaters, he searched for signs of a problem. But there was nothing wrong. Instead of a grimace, Jenny's mouth had formed an O. Her eyes had widened as the batter turned a chocolate brown. He laughed softly. Warmth spread through his chest at her clear enjoyment of something he admittedly took for granted too often. Thankful for the reminder of the simple pleasures that came from baking, he let his guard down for just an instant.

And in that moment, their eyes met.

Nick didn't even try to look away. Time slowed and seemed to stretch while he lost himself in the depths of Jenny's dark orbs. Or, maybe he found himself. He didn't know.

What he did know was that he didn't want the moment to end, didn't want to let go.

The soft whir of the mixer faltered.

Nick snapped to attention. While they were lost in each other's gazes, Jenny had let go of the spatula. And, as they were known to do, this one had gotten caught between the beaters. He snapped off the power.

In the sudden silence, Jenny blinked as if waking from a dream. She ducked her head, but not before Nick noticed the faintest hint of a smile that played across her lips. Whatever they'd shared, she'd felt it as much as he did. And while he told himself that was a bad thing, somehow, he couldn't help but be glad that the moment had affected her as much as it had him.

"Did I ruin it?" she asked, staring into the bowl.

"No, everything's fine." He grabbed the spatula by the wooden handle and tugged it free. "This happens all the time."

"Not to me, it doesn't," she murmured.

Sensing her words carried a double meaning, Nick cleared his throat for the second time that night. He wasn't quite sure how, but he managed to regain his equilibrium. Determined to hang onto it, he handed Jenny the spatula. "Let's finish up so we can put these in the oven." He didn't wait for her response, but hit the power button and began adding the rest of the dry ingredients to the mix. Once the cupcakes were baking, he set the timer and turned to her again. "Ready for the fun part?"

"I thought we were already having fun," Jenny protested, her eyebrows pulling down at the center.

"True enough," he agreed. "But everyone likes one part of baking over another. For me, it's the frosting." Crossing to the fridge, he pulled out a bowl of blended butter and cream cheese. He grabbed a fresh set of beaters from a nearby drawer and snapped them into place. "This time, I'll hold the mixer while you add the confectioner's sugar."

Jenny eyed the canister on the counter. "How much?"

He shrugged. "The frosting will form peaks when you've added enough."

"That doesn't sound very scientific, but I'm game."

She scooped up a heaping measuring cup of the fine powder. Before Nick had a chance to warn her to go slowly, she dumped the whole thing into the bowl, just like she had with the cocoa. Instead of pulling the sugar into the mix, however, the beaters kicked the loose powder into a cloud that sweetened the air.

"Uh-oh!" Jenny blinked as sugar began to settle. Soon, it coated their hair, arms and faces. It dusted their clothes in snowy white. The tiny particles rained down on the counter and the floor as heat climbed onto her cheeks. "That wasn't supposed to happen, was it?"

Nick swallowed and tasted sugar, but it was the distraught expression on Jenny's face that required his immediate attention. "Hey, sometimes things don't work out perfectly the first time you try something new. But it's not a problem. You'll do better next time."

"Seriously? I've practically destroyed your kitchen." In what must have been an attempt to clean herself up, she clapped her hands together. Her efforts merely stirred more white into the air.

Nick squinted through dusty lashes. Extra-fine sugar coated everything within a four-foot radius. "It's easy enough to clean up. A damp rag will do the trick." He grabbed one from the sink at the end of the counter. When he swiped it through the white dust, it left a clean streak. "See? Easy as pie."

"I never understood why people say that. I watched my aunt make pies once. There wasn't anything simple about it."

"The easy part comes when you eat it." He grinned and handed her a second cloth. "Dust yourself off, and we'll get back to work. We'll wait to clean the rest until we're done. Just in case"—he shot her a teasing glance—"you know, it happens again."

"Oh, you!" Jenny swatted at him with the rag.

Nick sidestepped just in time to avoid getting smacked. "Trust me. You're not the first to make that same mistake. You won't be the last." When Jenny finished blotting her face and arms, he pointed to her cheek. "You missed a spot."

"Here?" Jenny dabbed again.

"Nope. Still there." He grabbed a fresh cloth and moved closer. He'd nearly reached the stubborn sugar when a plaintive meow sounded at the door.

Nick froze. The noise had kept him from making a big mistake. No matter how good he told himself his intentions were, deep down he had to admit that he wanted to do more than brush a few sugar crystals from Jenny's cheek. Which could only lead to trouble. He reluctantly dropped back a step. "You know what? You have a lot more on you than I thought. Why don't you wash up in the ladies' room while I grab our cupcakes?"

Jenny's gaze shifted from his face to the ingredients that waited on the counter to be mixed. "But what about the frosting? I—"

He cut off her objection. He needed her to go, needed her to leave the room before he did something really dumb—like pulling her into his arms. "I'll finish up here. Trust me. It'll be better this way."

Or if not better, at least safer. For both of us.

The confusion that clouded Jenny's features cleared. Her arguments died, and she spun on one heel.

Nick clenched his teeth and watched her until she disappeared behind the swinging doors. Only then did he straighten.

Idiot. I'm an idiot.

He'd had one job to do—help a bride in need. But he'd ruined everything by falling in love. And he had fallen in love with Jenny. With her ready wit, her sparkling personality, how she went out of her way to be kind to everyone she met. He'd never known anyone like her, and he wanted them to spend the rest of their lives together. There was just one problem—she was engaged to someone else. Which meant, no matter how he felt about her, he couldn't act on his feelings. Not even a little bit.

His mouth set in firm lines, he forced his focus to the tasks at hand. Removing the cupcakes from the oven, he set them on a nearby cooling tray. That done, he turned his attention to the frosting. By the time Jenny returned, he'd incorporated the last of the powdered sugar into the buttery mix.

And his feelings? He'd buried those so deep that Jenny would never see them.

"What flavor do you want?" Determined to stick to the program and not get lost in Jenny's gaze, he handed her a tasting spoon loaded with frosting.

"Hmm." She delicately licked the sample. "Do we have to? I think it's perfect just the way it is."

"Okay," he agreed, looking anywhere but at her. "There's

nothing better than a chocolate cupcake with vanilla buttercream frosting. But then, I might be slightly prejudiced."

"You think?" Jenny teased.

He refused to get sucked in by the sparkle in her eyes. Setting his lips into a grim line, he demonstrated the proper way to fill a piping bag. But no matter how hard he tried to remain aloof and detached, he grinned when she spun perfect circles across the tops of each of the cupcakes.

"They look good enough to eat," she declared as she polished off the last cupcake with a delicate swirl.

"You can add toppings if you'd like." He pointed to a row of bins built into one wall. Each housed a different confection, ranging from crushed candy bars to candied fruits. "Or how about a dash of cinnamon?"

"I might have to try one before I can know for sure," Jenny said, clearly angling for a taste test.

"Spoken like a true baker." He lifted one of the cupcakes from the rack while Jenny did the same. By mutual agreement, they took their first bites at the same time.

"Not bad," Nick pronounced. The chocolate nearly overpowered the sweetness of the cupcake, but for a first effort, Jenny had done quite well. He glanced at her to see if she felt the same way and stilled.

She stood, her eyes closed, a expression of pure bliss on her face.

He'd always thought she was pretty, but seeing her standing there, her beauty shone brighter than it ever had before. There was a dreamy air about her that he'd expected to see when she spoke about her fiancé. It was a look he'd begun to wonder if she was even capable of. Yet, there she stood, right in front of him, practically rapturous over a simple cupcake.

His heart melted. All of a sudden, he couldn't fight his feelings anymore. His heart thudding, he decided to take a chance.

"Jenny?" he whispered and stepped closer.

Chapter Thirteen

The heady mix of chocolate and buttercream overwhelmed Jenny's senses. She closed her eyes. Sure, she'd had better cupcakes. Nick's daily specials had more complex flavors. The texture of this one wasn't nearly as fine. But she'd definitely give it an *A* for effort. Especially since it was the first one she'd ever baked by herself.

Well, with more than a little help from Nick, she corrected. She licked her lips. How could she thank him?

Air brushed softly across her shoulders. Something—or hopefully, someone—had moved nearby. Praying Nick had taken a step toward her, she pried her eyes open wide enough to peek out through her lashes. He had definitely moved closer. Her heart responded by kicking into high gear. A giddy thrill passed through her as the realization that she was about to be kissed struck home.

She tucked her bottom lip between her teeth and sighed. She couldn't kiss Nick until he knew her secret. She had to tell him the truth, no matter what the cost. Then, and only then, could she find out how he really felt about her, about them.

Music blared, and she flinched. Her eyes sprang open just

in time for her to see Nick double-stepping a hasty retreat. He didn't stop until his hips rested against the counter behind him.

Another blast of music struck. Recognizing the theme song from her cousin's last hit movie, Jenny firmed lips that had softened in preparation for a kiss that was so not going to happen. "Perfect timing," she muttered while a potent disappointment swirled through her chest. Fighting it, she reached for the device she'd stuck in her back pocket when she'd left the bed and breakfast. "Hello," she said, thumbing the button.

"Where've you been? I've been trying to reach you all day!" So much for the dulcet tones Kay used whenever she appeared before the cameras. Strident, her voice grated across Jenny's raw nerves like fingernails on a chalkboard.

"Really?" Figuring this was not a conversation she wanted Nick to overhear, she held up one finger, asking him to give her a minute. At his nod, she speed-walked through the swinging doors to the public side of the bakery. On the way, she pointed out a decided lack of voicemail to her cousin.

"You know I never leave messages." Although Kay didn't say as much, Jenny couldn't miss the implication that such mundane tasks were beneath someone who'd achieved her level of stardom. "So, where were you?"

"I was out," she answered on a long, low exhale. She'd spent the day wandering in and out of the shops on Honeymoon Avenue and thinking about Nick. She probably should have returned Kay's missed calls, but her feelings for the baker were too new, too fresh to share with anyone, much less with the cousin who'd sent her to Heart's Landing as a pretend bride. "I planned to call you when you got home from the studio tonight."

"But I needed to reach you right away. We have a *huge* problem."

"What now?" She didn't have any problems other than a cousin who'd just interrupted the most important moment of her life. Honestly, sometimes Kay's flair for the dramatics rubbed her the wrong way. This was one of those times.

"It's a crisis. And you're the *only* one who can fix it."

Phooey. Just when she thought things had been going so well. Kay hadn't ordered a single change to the wedding plans in nearly a week. She should have known it wouldn't last.

"It's the cake. It's all wrong."

Say what?

Jenny squeezed her eyes tight. Nick had designed a stunning, multi-tiered creation that Kay's guests were sure to rave over. She pointed out what they both already knew. "It's exactly what you said you wanted."

"And now I don't," Karolyn said, her voice petulant. "Everyone in Hollywood is on this new diet. They'd rather die before letting one drop of sugary icing touch their lips. We can't. We just can't. I'd be mortified."

"Karolyn," she said, trying to make her cousin see reason, "your wedding is a special occasion. People make exceptions for events like this. Think of Thanksgiving or Christmas. You wouldn't serve Thanksgiving dinner without pumpkin pie, would you?"

"No, but—"

She rushed on. "What about Christmas? Remember how we used to leave cookies and carrots for Santa and his reindeer? You can't have Christmas without gingerbread men, can you?"

"I guess not."

She crossed her fingers in the hope that she was getting

the point across. "It's the same with weddings. Because it's *your* wedding, your guests will expect something spectacular." Nick's rich icing piped to match the lacy pattern of Karolyn's dress was just the ticket.

"What I want is beside the point. People are flying across the country to see me walk down the aisle. The least we can do is serve them something they'll want to eat. We have to make allowances."

Jenny shook her head. "There's no such thing as a sugar-free, carb-free cake." Well, there was, but it looked and tasted like cardboard.

"I've made up my mind," Karolyn insisted. "I want a naked cake."

"I don't even know what that is." Jenny rubbed her head. Behind her eyes, a drummer pounded a familiar beat.

"It's exactly what it sounds like, a cake without any frosting. Hang on. I'll send you a picture."

Seconds later, her phone dinged to signal an incoming text. Jenny swiped it and stared open-mouthed at the bare edges of cake layers glued together by a thinnest layer of icing. Someone had tucked flowers between the tiers, but without water to keep them fresh, the blossoms had wilted. The whole thing resembled the last item on the bake sale table at the church bazaar. "You can't be serious," she gasped.

"Oh, but I am." Kay's voice dropped. "You need to make this happen."

"But N—the baker. He'll have a conniption."

"I don't see why. It's a lot less work for him, and he's still getting paid the same amount. He'll probably thank you."

Her cousin obviously didn't know Nick. Jenny pictured the storm clouds that would gather in his eyes when she broke this piece of news to him. He was going to hate it. "I don't think—"

"What you think doesn't matter. This is what I want." Kay's voice turned deadly quiet. "I'm depending on you to make it happen."

For a moment, the weight of three thousand miles stretched between them. At last, Jenny shook her head. Between a rock and a hard place—that was exactly where she was. Though she refused to let Kay turn her into one of her many yes-men, she *had* sworn to give her cousin the wedding of her dreams. She could at least present this latest idea to Nick. "I'll do my best," she said without making any promises.

"What's going on with you lately?" Kay asked on the heels of her answer. "We used to be simpatico. Most of the time, you knew what I wanted before I did. But we're not on the same page anymore. It's like you're not even trying to understand me," she said, ending on a breathy sigh.

Jenny bit down on the first response that popped into her head. Her cousin probably wouldn't appreciate her pointing out how different the wedding was now from the intimate family gathering she'd first planned. That alone had caused some friction between them, but there were other factors at work, as well. Other people weighing in with their opinions. "Aunt Maggie is there with you. I'm sure she's been a big help. But it's only natural that she'd have a few suggestions about the festivities. And then there's Chad. He has his own ideas about how things should be done. They're great, but I'm having a hard time keeping up," she admitted. "And I'm not the only one. All these changes have the people I'm working with spinning in circles."

"It doesn't help that I keep calling with more demands."

Kay's voice softened. "You probably think I've turned into Bridezilla."

Jenny heard the faint stirrings of insecurity in her cousin's laugh. Knowing how quickly one of Kay's mercurial mood swings could lead to a dramatic meltdown, she struggled to stay calm and collected. "If there's one thing I've learned by coming to Heart's Landing, it's that every bride wants her day to be special. I'll do my best to make your wedding everything you want it to be, but we can't get so wrapped up in the details that we lose sight of what's really important. This is a celebration of the love you and Chad have for each other."

"You always know just what to say. I miss having you here." Karolyn's voice grew the tiniest bit melancholy. "It's never going to be just you and me again, is it?"

"Things will be different," she agreed, "but you have Chad now. He's a keeper."

"He is that." Kay chortled.

"And, soon, you'll be starting your new lives together."

"I can't wait! In less than a week, I'll be Mrs. Chad Grant."

Thinking of the changes the marriage would bring, Jenny smoothed one hand over her hair. Once the newlyweds returned from their honeymoon, there'd be households to combine, schedules to mesh, and tough staffing decisions to make. The married couple wouldn't need two housekeepers, two cooks.

Or two personal assistants?

She gulped. Losing her job was something she hadn't wanted to think about. Worrying about it now wouldn't do any good. Karolyn would make the decisions when the time came and, no doubt, she'd do whatever was best for her career.

Jenny tapped her finger to her chin. She had other wedding details to discuss with her cousin while she still had Kay's attention. "How'd your appointment go with Madame Eleanor? Did you find a wedding gown?"

"I did! Oh, Jenny, you should see it! It's perfect. It's the most beautiful trumpet-style gown with what Madame Eleanor called a royal train. The cap sleeves are a gorgeous see-through lace, and the neckline plunges way down in front. The back—oh, you should see the back—it hugs me in all the right places, if you know what I mean."

After helping the movie star dress for countless awards shows over the years, she wasn't a bit surprised to hear that Kay had selected a form-fitting gown.

"There's just one little problem."

"Oh, yeah?" Jenny relaxed. Whatever it was, it was Madame Eleanor's to fix.

"My gown isn't exactly made for dancing. I'll probably bust out a seam if I so much as breathe wrong. I need a second dress for the reception."

No problem. "Madame Eleanor would be only too happy to sell you another one."

"She would."

Sensing trouble, Jenny stiffened. "Why do I think there's a but at the end of that sentence?"

"My gown needed some alterations. Madame couldn't handle those, plus the fittings for my second dress. But I spoke with the owner of Dress For A Day. She has the gown I want in stock, and she's put her seamstress on standby. I need you to go there, try the dress on, and buy it for me."

Jenny rubbed her forehead. Working for a Hollywood mega-star, she'd handled some strange requests. But this had to be one of the oddest. "How is that even going to work?"

Kay paused. "We're practically the same height. And the dress laces up in the back, so it's very forgiving. It should look the same on both of us as long as you haven't, like, gained thirty pounds or anything since you've been out there."

"Not hardly." She might have eaten a dozen cupcakes, but between the stress of arranging the not-so-simple wedding and her daily workouts on the B&B's treadmill, she'd burned off every one of the extra calories. "That's one thing that hasn't changed."

"Okay, then. This will be easy."

"Uhh…" There were a lot of words she'd choose to describe trying on her cousin's wedding gown. Easy wasn't one of them, but she stopped herself before she could protest. In California, whenever Kay needed a special dress, she'd picked up the phone and called her cousin's favorite designers. Within hours, their assistants would wheel racks of options into the house. To help narrow down the choices, Jenny had often modeled their top picks.

Trying on a wedding gown wouldn't be that different, would it?

"Sure," she said, glad Kay had finally given her a task she could accomplish without upsetting half the shopkeepers in Heart's Landing. "Any particular instructions?"

"Well, the one I want has a mermaid silhouette. Strapless, of course. I plan to dance the night away, so make sure it's not too low in front. A wardrobe malfunction would ruin everything. I'm sending you a picture of it now."

As her phone chimed an incoming text and the image scrolled across the screen, Jenny tried to imagine dancing in a dress that called for industrial-strength Spanx despite a corset-laced back. "Better you than me," she murmured, thinking the gown wasn't her style in the least.

"What's that?"

"It's going to look beautiful on you," she assured her cousin.

"Thanks, Jen. You're one in a million. Just call the shop tomorrow and see when they can fit you in."

Jenny swallowed a long-suffering sigh. She should have known better than to expect Karolyn to schedule an appointment. Dutifully, she added it to her list of things to do.

"I owe you a big hug when we see each other. I miss you so much!"

"Speaking of seeing each other, it won't be long now." Even though Kay had copies of the itinerary on her phone, it never hurt to remind her cousin of the schedule. "You and Chad, your attendants, and Aunt Maggie are flying out of LAX Thursday night. Your plane gets in at ten on Friday. I've arranged for limos to pick everyone up. The driver will take you straight to the Captain's Cottage where you'll spend the weekend. I'll meet you there. We have a lot to do, so be ready to jump right into it." Mentally, she added time for a fitting to a list that included the rehearsal dinner and assembling the gift bags.

"Uh-huh. I'll run everything by Chad and get back to you. We'll talk later. I've got to dash now. Ciao."

Listening to dead air, Jenny shifted uneasily. She couldn't put her finger on the exact cause, but something Kay had said didn't ring true. She tugged on a loose strand of hair. Whatever her cousin had up her sleeve, she'd find out in due time. For now, she had more immediate problems. Her stomach sinking, she flipped to the picture of the naked cake.

She tsked. The ugly layers looked worse that they had the first time. "Nick will never forgive me for this," she whispered. Gathering her courage, she drew in an unsteady breath and prepared to tell him about the most recent change of plans. "Nick," she called, plunging through the swinging doors long before she was ready. "We have to talk."

Just talk. Their almost-kiss had evaporated like the morning dew the instant her phone rang. She and Nick wouldn't pick up where they'd left off. In fact, she'd count herself lucky if he didn't cancel her entire order once he heard her latest demands.

Nick was nowhere to be seen when she walked into the kitchen, but he'd obviously been busy while she was in the other room. The bowls and implements that had littered the counters had either been washed, dried and put away, or loaded into the dishwasher. Every trace of powdered sugar had been removed from gleaming countertops. Except for a tray holding ten cupcakes on one end of the counter, no one would ever guess they'd spent two hours making a mess of things.

The soft squeak of a door opening and closing drew her attention to the back wall. Warmth flooded her when the tall baker appeared. She gave him her best smile. "I was wondering where you'd gotten off to."

Crossing the room, Nick brandished an empty tin can. "Had to feed the cat. I've sort of adopted a stray. That was her crying in the alley."

Without warning, tears stung Jenny's eyes. A lesser man would have lost his temper when she'd plowed into him the day they'd first met. Nick hadn't. In fact, from that moment on, he'd plied her with cupcakes, helped her line up appointments, offered advice, and given her a place to hang out when the other shopkeepers looked at her like they couldn't decide whether to wring her neck or ply her with tea and sympathy. When she'd needed a break from the pressure of planning a wedding, he'd even adjusted his busy schedule to spend time with her. The man who did all that fed stray cats, too? Without a doubt, he was one of the best people she'd ever met.

Yeah, and how had she repaid his kindness? She hadn't been truthful with him. She'd kept so many secrets since she'd come to Heart's Landing, she was having trouble keeping her story straight. But there was no way out. With the wedding so close, she had to protect Karolyn's identity a few days longer. And that meant she had to lie to Nick again. Only, this time, she'd hurt him in the process.

Hating what she had to do, she held up her phone. "Listen. I, uh, I just spoke with Bob."

"I figured." Clouds shuttered Nick's expression as he pitched the can into the trash can and washed his hands.

"He, um, we—we want to do something a little different for the wedding cake."

At the sink, Nick's shoulders stiffened. "What's wrong with it?"

"Nothing. It's just..." This was harder than she'd thought it would be. She drew in a steadying breath. "He wants a naked cake. I tried to talk him out of it, but he's adamant." Unable to face the baker, she stared down at the image of the cake Kay insisted on serving at her wedding.

"No. I won't make it."

Stunned by his flat refusal, she resorted to the only leverage she had left. "Then I'll cancel the order and find someone who will."

"At this late date?"

Jenny sighed. He was right. With the wedding only days away, she'd never find another baker on such short notice. Instead, she'd have to reason with the one she had. "So, you'll make the naked cake for me?" she asked sweetly.

"No. I can't," Nick said, his voice flat.

A spark of hope lit in Jenny's chest. She stared up from her phone. "You *can't* make one? Or you won't?" Furtively, she crossed her fingers. Nick was the best baker in the entire area. If he said he didn't have a clue how to make a naked cake, she'd simply tell Karolyn it couldn't be done.

"I can. I've made them before."

"Oh." Her heart sank. So much for taking the easy way out.

"They're fine for serving small groups, like a dinner party or a small gathering. Anything more than a two-, possibly a three-tier cake, and it loses what little elegance it had to start with."

"I see," she said, disappointed. She didn't imagine that explanation would go over well with her cousin.

"But that's not the real reason I won't make one for your wedding. There's something more important."

"Yes?" What could that possibly be? Not trusting her voice, she let her eyes ask the question.

"You," he said simply. "You love frosting. When you ate that cupcake earlier, you were euphoric. Tell me I'm wrong."

There was no sense lying about that. Not when the rich taste of buttercream still lingered on her tongue. Nothing she'd ever tasted, not even the desserts in the five-star Parisian restaurants she'd dined in while Karolyn had been on location last year, could hold a candle to one of Nick's cupcakes. She kicked out a foot and scuffed the heel on the floor. "No, you're right."

"So, why would you want a cake without frosting?"

Because it's not my cake. Not my wedding.

Prepared to jump into the conversation, the words poised on the tip of her tongue. Every fiber of her being urged her to tell Nick the truth. But she couldn't. Despite the guilt that twisted her insides into a pretzel, she clamped her mouth shut. Kay and Aunt Maggie were the only family she had—she couldn't betray them. If she confessed her secrets to Nick and the word got out, the paparazzi would descend. They'd turn Kay's wedding into a media circus and ruin everything. She couldn't let that happen, couldn't let her family down, not after all they'd done for her. With no other choice, she resorted to the one tactic that had worked in the past. "Bob wants it that way," she said, shifting the blame to her nonexistent fiancé.

This time, though, Nick persisted. "What about what *you* want? Isn't that just as important?"

"It is, but…" Her voice trailed off. Jenny grabbed a napkin and blotted her eyes. The wedding cake she'd ordered cost a bundle. She couldn't believe Nick would risk losing the sale just to make her happy. But he didn't understand, and she couldn't make him without betraying her family.

"No buts," Nick said using a tone that brooked no argument. "It's about time you got something you wanted out of this wedding. If you can stand there and tell me you honestly want a plain almond cake with no icing, I'll make it for you. But you're going to have to tell me that's what *you* want. Not your fiancé. Or your mother-in-law. Or your guests. Just you. What do you want?"

Jenny's resistance melted like butter on a hot stove. "I want frosting," she whispered. "Lots and lots of frosting."

"Okay, then." A slow smile worked its way across Nick's face. "That's what you'll get."

Jenny ran her tongue over her bottom lip. Nick's creation was sure to be as tasty as it was beautiful, but that still didn't give Kay what she wanted. Her gaze drifted to the cupcakes they'd just made, and she resisted giving herself a swift kick. Of course. The solution was so clear, she was surprised she hadn't thought of it earlier.

She peered up at Nick. "You make cupcakes to match the cake for the bride and groom, don't you?" She knew the answer as well as she knew the colorful stains on one of her favorite jackets. The day they'd met, Nick had been on his way to deliver a forgotten batch of miniature cakes when she'd collided with him.

"I do." Nick blinked. "Quite often, the wedding party doesn't have a chance to eat during the reception. I always decorate a dozen or so for them to enjoy later."

"What if this time, you made the cupcakes, but you didn't frost them?"

"Naked cupcakes?" Nick's lopsided grin dipped to one side. "It's a good compromise. I like how you did that."

She crossed her fingers and hoped Karolyn would see it that way, too. Whether her cousin did or didn't, it was the best solution she could come up with to resolve the latest wrinkle in Kay's wedding plans.

But thinking of wrinkles led to thinking of wedding gowns, which, in turn, reminded her that she'd added more places to go and people to see to tomorrow's busy schedule. "I'd better get back to the B&B," she said, not bothering to hide her regret.

"You're sure?" Nick's glance drifted to the clock on the wall. "It's early yet."

"Much as I'd like to stay longer, I need to make an extra stop first thing tomorrow morning. That is, if I can even get an appointment." She couldn't help the way her shoulders drooped. Kay had conveniently overlooked that important detail. "It seems I'm suddenly in need of another wedding gown."

"Another dress." Nick felt questions crowding his mouth, vying to get out. Why on earth would Jenny need another gown for her wedding? She was only walking down the aisle once, which—in his book—was already one time too many. He tamped down his frustration with yet another useless reminder not to question the actions of a true Heart's Landing bride-to-be.

"It's not that unusual." Jenny stood, her arms akimbo. "The one for the ceremony is really more for show. It'll look stunning in the pictures, but it's not made for sitting down. It's definitely too snug for dancing at the reception. For that, I need something a little less structured."

The idea of down-to-earth Jenny walking down the aisle in a clingy dress took his breath away. He swallowed and rubbed his eyes. Focus. He had to focus on the current problem. "And you're just deciding this now?" A bad feeling rumbled through his gut. He'd narrowly averted disaster with her cake. Shopping for a new gown at this late date sounded suspiciously like there'd been another huge change in Jenny's wedding plans.

"It was, um, Bob's idea." Jenny stared down at her feet. "He thinks I should wear something in a different style for the reception. I've already chosen the second dress—I just have to try it on to be sure it's the right one. The thing is, I hate to go to that appointment alone. I'd ask the maid of honor to go with me, but she won't get here until Friday. I'm afraid to wait that long."

"You think?" He didn't know much about buying dresses,

period, but he'd walked through his mom's living room a time or two and found her glued to a TV show about bridal gowns. In every episode, the bride and an entire entourage descended on the salon months before the actual wedding date. "You're right. Someone needs to go with you. Is there anyone you can ask?"

"Everyone is so busy preparing for the wedding, I hate to ask them to take the time to go shopping with me. But I do want a second opinion."

Jenny looked forlorn and unsure of herself, standing there studying her toes. Here she was, trying to make the best of a difficult situation, and he'd just added to her troubles instead of helping her like he should.

Guilt and responsibility teamed up to aim him toward the obvious decision. Not that he had much choice in the matter. He'd already promised to keep a close watch over the town's wayward bride, hadn't he? "Look, you could pour everything I know about fashion into a measuring cup and have room to spare, but I'll come if you want me to."

"Really?" Tears sparkled in the brown eyes Jenny turned on him. "It won't take long, honest. I know exactly what I'm going to buy. They're holding it for me at Dress For A Day."

Understated elegance was the theme at the bridal salon on Boutonniere Drive. Though the shop had initially catered only to local brides, the owner gave every client the star treatment. As a result, the store's reputation had spread in recent years. Now, it wasn't unusual to see cars sporting license plates from Boston or even New York parked in the parking lot.

"That's Cheri Clark's place. She's one of my best customers."

"A bridal salon?"

"She orders dozens of petit fours to serve to her clients. Why don't I call her now and make sure she has an opening?" Not that there was any doubt. Cheri, like every other shopkeeper in town, would go an extra mile for a true Heart's Landing bride.

"You'd do that for me?"

"Sure. I'll get right on it." Nick turned away, unable to watch in case the threatening tears spilled onto Jenny's cheeks. Afraid he wouldn't be able to resist wiping them away if that happened, he ducked into his office, where he took a minute or two to regain his own composure before he selected Cheri's number from his contacts list.

Once he'd explained the situation, the long-time resident of the area was quick to offer her help.

"So, you can fit her in?" he asked, half afraid, half hoping the shop owner would turn them down.

"Nick, I earn my living by supplying gowns to brides who, for one reason or another, show up in Heart's Landing without one. Of course I'll work with your friend. If I'm not mistaken, I already have one on hold for her. A Sophie Olsen," she said, rattling off the name of a designer so popular even he'd heard of her. "Is that right?"

He gave his head a barely perceptible shake. He should have known Cheri would be up to the task. The woman hadn't so much as taken a beat when he'd asked about a last-minute purchase. Poking his head out the door, he passed the question along.

"Ask her if it's a strapless mermaid," Cheri added. "In a size four."

He hadn't watched all those shopping shows with his mom without learning a thing or two about dresses. Though Jenny would look stunning in a flour sack, the gown she'd chosen was so far outside her normal wheelhouse he couldn't picture her in it. When the shop owner confirmed that she did indeed have the gown on hand, he bit down hard over a groan and issued a silent vow that he'd support Jenny's choice, no matter what.

Returning to the kitchen, he announced, "We have an appointment at ten o'clock tomorrow. Cheri is going to work with you herself. You'll be in good hands."

"Oh!" Stars burst in Jenny's eyes. "You're my hero!"

He barely had time to think, definitely didn't have time to react before she flung her arms around his neck. Her soft curves pressed against him in an embrace that was everything he could possibly want. No one could blame him for reaching for her, his hands circling her narrow waist, his heart galloping. Not when he finally had her in his arms, right where he'd wanted her to be from the first moment he'd laid eyes on her.

Except the circumstances couldn't be worse. Here he was, holding onto the first woman he'd developed feelings for in ages and she was engaged to someone else. Was, in fact, thanking him for helping her shop for the dress she'd wear to marry another man.

The realization struck like a blow to his belly. Air hissed through his teeth. The fingers that had held Jenny straightened. Somehow, his hands found her shoulders. With a strength he didn't know he had, he gently pushed her away from him.

"I'm sorry," he said, missing her touch far more than he should. "That shouldn't have happened. We can't— I can't—"

"It's okay. It really is." Jenny's blue eyes bore into his. "We need to talk. There's something I should have told you, something I need to tell—"

Nick held up a hand, stopping her. He couldn't think. He

could barely breathe. He certainly couldn't let Jenny finish. "I think you'd better go," he said, his voice hoarse.

"But I— Can we talk?"

"Not now. Not tonight." He refused to meet Jenny's gaze. He couldn't bear to see the hurt that colored her features. He nearly couldn't handle the confusion in her voice.

His stomach twisted. She hadn't intended her hug to mean anything more than an exuberant thank you. He was the one who'd taken advantage of the situation. That was something he shouldn't have done, something he'd never let happen again.

Turning away from her, he spoke over his shoulder. "It's going to take me a little while to lock up the shop for the night, and I need to get an early start if I'm going to meet you at Dress For A Day tomorrow."

"If that's what you want."

He didn't have to see her face to know he'd hurt her. But in this case, he had to do the right thing for both of them. He and Jenny had spent so much time together over the past couple of weeks that she was confused. That was all. She'd see things in a clearer light by morning. When that happened, he didn't want her to have any regrets. Not on his account. No matter how much he cared for her.

Not even if he was head-over-heels in love with her. Which he was.

"I think it's for the best. We're friends. I don't want anything to jeopardize that."

He wasn't sure how he was going to get through the next few days without letting his feelings show, but he'd manage. No matter what it took. And right now, that meant refusing to watch as Jenny slowly walked across the bakery floor and out the door.

After she'd gone, he leaned over the counter, his heart as heavy as a lump of dough that refused to rise. He'd made a mistake, a terrible mistake. Any red-blooded man would've done the same thing, but it had been a mistake all the same. One he could never repeat.

Which didn't let him feel one iota better about the situation.

Giving up on sleep, he never even bothered to go upstairs. Instead, he planned to get a jump start on the next day's orders. But solace eluded him. Not even the quiet of the bakery, the silky feel of flour sifting through his fingers, could ease the heaviness in his heart. Still, he had to maintain the facade of friendship with Jenny for a few more days. He didn't have any other choice. He couldn't ruin the wedding of a true Heart's Landing bride any more than he could confess his true feelings to her.

Even if he regretted not taking the chance for the rest of his life.

Chapter Fourteen

On Wednesday, Nick slipped inside Dress For A Day well before Jenny's scheduled appointment. He waved hello to a woman who wore a white shell under a black blazer. Her black pants and shoes completed a fashionable outfit that provided stark contrast to the white gowns that hung… everywhere. "How are things?"

"It's going to be a really good day." Cheri Clark rubbed her hands together. Lips painted a cheery red widened. "I can't wait to get started. It's not often I get to help a true Heart's Landing bride. What do we know about her?"

"Well." He stopped before he blurted out that Jenny was perfect. She wasn't. The pressures and demands of planning her last-minute wedding had left her on edge. More than once, she'd shed a few frustrated tears. For someone who didn't make a move without consulting her calendar, she hadn't put a whole lot of thought into what she wanted for her wedding. In that regard, her mind was as capricious as foam on a wave. But, despite the fact that she'd driven every vendor in town to distraction, she'd never lost her temper and always went out of her way to treat the everyone with respect. Her infectious smile teased laughter from those around her.

Her kindness and concern drew everyone around her to her. Even an old grump like him.

"She's special," he finished.

"That's not very specific." Cheri glanced toward the door. There was no sign of the salon's newest customer. "I hear she's trouble."

The description set Nick's teeth on edge. "She's had a few problems." He'd concede that much, but no more. "Some of the other shopkeepers say she can't make up her mind, but it's not her fault. The guy she's engaged to, he's the one who keeps making changes. Like today." He gestured toward the racks of white dresses. "It was his idea to buy a second wedding gown. Something he just sprang on her last night. It's been like that the whole time she's been here."

"Hmm." Cheri brushed an imaginary fleck of lint from her jacket lapel. "She might be a true Heart's Landing bride, but it doesn't sound like she's marrying a Heart's Landing groom."

"Is that even a thing?" He'd never heard the term before, but it made sense. For every bride, there had to be a groom. He'd had his doubts about Jenny's since the beginning. But was that because Bob was wrong for her, or because he wanted her for himself? His brows tied themselves into a tangled knot. He glanced up to find Cheri starring at him speculatively.

"Tell me again why you're involved in this?"

He'd been asking himself the same thing. Of course, admitting that he'd fallen in love with the bride-to-be was out of the question. He reached for an answer that had nothing do with his personal feelings. "Mildred and the others asked me to take charge of her, keep her from making any more changes to the wedding plans. I'm only doing what they asked me to do."

Though, after last night, he was pretty sure Jenny and he would both be better off if he stayed away from her. Very far away. There was only one problem with that plan—he'd tried it and failed. He could no more keep Jenny at arm's length than he could serve a naked cake at her wedding.

Hair the color of wheat bleached by the sun tilted at an angle as Cheri studied him through narrowed eyes. "You're not falling for this girl, are you, Nick?"

Too late. He already had. But that was information he'd carry with him to the grave. "Who, me?" Struggling for an innocent air, he held out his hands. "Not a chance."

"Good to know. 'Cause if the job ever gets to be too much, let someone know, okay? No one wants to see you get hurt."

He was pretty sure it was also too late to avoid that. Nevertheless, he gave his head a firm shake. Not only would his own moral compass prevent him from crossing a line with a bride-to-be, he had to think about his town. There was too much at stake for him to let his feelings for Jenny interfere with her wedding. And with that, he steered the conversation into safer waters. "So, do you have this dress she's interested in?"

Cheri straightened marginally. "I do. The funny thing is, you said she found out about it last night. But someone requested the dress for her a couple of days ago."

"The fiancé, probably." Nick's hand fisted. "I've never met the guy, but the more I hear about him, the more unbelievable he sounds." What did Jenny see in him?

"No, it was a woman. I took the call myself."

"Huh." Was this Bob character so busy that he couldn't

even make a phone call? His opinion of Jenny's fiancé sank another notch. Not that it mattered. Cheri had the dress. That was the important thing.

A knowing look warmed Cheri's expression. "It, along with a few hand-picked selections, are in the back. I find my clients are usually happier with their final choice when I give them several gowns to choose from."

Nick nodded. Cheri's reasoning had a certain logic. Wasn't that why he filled the bakery's display case with different kinds of cookies? Although his customers invariably chose the same favorites over and over, they liked having options.

It was too bad love didn't work like that. If it did, he'd confess his feelings for Jenny and give her another option. Then, maybe she'd choose him instead of Bob.

Careful now.

That sounded an awful lot like he'd walked right up to that line everyone talked about and was thinking about crossing it. Wasn't that something he'd just sworn he'd never do?

Karolyn could keep her tight-fitting gowns with their plunging necklines and revealing backs, Jenny thought as she studied the white dress on display in one of the windows facing Boutonniere Drive. Embroidered flowers dotted the skirt's billowing layers. More decorative stitching climbed from the narrow waist to the rounded neck and onto the shoulders of the sleeveless bodice. She sighed. When it came time to choose her own wedding dress, she wanted one like the one in the window, one that made her feel like Cinderella going to the ball.

That was, if she ever found her Prince Charming. She'd thought Nick was the one last night in the bakery. For one split second, she'd dreamed of how he'd react when she told him the real reason she'd come to town. She'd imagined seeing the knowing little smile he often wore spread across his face. How he'd draw her into his arms and tell her he understood. Next, they'd confess their love for each other. She'd even thought about the life they'd build together right here in Heart's Landing. She'd start her own business. He'd continue making the best cakes for miles around. They'd buy a quaint little cottage on the bluff above the ocean, raise a family, and spend their lives loving one another.

But then, her dreams had come crashing down. Nick wasn't her Prince Charming. He never would be.

She should never have hugged him like she had. In her excitement about Kay's dress, she'd reacted without thinking. Once she was in Nick's arms, she'd wanted nothing more than to have him hold her and pull her closer.

But he hadn't. Instead, he'd made it clear that he wasn't looking for that kind of relationship. At least, not with her. His reaction had dashed any hope of ever sharing more than a casual friendship with the man she'd fallen in love with.

She still didn't know quite what had happened afterward. Her heart aching, tears blurring her vision, she must have walked to the B&B and climbed the stairs to her room. There, she'd tossed and turned all night. This morning, she'd nearly called the man who'd broken her heart, nearly told him that she no longer needed his help this morning.

But she hadn't. She was stronger than that. She had to admit Nick had taught her that lesson. He'd urged her to trust her instincts, to believe in herself. So, determined to make it through this final appointment without breaking down, she squared her shoulders and dotted concealer over the dark circles under her eyes. She wouldn't let Nick see how badly he'd hurt her. After today, she'd never have to see him again.

Well, not until the wedding. Not that he'd give her a second glance once the truth came out. By then, the entire town would be swept up in the thrill of having Karolyn and Chad in their midst. With not one but two celebrities to fawn over, everyone would forget about her.

Nick included.

She gave the gown in the display window a final, wistful glance, grasped the brass handle on the door, and let herself into Dress For A Day. Strategically placed in out-of-the-way spots, sprays of cream-colored flowers sat in crystal vases atop tall stands. Their smell perfumed the air. The moment she stepped onto the runner of soft burgundy that led from the entryway to a viewing area where couches and chairs had been artfully arranged around floor-to-ceiling mirrors, she understood why brides up and down the East Coast raved about the salon. Soothing ecru walls highlighted the dresses that hung from wooden hangers in deep-set alcoves lit by recessed lighting. No matter which direction she faced, bridal gowns beckoned her to come closer, to touch, to feel.

She lingered at the entryway, taking it all in while her eyes adjusted from the bright glare of sunshine outside to the low lighting. She'd barely had time to tuck her sunglasses into their case when she spotted Nick striding toward her. The diminutive woman at his side matched him step for step.

Nick.

She eyed the man who insisted on being her friend and nothing but her friend. Stiffening, she erected barriers around her heart to guard against the empty apologies he'd probably offer for the way things had ended between them last night.

"Good morning, Jenny." Looking remarkably well-rested, his face crinkled into a smile.

She arched one eyebrow. Apparently, they weren't going to pick up their conversation where it had left off. So be it. She hadn't slept a wink, but if he wanted to pretend nothing had happened between them, that was fine with her. And it would stay fine, no matter how much her pulse jumped at the sight of him. She modulated her tone. "Morning, Nick."

Nearing, he handled the introductions with the cheery nonchalance of a casual acquaintance. "Cheri, this is Jenny Longley. Jenny, Cheri Clark, the owner."

Despite her tiny frame, Cheri enveloped her hand in a firm grip while they exchanged the usual pleasantries. Like a reporter drafting a story, Cheri asked the standard who, what, and when questions about the wedding and nodded her approval in the appropriate places. When the conversation started to lag, the woman suggested they get started.

"Nick, have a seat right there," Cheri said, directing the baker to a couch and chairs in front of a three-way mirror. "Jenny, can I offer you anything before we try on the first gown? A mimosa? Something sweet to nibble on?"

"No, thanks." She needed to get this over with and get on with her day. With Kay and the entire wedding party set to arrive bright and early Friday morning, she had a long list of final preparations to handle in a limited amount of time. She couldn't afford to start the day off with champagne. As for the treats, she eyed the petit fours and told herself she'd lost her taste for anything from I Do Cakes.

"Well, let's see what you think about this gown, then. Shall we?"

In a dressing room painted the same soothing ecru as the walls in the viewing area, Jenny slipped out of the yellow sundress she'd worn and wrapped herself in a soft lavender robe someone had thoughtfully hung on the back of the door. She'd barely finished before Cheri returned with the dress Kay had ordered. Standing on tiptoe, the owner hung the gown on a display rack and stood back.

"Isn't it lovely?"

"It's quite something." The gown was even more form-fitting than she'd feared. Doubly glad she'd skipped the second cupcake at I Do Cakes last night, Jenny skimmed one hand over her thigh. Even the Spanx she'd wiggled into this morning might not be enough to let her pull the tight fabric down over her hips. Suddenly worried, she longed to tug on a strand of hair but had to settle for giving her smooth chignon a pat.

"It's not what you expected? I assure you, it's the one you requested." Cheri fluffed and fussed with the layers of satiny fabric that started around mid-thigh. She turned over a discreet ticket. "And it's in your size."

"It's not that. It's—" She stopped herself. The dress was about as far from what she would choose for herself as she could get, but this wasn't the time to share that tidbit of information. She needed to protect Kay's secret for two more days, until her cousin delighted everyone in town with a grand entrance. She could manage that much, couldn't she? She schooled her features and summoned an awed tone. "It's lovely," she agreed.

Cheri's pensive expression said she wasn't entirely convinced by her client's reassurances. "It can be hard to imagine yourself in a dress when it's on the hanger," she offered. "Let's try this one on and see how it looks."

The dress was pretty enough, but so skin-tight that Jenny needed—and gratefully accepted—Cheri's help in shimmying into it. Once she had it on, she ran a hand over the rich fabric. She didn't have to be a fashion expert to see it had been exquisitely made. The lace and beadwork alone had to be worth a king's ransom. Which was appropriate, since by the time they squeezed and tucked and nudged her into place, she felt like she'd been encased in a tight-fitting suit of body armor.

"That's right—nice and tall. Throw your shoulders back. There." Cheri gave the corset a final tug, then moved to the other side of the dressing room. "You look fabulous. It fits you perfectly."

Jenny studied her image in the mirror. Kay's flair for the dramatic called for something extraordinary. With a sweetheart neckline and a back that redefined the term "backless," the gown certainly fit the bill.

"Are you ready for the three-way mirror?" Cheri asked.

Walk out there wearing this?

Honestly, she'd rather curl up and die, but she didn't have much choice. No matter how ill at ease she felt, she'd agreed to play the part of an enthusiastic bride-to-be. And what bride spent thousands of dollars on a wedding gown without seeing it from every angle?

Fighting an urge to cross her arms across her chest, she trailed Cheri into the main room. On the dais, she strutted from one end of the platform to the other. Determined to carry out her role, she gave her image in the mirror a cursory glance. A thousand tiny crystals sewn into the fabric sparkled. The layers of silk that formed the mermaid's "tail" rustled. As much as the dress was so not for her, she had to admit her cousin would love it.

"Yes." She nodded her approval. "This is the one." She

had turned, intending to make a beeline for the dressing room, when Cheri held up a hand.

"Wait now. Don't you want a second opinion?"

Oh, yeah. Nick again.

Either by design or haste, she'd overlooked the man who'd broken her heart. He sat on the edge of the couch, his body tense. Seeing his clenched jaw and fixed blue eyes, she straightened the tiniest bit. It'd take a very special dress indeed to put that particular mix of regret and desire on Nick's face. She'd seriously underestimated the impact of the one she wore.

"Well?" She skimmed one hand over her hips. Her lips in thin lines, she stared at Nick over her reflection in the three-way mirror.

His face hardened. He crossed his ankles. "Well, what?" he challenged.

"Does it fit?" She cocked one hip and anchored her hand there, knowing full well that the movement tugged the fabric tighter.

Conceding defeat, Nick swallowed. "Like a glove."

"Uh-huh." Despite her efforts to hide it, a smile tugged at her lips. When it came to things she hated, breaking in a new pair of leather gloves was at the top of a very short list.

"Well, that settles it, then. I'll take it." She turned to Cheri, who lurked in the shadows. "You'll have it ready for a final fitting Friday morning?" Although the dress didn't require alterations, Kay would no doubt expect to try it on the minute her plane landed.

"Yes. We can definitely do that," Cheri said all smooth assurance.

From his position on the couch, Nick coughed. "Wait a sec. That's it?"

"That's it." Poised at the edge of the dais, Jenny lifted the skirt off the floor. "We won't take up any more of Cheri's valuable time."

"But there are bunches of gowns you haven't even seen yet." Nick's gaze wandered the sea of white. "You aren't going to try on any of them?"

"You don't think this one looks good on me?" Sometimes, she simply didn't understand men at all. A minute earlier, he'd given this dress two thumbs up. But now he wasn't satisfied?

Nick shrugged. "I'm just saying, we're here. You might as well see if there's something else you like."

Something more to my taste?

She had to admit, it was a tempting offer. Gowns crowded the recessed alcoves. They hung in long racks along the walls. Surely, with so many to choose from, she'd find the one that was right for her. She fought an urge to leap from the dais and start pulling dresses off their hangers. She hadn't come to Dress For A Day to find a something for herself.

She motioned to the shop owner. "Cheri has already done us a tremendous favor by fitting me into her schedule today. I shouldn't take up more time when I've made up my mind."

Cheri's discreet cough argued the point. "Nothing is more important than helping you find the gown that's exactly right for you. Most of my brides try on several before deciding which one they want."

Jenny's resolve wavered. "If you're sure you don't mind..."

"I'm positive. Once you're married, you may never have the opportunity to try on bridal gowns again. Why not take advantage of this chance?" Cheri tapped a pensive finger to her chin. "I have a couple of dresses that would fit you just as fabulously as this one. Maybe even more so."

"If you insist." The beginnings of a smile crept across

Jenny's face. Now that she was committed, she might as well enjoy the moment. Excitement curled in her belly and spread outward. She leaned in conspiratorially. "So what shall we try on first?"

"I have a beautiful ball gown in your size. You'll look like a princess in it."

Her anticipation building, Jenny accepted the shop owner's hand while she stepped down from the dais. In the dressing room, the skin-tight layers of satin and lace came off much faster than they'd gone on. Thankful to be able to draw a full breath again, she sank onto a waiting chair while Cheri immediately whisked Kay's gown out of sight and into another part of the salon. She'd barely had time to relax before the shop owner was back, this time carrying a different confection in white satin and gauzy fabric.

"This is another Sophia Olsen." Cheri grunted softly as she stretched over the billowing skirt to hang the dress on the display stand. "But as you can see, it's quite different from the first one. It features Battenberg lace on the bodice, off-the-shoulder sleeves, a fitted waist, and a stunning chiffon skirt."

"I don't know." Jenny treated the gown to a pensive study. There had to be a dozen yards of fabric in the skirt alone. "It looks like something you'd wear if you were getting married in a castle. A big one." She could imagine the future Queen of England gliding down the aisle of Winchester Cathedral in a gown like this one.

Cheri had an answer ready. "The only question should be whether you like it or not. If you do, try it on and see how it fits. At worst, letting me see you in this dress will help me narrow down the choices for the next gown I show you."

That made sense, and soon she stood still as Cheri fastened the last of a long line of buttons that ran down the back. "You're right. I do feel like a princess. All I need is a tiara."

"We have those if you want," Cheri said, though doubt colored her words.

"No. I was just joking. Let's see what it looks like out there." The gown's more conservative lines made it easier to think about parading in front of the three-way mirror.

Though she told herself Nick had forfeited the right to voice an opinion by rejecting her the night before, she cast a surreptitious glance in his direction as she stepped from the curtained area. She smothered a smile when he sat at attention. She negotiated the step onto the dais while she pretended not to notice how his eyes tracked her every move.

"It is a sweet dress. I like this part." She ran her fingers lightly over the lace-covered bodice. Moving down, she fluffed out the full skirt. Delicate appliqués climbed halfway up the gauzy material. Speaking more to herself than anyone else, she pointed to the hem. "But, honestly, I think it's a little bit much."

"Really? You could dance all night in that one." Nick remained perched on the edge of the cushions.

"She's right," put in Cheri. "This gown fits you perfectly, but the skirt overpowers your frame. I'd suggest something that shows off your figure just a bit more, and I have just the thing. It's another Olsen. Brand-new. It came in yesterday, and it's one of my favorites. I think you'll love it."

Jenny shifted her weight from one foot to the other. It couldn't hurt to try on just one more gown, could it? She lifted the billowing skirts to mid-calf and stepped off the dais. "Okay, but this will have to be the last one. I really have a full schedule today."

Once again, Cheri wasted no time in helping her trade

one gown for another. In minutes, Jenny stood before the mirror in the dressing room while the shop owner fastened the final clasp.

"Oh," she cried, seeing her reflection. Off-the-shoulder sleeves led to a modest scooped neck decorated by scalloped edging that reminded her of the day she and Nick had spent at the beach. The close-fitting bodice softly cupped her curves. Below it, a wide satin belt circled her waist. Decorative lace dripped down to form points in a flaring skirt. From top to bottom, the dress was sheer perfection.

"I thought you'd like it." Tiny crows' feet at the corners of Cheri's eyes crinkled as she smiled smugly. "Shall we?" She held the dressing room door open.

"That's it. That's the one." In case she hadn't noticed how he slowly rose to his feet while she glided across the carpet, Nick's hoarse whisper left no doubt of what he thought about the dress.

"You think so?" Jenny spun in a circle. "I love it," she cried as the skirt flared out. "I feel like I'm walking in a cloud."

"It's as perfect as icing on a cake." Nick nodded thoughtfully.

Jenny chortled. Only a baker would draw the comparison, but he was right. The dress was everything she'd ever wanted in her wedding gown and more.

Cheri hovered. "It wouldn't need a single alteration. We could press and steam it and deliver it straight to the Captain's Cottage."

Except I'm not the one who's getting married.

Regret swooped in and stole the joy right out of moment. Jenny's stomach twisted painfully. She splayed her fingers across the layers of chiffon. "Oh, I'm not buying this." She let the rich fabric of the skirt sift through her fingers. "I'm getting the first one I tried on."

"But…" As if he'd had the wind taken out of his sails, Nick sank onto the cushions.

"You are?" Cheri's brows knitted. "You just said you loved this gown. Why wouldn't you get the one you like the best?"

Jenny swallowed. Like so many of the changes she'd made to the wedding plans since her arrival in Heart's Landing, Nick and Cheri would never understand why she had to choose one particular dress over another. As much as she wanted to explain it to them, she couldn't. Not without betraying Kay's trust. Instead, she forged ahead. "I have my reasons. I know what I'm doing."

From his position on the couch, Nick lifted one shoulder in a shrug she would have found endearing before he'd broken her heart. "You know your fiancé better than any of us." He stared at the carpet. "If you think he'll like the other one best, then who am I to argue?"

In a move that said she'd been dealt a surprise or two from brides in the past, Cheri straightened. "Don't you worry your head about a thing, my dear. You're going to be such a beautiful bride, it doesn't matter which dress you choose."

If only that were true. "Then it's settled. Let me get out of this gown and I'll get out of your hair."

Jenny cast a last, lingering glance at herself in the mirror. She didn't have to look twice. The expression on Nick's face when she walked out of the dressing area had said it all—if he loved her the way she loved him, this would be the dress she'd wear when she walked down the aisle. But he didn't love her, and suddenly, she couldn't stand to have the gown on a minute longer. Reaching for the zipper, she dashed down the hallway toward the dressing area.

Chapter Fifteen

Oh, man. How dumb was that?

He'd let himself forget, just for a moment, that Jenny was marrying someone else. When she'd walked out of the back of the store wearing that last gown, he hadn't been able to help himself. He'd practically heard the DJ introducing Mr. and Mrs. Nicolas Bell to the guests at their wedding. Like the hero in countless movies, he'd hold out his arm for her, lead her onto the dance floor and press her close while the band played their favorite song.

Then, fate had slapped him in the face with a cold bucket of *I'm not buying it.*

He wasn't Jenny's Mr. Right. She had chosen the other guy, like she'd chosen the other dress. He'd been stupid to think things would work out any differently.

But that was exactly what he'd been thinking, wasn't it? That somehow, some way, she'd choose him. That when the time came to say, *I do*, she'd tell Bob, *I don't.*

Yeah, that was never going to happen. He saw that now. She'd made her choice. She'd stick with it.

An empty, hollow feeling spread through his gut. By sheer force of will, he held it together until Jenny disappeared into the dressing area with Cheri. When he was unable to resist any longer, he reached for one of the slender glasses of mimosa. He chugged the mixture of juice and champagne down in a single swallow. Reaching for another, he stilled his hand. He didn't need anyone to tell him what would happen if he combined alcohol and a sleepless night on an empty stomach. He couldn't afford to lose his cool today. Not on the day he'd put the finishing touches on Jenny's wedding cake. The cake he'd serve following her wedding to another man.

He hung his head and somehow managed not to howl.

It took every ounce of strength he had, but somehow he pulled himself together by the time Jenny turned to face him on the sidewalk outside the dress shop a few minutes later.

"Thanks for coming with me today, Nick," she said, her voice and demeanor decidedly cool. As if he needed another clue, she extended her hand.

"Glad to do it." He grasped her palm in a polite shake. "So, what's on your agenda for the day?"

"I have to give the vendors their final payments and see a few people, but nothing you need to bother with. I'll check on the flowers with Mildred. Alicia asked me to drop by the Captain's Cottage to go over a few adjustments to the seating chart. I need to finalize pickup times with the car service. That sort of thing."

"Just the usual, last-minute confirmations, then? No changes?" He crossed his fingers. People were counting on him to keep a certain wayward bride on track. He couldn't let them down, no matter how much he suffered for it.

Jenny's lips parted. Instead of answering, though, she looked toward the opposite end of the street just as a horse-drawn carriage turned the corner onto Boutonniere. Her gaze fixed on the carriage. As still as one of Captain Thaddeus's stone hearts, she tracked the buggy's movement from one end of the broad avenue to the other. Her trance lasted until the wheels disappeared around a bend in the road. At last, a breath shuddered through her.

"Jenny?" His heart squeezed painfully at the unshed tears glistening in her eyes.

Like someone waking from a dream, she rubbed one hand over her face. "I'm sorry. You were saying?"

"We were talking about your big day when you went, well, blank for a minute. You're not under the weather, are you? You're drinking enough water?" She wouldn't be the first bride to overlook the need for food and water. Even in Rhode Island, dehydration could be a problem.

"I'm okay. Really, I am." Jenny brushed one hand over her eyes. "I love horse-drawn carriages. The pageantry. The elegance. I kind of lose it whenever I see one."

He thought her answer was a bit forced, her smile a bit too bright, but he could no longer assume he knew her moods, her wants, her dreams. Not when he'd judged the situation between them so badly. Not when she was marrying someone else. Scuffing his foot, he focused on the things he did know. That, for instance, Jenny had scheduled her own carriage ride. "What time will your driver pick you up for the ceremony on Saturday? I'll be sure to wave as you ride past the bakery." And not just him. He'd have the entire staff line the sidewalk.

Jenny ducked her head. "No horse-and-buggy for me."

"Seriously?" Just when he'd thought she couldn't surprise him anymore, she accomplished the impossible. He leaned forward. "Why not, when you're so obviously carried away by them?"

"Nice pun," she quipped, her mouth slanting up as

she raised her head. "But that wasn't something Bob and I wanted."

Humph. Bob, again. He should have known.

He traced the outline of his cell phone. This was one problem he could solve. With a single phone call, he could give the girl of his dreams her heart's desire on her wedding day. A carriage ride through town following the ceremony could be his present to the happy couple, his farewell gift.

There was just one problem, but it was a biggie. He couldn't watch Jenny and her Mr. Right ride straight down Procession Way and out of his life forever. Not without breaking down, he couldn't. He was strong, but he wasn't that strong.

The solution came to him in an instant. It seemed so obvious, he wondered why he hadn't thought of it right away. It was about time young Jimmy oversaw his very first wedding. Jenny's was the perfect place for him to start. Taking charge of the cake for a true Heart's Landing bride would give his assistant a chance to shine while sparing him a painful farewell.

Nick mentally patted himself on the back for coming up with such a brilliant idea. His plan only had one little flaw, he realized. He was in for a heartache no matter what.

Jenny dragged her fork through the tasteless lentils. She didn't bother stirring the unappetizing mound of brown soba noodles. Some julienned carrot, a spicy sauce, or a handful of pine nuts might have dressed up the side dish, but the strands of buckwheat pasta sat unadorned and cold on her plate. She lowered her knife and fork to the plate, a sign she had finished her meal.

"You're not going to eat any more than that?"

Great. Just what she needed, a waitress who felt entitled to chastise her for not cleaning her plate. She'd had her fill of people telling her what she could and couldn't do. She pushed the offensive dish aside. "I'm done."

So done.

Done with trying on wedding gowns she'd never wear. All but finished with the items on today's To Do list. Most of all, so over her cousin's latest suggestion to change, change, change one more thing about the wedding. This time, Karolyn had insisted on switching the location of the rehearsal dinner to a vegan restaurant north of Newport. Something that—now that she'd been there and done that—wasn't going to happen. Not only would the drive add several hours to a schedule so tight it squeaked, the food simply didn't live up to the hype. She shrugged. The pickiest eaters in Karolyn's wedding party would just have to fill up on tossed salad and the restaurant's old-world style bread drenched in olive oil and herbs while the rest feasted on top-notch Italian cuisine. She was sticking with her first choice, Bow Tie Pasta.

Waiting for the bill, she rubbed her forehead as worries about the days ahead troubled her thoughts. She'd have to sweet-talk like a Southern belle to keep the star-studded wedding party on track throughout their busy day on the eve of the wedding. The rush would start the moment she greeted the new arrivals at the Captain's Cottage. From there, she'd whisk Kay off to a final fitting before dropping her off at Perfectly Flawless. Massages and facials would help the bride and her attendants recover after the long flight from L.A. The rehearsal and dinner would follow. Later still, they'd assemble the gift baskets.

Had she crammed too much into one day? She gave her

head a small shake. Kay hadn't left her much choice. They'd simply have to get it all done.

Speaking of getting things done, though, now that she'd decided in favor of Bow Tie Pasta, she'd have to stop by the restaurant and make the final payment. Thank goodness she hadn't cancelled those reservations like Kay had wanted her to. She supposed she had Nick to thank for that. Ever since they'd met, he'd been encouraging her to trust the decisions she'd made, stick with her original choices. This time, she had.

For a second, she pictured his face when she shared the news. He'd be happy for her, no doubt. To celebrate, he'd serve her one of his delicious cupcakes.

Her empty stomach clenched. She balled the paper napkin in her lap.

There'd be no more afternoon visits to the bakery. No lingering talks with the baker over tea and cupcakes. No. More. Nick. He'd made his position very clear—he didn't love her like she loved him.

"Dessert comes with your meal. How about a non-fat, gluten-free, black bean brownie with organic prune topping?" The waitress plunked an overpriced bill on the table.

Jenny fought the urge to clamp a hand over her mouth. She couldn't think of anything worse.

Unless it was spending the rest of her life without Nick in it.

Chapter Sixteen

Her broken heart safely hidden behind sturdy barriers, Jenny reached the end of the wide walkway in front of the Captain's Cottage. She turned and retraced her steps to the entrance. Where were they? Her heels tapped out the question on the concrete like an operator tapping out a message in Morse code. She mounted the steps to the front door and, from the higher vantage point, checked the horizon. Beyond the spot where the road disappeared around a bend, trees swayed in the mid-morning breeze. Otherwise, nothing moved. Certainly not the town cars she'd hired to ferry Karolyn, Chad, their attendants, and their closest relatives from the airport to Heart's Landing.

She tromped down to the sidewalk where she completed another circuit. When there was still no sign of the arriving party, she whipped out her phone.

"Global Limo Service." The receptionist answered on the first ring. "How may I assist you?"

"This is Jennifer Longley. I need to check the status of a pickup from Terminal V at Boston Logan." Quickly, she provided the necessary details, including the expected arrival time of Karolyn's private jet.

"I'll look into that for you, Ms. Longley. Please hold."

Jenny tapped her toe. A mercifully short time passed before the woman came back on line.

"Ma'am? The drivers are waiting at the gate. Their passengers haven't arrived yet."

"Thank you. I'm sure their flight will land soon." Why hadn't Kay called to let her know about the delay?

On the other end of the line, the receptionist cleared her throat. "I'm sorry, but we'll have to add a surcharge for the extra time."

"Of course." She didn't even flinch. Whatever the cost, her cousin would cover it. "I'll make some phone calls. Just don't let the drivers leave. It's important that my party makes it here today."

"Will do. Is there anything else I can help you with?"

There wasn't, and Jenny ended the call. She considered her next move on another trek around the sidewalk. Frequent checks of the news and social media assured her there'd been no plane crash. With that worry put to bed, she punched in the number for Kay's home in Beverly Hills. She froze when someone answered on the second ring.

"Karter residence."

"Aunt Maggie?" What was her aunt doing in California? Why wasn't she on the plane? Or better yet, getting settled into her suite in the Captain's Cottage? Unease churned in Jenny's stomach. She braced for answers she'd probably hate. "What happened? Why aren't you here?"

"I guess you haven't spoken with Karolyn?" Aunt Maggie made a dismissive noise. "That girl. She never changes. Has to do everything at the last minute. You, you're the opposite. Everything planned out in advance. Usually with a back-up in case something goes wrong. How you two both grew up together and turned out so differently, I'll never know."

"Both approaches have their plusses and minuses." Hers tied her to a rigid schedule, though lately, she'd discovered the world wouldn't end if she ignored her To Do list long enough to go for a walk in the park. Out of habit, she defended her cousin. "Kay has her good points. She has more talent in her little finger than most people have in their entire bodies."

"True enough. She put those skills to good work, and look where it's gotten her. She's done quite well for herself."

That was an understatement if she'd ever heard one. But it didn't explain why she and Karolyn weren't headed to Dress For A Day for her cousin's final fitting. "Aunt Maggie, your flight?"

Instead of answering, her aunt continued to ramble. "You may not be an actress, but I always thought you'd go places, do things with your life. I guess you're content working for Kay, though?"

The back-handed compliment landed like a lead weight in Jenny's stomach. She pulled the phone away from her ear and stared at it. Had her aunt really meant to say she'd failed to live up to her potential? She swallowed. "I thought you wanted me to work for Kay, Aunt Maggie. You asked me to help her out right after graduation."

"I didn't mean forever, dear."

Well, no, but… Tears stung her eyes. "I owe you and Kay so much for all you've done for me. Helping out was my way of paying back."

"Sweetheart. You don't owe me, or Kay, a thing. You never have. When your parents died, I wanted you to come and live with me. It was like…"

Jenny heard the strain in her aunt's voice and gripped the phone tighter.

"It was like having a little bit of my sister with me again."

Oh!

Jenny stared hard at the horizon. All those years ago, a freak train wreck had changed her life forever, but she'd never considered how much her aunt had lost that night. "I—I don't know what to say."

Aunt Maggie's voice firmed. "One of these days, you're going to strike out on your own. When you do, I'll be one of the first to cheer you on."

"I appreciate that, Aunt Maggie. Maybe more than you know." A thready sigh shuddered through her. She'd need time to absorb everything she'd learned from her aunt. Sometime this weekend, she'd make an opportunity for the two of them to sit down and have a longer chat. Right now, though, a series of appointments and events stretched across the next twenty-four hours like stepping stones across a pond. Only, Kay was in serious danger of missing the first step that would culminate in her walking into the grand ballroom of the Captain's Cottage tomorrow and exiting a short while later as Mrs. Chad Grant.

"So, where is my talented, disorganized cousin?" Hoping Kay's plane was even now circling the airport, Jenny crossed her fingers.

"Hang on. I'll get her."

She's still in California!

The realization struck another blow to her stomach. She doubled over, her carefully built schedule imploding like a building on the set of a disaster flick. At the very least, the fitting and appointments at Perfectly Flawless were out. Would the bridal party even arrive in time for the rehearsal dinner?

She checked her watch. If Karolyn left for the airport within the hour, they could still run through the ceremony before their dinner reservations.

"Oh, Jenny. I'm so glad you called." Talking a mile a minute, Kay blurted, "Ever since the news of our engagement got out, reporters and photographers have camped out on the street outside the gates. It's like a zoo here, only I'm the one on display! Can you make them go away?"

She could no more control the paparazzi than guess what stunt her cousin would pull next. Tired of Karolyn's shenanigans, she spoke through clenched teeth. "I'm in Heart's Landing. Where you sent me to plan your wedding. Which, in case you've forgotten, is happening *to-mor-row*. Only, I'm short a wedding party. Why are you still in L.A. when you're supposed to be here?"

"Right. About that." As if her cousin had clamped a hand over the receiver, the voice in Jenny's ear grew distant and muffled. She tapped her foot until, at last, Kay picked up the conversation where she'd left off. "Chad and I decided we'd fly in tomorrow with the rest of our guests."

"Wait! What? No, Kay." Hating the whiny sound of her own voice, Jenny pulled the phone from her ear and counted to ten. Staring up at the sky, she decided it was probably a good thing she wasn't close enough to grab her cousin by the neck. As it was, she could barely speak. "The rehearsal is this evening. The rehearsal and the rehearsal dinner. And—"

"I know. I know. And I'm sorry. But it didn't feel right to leave our friends to fend for themselves on the flight."

But it was okay to leave *her* hanging? "It's not like they're going to suffer," she protested. She'd flown with Kay enough to know everyone on board would be treated to first class service, a coast-to-coast open bar, movies, meals. "They'll have everything they could possibly want."

"But what they want is to spend time with Chad and me. Besides, I can't fly to Rhode Island tonight. I have other plans."

Other plans? Plans more important than your wedding rehearsal?

Jenny stalled, trying to find a way to get her cousin to change her mind. "What about the restaurant? I reserved one of their private dining areas."

"Oh, just cancel the reservations. People do it all the time."

"Kay, be reasonable." She thought of the cooks and kitchen staff at Bow Tie Pasta. "Do you have any idea how much prep work went into preparing for twenty-five VIP's? People have put a lot of effort into making sure everything is perfect for your rehearsal and your wedding. You can't just change your mind at the drop of a hat." When Kay didn't answer, she added, "Even if they could fill those seats at the last minute, I've already paid the bill."

"I don't suppose they'd give us a refund."

"Have you completely lost your mind?" Jenny gulped. She'd pushed too hard. Listening to dead air, she half expected Kay's next words to be, "You're fired!"

"You're right. I'm sorry," came the words she least expected to hear. "I've been a pain, and you have every right to be upset with me. I've asked too much of you."

Jenny swallowed. The abrupt change of direction threw her off guard. "It's okay," she said, calming. "Weddings are stressful." She should know—she'd been at her wits' end over this one, and it wasn't even hers.

"No. I'm *really* sorry. Mom's been on my case about taking advantage of people. Especially you. She says I don't hear the word *no* enough." Kay's voice dropped to a conspiratorial whisper. "I think she might move into the guest house once Chad and I get back from our honeymoon. I bet I'll hear *no* plenty then."

"Whoa, that'll be different." The image of her mega-star cousin being bossed around by her aunt made her smile. But with Aunt Maggie there to run Kay's life it sounded like she might be out of a job sooner than expected.

Needing some time to sort out how she felt about that, Jenny steered the conversation back to the topic at hand.

"So, the rehearsal is out. But you can wing it. Remember the wedding in *The Blossom Point*?" In the blockbuster movie released the previous fall, Karolyn played a girl whose rocky courtship had finally concluded with her walking down the aisle in her mother's hand-me-down wedding dress. Viewers across the country had reached for tissues as the closing credits had rolled across the screen. "Just think of that scene tomorrow, and you'll do fine. Better than fine," she corrected. "Because you'll be marrying Chad."

"Thanks, Jen. I knew I could count on you."

Maybe that was part of the problem. Jenny exhaled a ragged breath. Maybe Nick had been right again, and she'd been too accommodating. That was something else she'd have to change when—and if—she returned to California. But for now, they had a wedding to get through. "I'll see you tomorrow, then. The flight still gets in around eight?" She'd arranged for a dozen busses to ferry the guests to Heart's Landing.

"I guess." Karolyn's voice grew distant. Jenny caught snatches of effusive greetings and the rustle of fabric before her cousin said, "Hey, I have to go. Haley and Sue just got here."

"Sure." Jenny nodded. Haley, her cousin's bestie, and Chad's sister Sue were in the wedding party.

"We're getting facials, then they have some sort of bachelorette party in the works. So, see you tomorrow?"

"Yeah. On your wedding day. Don't worry about a thing."

"Oops. The girls say I have to hang up now or they'll steal my phone." Kay's voice dropped to a whisper. "I'm sure everything will work out perfectly. It always does when you're in charge."

Jenny listened to the click that indicated Karolyn had ended the call. She wished she shared Kay's confidence. But, in less than twenty-four hours—without trying on the gown she'd chosen for her reception, without ever taking a peek at the location for her wedding, or running through her lines even once—her cousin planned to walk down the aisle in front of some of the industry's top movers and shakers. So much could go wrong with that plan that Jenny couldn't bear to think about it.

She sank onto the steps of the Captain's Cottage. In rapid succession, she cancelled the appointments at Dress For A Day and Perfectly Flawless. Her next call went to Mildred, who agreed to deliver the floral arrangements for the rehearsal dinner to the Captain's Cottage. If nothing else, they'd use the flowers to brighten nooks and alcoves throughout the mansion. She worked her way down a list of musicians and drivers until, near the end, she spotted an item that nearly gave her heart failure.

"The gift bags." Two hundred and fifty of them, to be precise. Each one empty and waiting to be filled by a bridal party that had decided they had better things to do.

Now what? She shook her head. This was exactly the kind of problem she and Nick used to discuss at I Do Cakes each afternoon. She'd walk into the bakery with the newest wrinkle in Kay's wedding hanging like an albatross around her neck, and somehow over coffee and a cupcake, he'd set her free.

She wished she could turn to him now.

But she couldn't go to him for help. Couldn't turn to the one person in Heart's Landing she trusted to come up with a solution whenever Kay threw a stumbling block in front of the wedding plans. She and Nick were never going to find happiness together. They weren't even speaking to each other.

Her face fell. The barriers she'd erected around her broken heart weakened. Another round of tears threatened. She fought them down.

Dusting her hands together, she reached a decision that was long overdue. No matter how the future played out between her and Nick, no matter how badly Kay had messed up the plans for the rehearsal, she was done with letting her will-o'-the-wisp cousin determine her future. It was time to move on. She hadn't nailed down the particulars yet, but she'd work on it. She might even come up with a plan tonight. In the meantime, she needed to speak with Alicia about cancelling this evening's rehearsal and get to work on those gift bags. Moments later, she knocked on the event coordinator's door.

"Jenny! Come in. Come in." Alicia rose from the chair behind her desk. "Is Bob with you?" The coordinator glanced over Jenny's shoulder as if she expected the nonexistent groom to appear in the doorway. "I've been so looking forward to meeting him."

"Bob—" Her tongue tripped over the name of her mythical fiancé. She rubbed her head, tired of the pretense. According to the plan that lay in ruins, she should be introducing

Karolyn to the star-struck citizens of Heart's Landing right about now. But here she was, still stuck with keeping her cousin's secret for another day. She cleared her throat. "I'm sure he'd love to meet you, too. Unfortunately, there's been a delay. He and the rest of the wedding party weren't able to leave as soon as they'd hoped. I'm afraid they won't get here till tomorrow."

"I see." Alicia's eyebrows might have climbed to her hairline, but otherwise she did a good job of controlling her shock. "You poor thing," she gushed, stepping forward. "I know how much you were counting on his arrival tonight. I suppose this means the rehearsal is off?"

Jenny took a big breath and exhaled it slowly. "Yes. I've notified the minister and called Mildred. She'll bring the flowers here."

Alicia ventured a tentative, "And the wedding?"

"Oh, it's still on," she rushed to reassure the woman. Kay might waffle when it came to having a plan and sticking to it, but her cousin and Chad Grant were in love with one another. That much, she knew for sure. "Everyone should get here by ten tomorrow morning."

Alicia's head swung back and forth in wonder. "Seriously, Jenny. I don't know many brides who could handle this as well as you have. Not only did you pull your wedding together on very short notice, you've taken every curve and upset in stride. You've done an amazing job." Alicia glanced around the room, her focus coming to rest on a family photograph. "I don't suppose there's any chance you and your new husband will decide to settle here, is there? Because I could use someone with your skills to help me run this place until I retire in a couple of years."

Her pulse jumped. That sounded an awful lot like a job offer and what might be an answer to her prayers.

As much as she wanted to talk more, though, she'd promised her cousin she'd keep her secret until Karolyn arrived in Heart's Landing. And that meant, any talk of her future would have to wait until after the wedding. "If circumstances were different, I'd jump at the chance." She glanced down the hall to the room where boxes were stacked from floor to ceiling. "But right now, I need to see about the gift bags for our guests."

"You're going to do those yourself?"

She brushed a loose strand of hair behind her ear. "I guess it wasn't such a good idea to count on putting them together with my bridal party." She straightened her shoulders and aimed for levity on her way to the door. "It's going to be a long night. But with all that chocolate, I'll have plenty of fuel to keep me going."

Leaving Alicia's office, she headed for the room where wine crates lined the walls and towering stacks of boxes from Favors Galore covered two of the six tables. She eyed the cartons of tissue paper and ribbon that had been piled in one corner and sighed. Like she'd told Alicia, the job wasn't going to do itself.

She grabbed a bag and a handful of tissue and went to work. Minutes later, she finished off the first of the gift bags with ribbon. "One down. Two hundred forty-nine to go," she murmured. She checked her watch and groaned. At this rate, Karolyn and Chad would be on their honeymoon by the time she finished.

"Where are you? I thought you were watching out for this girl."

"Hold on." The mixer had practically drowned out Alicia's voice. Nick turned the dial. Quiet descended on I Do Cakes' kitchen. "Now, what was that again?"

"I asked where you were, although from the sounds of things, I know exactly where you're not. You're not here—watching out for Jenny—like you're supposed to be."

Nick bristled. He'd done exactly what everyone had asked him to do, and what had he gotten for his efforts? Nothing. He'd given Jenny his heart, and she'd tossed it aside, scratched his name off her list of favorite people, and made it perfectly clear that she wanted nothing further to do with him. "She's no longer my responsibility," he replied firmly. That had ended the moment Bob had stepped off the plane. "I did everything I was supposed to."

"Then why is she alone in the conference room, putting together gift bags for her wedding without a single person to help her?"

"I don't know anything about that, Alicia. If you want answers, talk to her fiancé." According to the schedule, Bob and the rest of the wedding party had arrived earlier this morning. By now, the happy couple should be walking about Heart's Landing arm-in-arm. Which explained why he'd hunkered down in the bakery, determined not to so much as stick his nose outside until this particular wedding was over and Jenny was out of his life forever. Not that he had any intention of telling that to Alicia. Or anyone else, for that matter.

"You're not hearing me, Nick. The point is, Bob *isn't* here. Jenny said his flight was delayed, and he won't be able to get here till tomorrow. In the meantime, she's trying to assemble those gift bags by herself."

Nick wiped a dab of frosting from his hand and frowned. Like the cake he'd burned, the caramel he'd scorched, and the marzipan he'd ruined after seeing Jenny on Wednesday, he would toss this batch of frosting in the trash. This time, he'd let the butter sit too long at room temperature. It had separated, leaving a slick, oily residue on his fingers that felt as wrong as Jenny's wedding.

But that situation was no longer his problem. After they'd spoken outside Dress For A Day, he'd made a promise to himself. From now on, he'd stay as far away from Jenny as possible. She'd made her choice, and it wasn't him. No matter how much it hurt to think of her in the arms of another man, he had to respect her wishes.

Or did he?

The man Jenny planned to marry had let her down. It hadn't been the first time. Nick was afraid it wouldn't be the last. He couldn't be certain of that, of course, but he was sure Jenny needed a friend. Could he be that for her? Could he ignore the empty hole where his heart used to be long enough to help her one last time?

"That's too big a job for one person, Nick."

Alicia's not-so-gentle reminder was just the nudge he needed. "I'm on it."

Of course, there was always the possibility that Jenny would take one look at him and say, "Thank you very much, but no thanks." To keep that from happening, he needed reinforcements. He reached for his phone. In minutes, he'd enlisted several volunteers who were more than happy to pitch in and help a true Heart's Landing bride out of one more jam. After all, Jenny might refuse to let him lend a hand, but she couldn't very well refuse an army.

Now, all he had to do was hide his broken heart for a few more hours. Long enough to help the woman he loved put the finishing touches on the preparations for her wedding to someone else.

He gulped.

Helping Jenny was going to be harder than he'd thought it'd be. A lot harder.

Chapter Seventeen

In the conference room of the Captain's Cottage, newscasters chattered on the television mounted on the wall behind Jenny. Leaning away from the table, she stretched. It hadn't taken as long as she expected to settle into a routine. Grasp the handles. Shake a fresh bag open. Layer enough tissue into the bottom to cushion the wine bottle. Wedge the candy in beside it. Top with more tissue. Tie the whole thing off with a ribbon. Voila! Ten down, another two hundred forty left to go.

She stiffened as footsteps sounded on hardwood floors in the hallway. Voices rose above the comforting noise of the TV. Seconds later, she laughed at herself. Did she honestly think a band of pirates had invaded the Captain's Cottage? That might have happened in Thaddeus's day, but not now. Most likely, it was just another bridal party gathering for their wedding.

Except, Karolyn had rented the entire mansion for the weekend, so why were throngs of people roaming the halls?

At a knock at the door, her heart rate doubled. She brandished a wine bottle like a club. "Who is it?"

Rather than replying, the new arrivals took their lives in their hands. The door sprang open.

When a familiar face filled the gap, Jenny lowered her would-be weapon, but she didn't try to hide her confusion. "Mildred? What are you doing here?"

Lines around the florist's eyes crinkled. "I—we—heard you had quite the project on your hands and could use some help. I brought extra scissors." She stepped into the room.

"We brought wine." Ashley crossed the threshold on Mildred's heels.

"And glasses." Brandishing a stack of paper cups, Alexis joined her sister.

"I brought my curling scissors—they make great bows." Cheri edged past the twins.

"Janet sends her regards." JoJo aimed an ever-present camera at the stacks of supplies. The shutter clicked. "She wanted to come, too, but she's up to her eyeballs in prep for tomorrow's festivities."

"I brought my boss." Alicia crowded into the room that had rapidly filled with people. "He's pretty good at lifting and toting. If you need anything moved, he's your man."

"I'm Jason," said a tall, dark-haired stranger who bore a striking resemblance to framed portraits of Captain Thaddeus Heart. "Just point me in the right direction."

"Nice to meet you." She would have said more, but her mouth stalled as Nick joined the throng.

"Sustenance." He lowered a brownie-laden tray to one of the empty tables.

Heartache, fresh and bright, stabbed Jenny's chest. She drew a ragged breath and turned to the people who'd opened their hearts to her while she'd been in Heart's Landing. "What are you doing here?"

"Everyone in town knew you'd planned on having your wedding party put together the favors for your guests tonight," JoJo explained as she lined up for her next shot. "When we heard their flight was delayed, well, we couldn't let you handle all this by yourself."

Touched, Jenny pressed one hand over the place where her shattered heart thudded. She could hardly believe these people—people she hadn't even known four weeks ago—would rush to help her. "You're doing this for me?"

Jason's head bobbed. "We always go the extra mile for a true Heart's Landing bride."

"*All* our brides," Alicia corrected. She aimed a stern look at her boss.

Jenny barely had time to wonder what Jason meant before Nick clapped his hands together.

"These bags aren't going to stuff themselves, folks. Let's get started." He shot her a pointed glance. "Jenny, what's first?"

She swept the crowded room. As many changes as she'd thrown at them over the past few weeks, no one in this room owed her a thing. Yet, they'd given up a big part of their day to help her out of a jam. And she had no doubt that Nick had arranged the whole thing. She shot a grateful smile at the man who'd broken her heart. Warmth spread through her when his lips curled up in return. Glad that they were at least on speaking terms, she fought back the sting of tears as she addressed the group. "You don't know how much I appreciate you being here tonight," she began. "I never thought—"

"Hush now," Mildred interrupted. "We're just helping out a friend. You'd do the same for any one of us."

"I would." Jenny blotted her eyes. Karolyn and Chad had found better things to do on the eve of their own wedding, but she could count on the friends she'd made in Heart's Landing. And they could count on her.

"Too much talking!" Ashley declared. "Let's get to work before everyone breaks out their hankies."

"I'll drink to that." Alexis pulled the cork from a wine bottle and poured cabernet into paper cups.

Within minutes, the group formed an assembly line of sorts. The room filled with the sounds of crinkling paper, the snip of scissors, and the lively chatter of friends, old and new. Deciding she couldn't let their sacrifice go unrewarded, Jenny found an excuse to slip away long enough to place a discreet call to Bow Tie Pasta. Pleased to free up more tables on a busy weekend night, the maitre d' agreed to deliver half the food Jenny had ordered for the rehearsal dinner to the Captain's Cottage and send the rest to a local soup kitchen.

By the time she returned to the conference room, the evening news had ended. On the TV, the hosts of an entertainment show expressed shock and horror at the breakup of one of Hollywood's longest romances.

"Sources tell us he's been seen around town with his latest co-star." A photograph of the aging movie star flashed on the screen. He stood with one arm draped over the shoulder of a beautiful young woman.

"Jenny, you're from L.A. Is any of this stuff true?" Ashley glanced up from the bow she was tying.

"Not as much as they want you to believe." The pose in question was from a script Karolyn had read before she'd turned down the part. Jenny pointed to the TV. "That picture was taken on set. He has his arm around her because that's what the role called for, not because he's in love with her. A lot of those reports are pretty exaggerated."

Another two hours passed before Mildred layered tissue

into the last of the gift bags and passed it to Alexis, who carefully placed the final wine bottle inside. Ashley added the remaining box of candy. Cheri tied the final bow, and a collective cheer rose throughout the room. Meanwhile, Jason flattened the last of the empty boxes for recycling while Alicia patrolled the area, picking up scraps of paper and ribbon.

After Nick placed the finished bag on the reception room table with the others, the waiters and waitresses from Bow Tie Pasta arrived. Bearing trays of lasagna, salad, and several pasta dishes, they streamed into the room. As wonderful odors drifted in the air, Jenny overrode a few half-hearted protests and ordered everyone, including the wait staff, to help themselves. Soon, laughter and conversation flowed along as people fixed plates and pulled up chairs around the tables.

Watching them while she waited her turn at the back of the line, Jenny drank in the scene. Warmth blossomed in the center of her chest and spread outward. She'd come to Heart's Landing to arrange her cousin's wedding. In the process, she'd made so many good friends, she never wanted to leave. Especially now that she and Nick had apparently declared a truce.

She eyed the tall baker, who chatted with Cheri as they filled their plates. Her heart was still broken, but maybe she and Nick could be friends. She could live with that. She'd have to if she accepted Alicia's offer to come and work for her here at the Captain's Cottage.

But.

The whole time she'd been here, she'd kept a secret from her new friends. They'd shared their pasts, their hopes for the future with her. In return, she hadn't been honest with them. She hadn't trusted them with her own truth. It was time to change that. If she wanted to be a part of this community, to live the rest of her life here in Heart's Landing, she needed to reveal the real reason she'd come here in the first place. And she needed to do it now.

A restless excitement rippled through her. From Alicia to her newest acquaintance, Jason, everyone in the room would be thrilled when they learned it was Karolyn Karter, not her, who'd walk down the aisle tomorrow. She eyed her wine glass. She needed to get everyone's attention, but tapping her knife on a paper cup wouldn't do the trick. Pushing away from the wall, she cleared her throat. "If I may, I'd like to say a few words."

Throughout the room, conversations and laughter faded until the only sound came from the television.

"Could someone mute that?" she asked.

Heads swiveled as people searched for the remote. Before anyone found it, an excited host on the entertainment show blurted, "This just in, folks—Karolyn Karter wed Chad Grant tonight in a Las Vegas wedding that took even Hollywood insiders by surprise!"

What?

That had to be a mistake, another example of reporters running with a story before they had all the facts. Karolyn would never…

Or would she?

The faces staring up at her from chairs and tables receded into the distance. Drawn to the television, Jenny stared over their heads at the screen mounted on the far wall.

"All of Hollywood has been following the romance that blossomed on the set of *Two Hearts on the Run* this summer. That love story culminated in the engagement of Karolyn Karter to her co-star Chad Grant six weeks ago. Since then, we've been chasing down rumors of a summer wedding, and tonight, our investigation paid off when we followed the two lovebirds to the Little Elvis Chapel in Las Vegas."

Karolyn wouldn't. She couldn't.

Jenny drew in a breath and got nothing. Her heart pounded. On the screen, the scene cut to flashing neon lights above a white clapboard church. Another talking head spoke into a microphone.

"The bride wore a stunning strapless gown by Sophie Olsen, while the groom dressed in traditional dark gray tux-and-tails for the intimate ceremony that took place only hours ago. A waiting limo whisked the happy couple off to the airport, presumably where they'll leave on their honeymoon, but not before the bride gave me this exclusive interview."

No! It couldn't be true. The story had to be a lie, didn't it?

The sides of the paper cup bent inward in Jenny's grip. Just like she'd been telling the others earlier, these reporters had aired a story before they had the facts. Although, she had to admit, the dress they'd described matched Karolyn's to a T.

Maybe her cousin had pulled off a publicity stunt designed to draw the paparazzi away from the real wedding. Yeah, that had to be it. Any second now, her phone would buzz, and Karolyn's laughter would fill her ear. Her cousin would no doubt brag about how she'd pulled one over on the reporters and the media types who dogged her every footstep.

Jenny reached for her phone, but the device's screen remained dark. On the television, a smiling Karolyn and Chad stepped forward to join the reporter. With the bright lights of Las Vegas twinkling in the distance, the camera zoomed in on the beaming bride.

"We couldn't wait another second to get married!" Kay squealed while the camera zoomed in for a close-up of the couple, surrounded by an entourage of giddy friends. Jenny swallowed hard as she spotted the familiar members of her cousin's wedding party. "I'm so happy to share this moment with our friends and fans on *Tonight's Entertainment TV*."

With that, Chad whisked his new bride into a waiting limo that merged quickly into the traffic on busy Las Vegas Boulevard.

Jenny's breath caught and her legs wobbled. Her teeth chattered. Much as she didn't want to believe it, she couldn't deny the picture of Chad and Karolyn decked out in their wedding finery. She stared at the screen, unable to breathe, unable to move. Tears rolled silently down her cheeks. This was no hoax. No publicity stunt. After the hoops she'd jumped through on Kay's behalf, after the upset and consternation she'd caused throughout Heart's Landing, her cousin and Chad had eloped.

"Well, there you have it." The reporter held a mic to his mouth. "Mr. and Mrs. Chad Grant have tied the knot Las Vegas-style."

Spots danced before Jenny's eyes. An urge to throw something swept her, but her hands shook so badly that she could barely hang on to the cup of wine she'd raised in a toast to her friends. Liquid sloshed over the edges. Her fingers lost their grip. The cup slipped from her grasp. It landed on the floor with a loud pop.

"Jenny?"

"Are you all right?"

"What's wrong?"

The concerned chorus rose from across the room. Jenny's shoulders slumped. The oddest sensation that someone had just pulled the rug out from under her left her unsteady on her feet. Her gaze dropped from the television to the troubled faces before her. From opposite ends of the room, Mildred and Alicia started toward her. Her movements stilted, she waved them back to their seats.

What was she supposed to say? How was she going to stand here and tell everyone that they'd wasted their time? That the wedding they'd worked so hard to pull off was nothing more than a farce? Pain stabbed her chest. It stole her breath.

She couldn't tell them. She couldn't explain something she hadn't even begun to understand herself. "I—I need a minute."

Clamping her hand over her mouth, she raced for the door. A sob escaped from between her fingers as she dashed down the hall to the ladies room. Once safely out of sight, she propped her hands on the cold porcelain. Her shoulders hunched. Tears streamed down her cheeks. They ran down her chin and splashed into the empty sink.

Had Kay intended to get married in Vegas from the beginning? Had the effort she'd poured into the wedding, the adjustments she'd made whenever Kay had changed her mind, the phone calls and the weeks of worrying over every detail been a ploy? Another part of an elaborate ruse her cousin had come up with to keep the paparazzi at bay? The idea was too painful to contemplate, and she hiccupped, unable to catch her breath.

She could hardly believe Kay had sent her here on what had amounted to a wild goose chase. It seemed ludicrous to think her cousin had spent thousands of dollars on a pretend wedding. But what else was she supposed to believe?

Why didn't I see this coming?

But she had, hadn't she?

She had to admit, right from the beginning, she'd had her doubts about Kay's decision to get married in Heart's Landing. Yet, she'd gone along with the plan. Had she really been surprised when her cousin's wedding had morphed from a small, plain wedding into an elaborate extravaganza? Slowly, she shook her head. She should have known better. Worse, she'd drawn everyone else in town into Karolyn's scheme. Now, they'd have nothing to show for their hard work. They'd never forgive her for her role in this fiasco.

Who was she kidding? She'd never forgive herself. She pounded her fist on the counter. Metal clinked. She wrenched the fake engagement ring from her finger and stuffed it in a pocket.

No more.

Before she'd come to Heart's Landing, she'd had a life. Sure, it hadn't been as thrilling as her cousin's. Maybe she hadn't felt completely fulfilled, but she'd chosen to put her family first. She'd had a job she was good at, a roof over her head. She hadn't had someone special to love, but she'd had hope, hope that one day she'd find her Prince Charming.

Then, Kay had sent her to America's top wedding destination, and she'd lost everything.

From the minute she'd set foot in the town where romance coated the buildings and dripped from the eaves, she'd felt like she'd finally found her place. She'd pictured the reactions of Mildred and the twins when Kay stepped out of her limo and thanked them personally for helping to plan her wedding. They'd have been thrilled. She'd seen herself working beside Alicia at the Captain's Cottage, helping other brides have their special day. She'd imagined what it'd be like to buy a quaint little house of her own, to build her future in Heart's Landing. She'd fallen in love with Nick.

But then, her dreams, like her heart, had shattered. Because, despite everything—the promises, the planning, the hours people had poured into her wedding, the expense—Kay had done the unthinkable. She'd betrayed them all.

Me, most of all.

She'd never be able to go back to L.A., never be able to work for her cousin again. Not after this. As for her dream of putting down roots in the town she'd come to think of as home, that had been crushed, too. Once her new friends realized they'd wasted weeks preparing for a wedding that wasn't going to take place—and that she'd been lying to them from the moment they'd met—they'd never forgive her. Alicia would withdraw her job offer.

As for Nick…she might as well face it. She'd given her heart to a man who didn't love her in return. Whatever small hope she had of rekindling their friendship, it had died the instant Karolyn and Chad had said, "I do."

And worst of all, she had no one to blame for her crumbling hopes but herself. It was all her fault. She'd known from the beginning that Karolyn's plans for a simple wedding were doomed to failure. Yet, she'd gone along, rolled with every change, kept her cousin's huge secret the entire time. In the end, she'd ruined everything and lost her one chance for friendship. For happiness. For love.

She closed her eyes. Her legs buckled, and she collapsed to the floor. More tears seeped through her lids and slid down her cheeks.

Nick was on his feet before Jenny made it to the door. "I have no idea what's wrong," he said, answering the unspoken question that circulated throughout the room. "But I'll find out. Trust me."

Questions, each more troubling than the last, raced

through his mind as he hustled down the hall in search of the woman who'd handed him his walking papers. Had she suddenly fallen ill? Had something on the evening news upset her? Had her fiancé called off the wedding?

He gave himself a swift chewing out for the thrill of hope that passed through him at that last one. He was resigned to the fact that they could never be more than friends. But what kind of friend wished her fiancé had practically left her at the altar? Not a good one, he admitted.

Besides, it hadn't happened. He might have pitched in like everyone else who'd rushed to Jenny's aid this evening, but he hadn't been able to stop himself from watching her every move. She hadn't received a single call, hadn't received any startling messages. There'd been nothing of note on the television other than the announcement that some celebrity had gotten married. No big deal.

He'd have sworn everything was perfectly fine up until a few minutes ago. With their help, Jenny had finished the gift bags in record time. She'd shown her gratitude by having Bow Tie Pasta deliver enough food for two armies. Then she'd stood, no doubt intending to thank everyone for coming out tonight. Not that she needed to. They'd fallen in love with the timid bride who'd gone from wishy-washy to certain in a matter of weeks. Even him.

Especially him.

But if she hadn't received bad news, what had upset her? Unable to figure it out on his own, he knocked on the door to the ladies' room. "Jenny?"

From the other side of the door, her voice rose above the sound of running water. "Go away, Nick."

Yeah, that wasn't going to happen. He propped one shoulder against the wall, determined to wait her out. Minutes passed. He tapped his foot and cracked his knuckles. He had nowhere else to go, nothing he'd rather do than be right here, in this moment.

At last the door crept open, and she stepped into the hall. Though she'd splashed water on her face, tears had created trails down her powdered cheeks. The black smudges under her eyes offered further proof that she'd been crying. Hard. Hard enough to turn her skin blotchy.

His heart squeezed painfully. His fingers curled. Whoever had done this to her, they'd answer to him. But first, he had to find out who, or what, had upset her. He wouldn't waste time trying to figure it out on his own. There was only one question to ask. Straightening, he stared at the woman he'd do anything to love and protect. "How can I help?"

She tried and failed to muster her composure. She pressed tissues against her damp eyes. Finally, a breath shuddered through her. She peered up at him through glistening lashes. "There's… there's something I need to tell you. Before I do, I want you to know that I tried to tell you earlier." Her eyes pleaded with him for understanding. "That night in the bakery—I'd made up my mind to tell you. But then, you—I got sidetracked." Her voice shook. Her head dipped. Her gaze dropped to the floor. "After that, it didn't matter anymore. But I, uh, I should have told you anyway."

"Told me what?" Whatever secret she was keeping, it would never change the fact that he was crazy in love with her. Or that it was impossible for him to ever let her know it.

"I came here under false pretenses."

Powerless to stop them, he felt his eyes narrow. "What, you aren't from California? You don't work for a big movie mogul? You're…" His mind filled in the rest with the least likely two words in the English vocabulary. *Not engaged?*

"I'm not getting married." Jenny threaded her fingers together. "I never was. It was all a lie." More tears leaked from eyes that wouldn't meet his.

"You're not?" His heart stalled. He tilted his head, trying and failing miserably to understand. "Why the act?"

"It was my cousin's idea, but I went along with it. She'd just gotten engaged and was scared to death that reporters and fans would ruin her wedding. She cooked up a ruse to keep that from happening. She knew I'd always dreamed of having a Heart's Landing wedding, so she sent me here to plan one. Only, it was hers, not mine."

As if she couldn't bear to look at him, Jenny studied the end of the corridor. "It was supposed to be so simple. I'd fly in, get everything set up, and leave. I wasn't supposed to be here long enough to fall in love. Not with Heart's Landing. Not with the people here. Not with…anyone else. But once word got out about Kay's engagement to Chad, everything snowballed into this huge production. I couldn't leave. I had to stay here to make sure everything was all set for their big day. From the very beginning, I hated not being able to tell everyone the truth. Most of all, I wanted to tell you."

"Why didn't you?" His mind reeled. His head felt too full. His heart, not full enough.

"I couldn't betray her. She's my cousin. She and her mom have done so much for me, I didn't think I could let them down. But then, tonight, when everyone showed up, I knew I couldn't keep this secret another minute. I decided to tell you—to tell everyone—the truth. That's what I was going to do, come clean."

"But then you ran out of the room."

"Because, after everything she—after everything *I*—put us through, Kay eloped."

"Kay?" He hit rewind on the last few minutes in the conference room. The television show. The ashen expression on Jenny's face when the host had broken the news. No wonder she'd looked like she'd been hit by a semi when the camera had focused on the newlyweds in front of the chapel. He brushed hair out his eyes as the first domino in the chain crashed into the next one. "Kay—Karolyn Karter is your cousin?"

"Yes." Jenny stared at the floor as if she wanted a hole to open up and swallow her. "She and Chad Grant ran off to Vegas and got married tonight."

"And the changes? The number of guests, the color scheme, the naked cake—they were all Karolyn's ideas?"

"Hers and her fiancé's. Yes."

"So there's no wedding. You were never engaged to Bob." His thoughts churned, slow and thick, like hand-beaten batter. It came down to one thing—*she* wasn't getting married tomorrow.

"No." Jenny shook her head. "I'm so, so sorry about everything I've put everyone through." She studied the door that led to the conference room. "How do I go back in there and tell them there won't be a wedding after the time they've spent on it, the effort they've put into it, the supplies they bought? The flowers. The food."

"You're not getting married." The words fell from his lips. Though his heart leaped at the idea that Jenny wasn't engaged to someone else, his brain was having a little trouble adjusting to this new reality.

A fresh round of tears seeped from under Jenny's eyelids. A powerful urge to swipe his thumb under her eyes rocked him. Not quite sure how he resisted it, he stumbled back. First one step, then another. Now that he knew the truth, now that he knew she'd lied, he needed to think, to sort out how he felt. He just, he couldn't do that standing here, not with Jenny within arm's length.

"I'm sorry," he said. "I'm going to need some time to process all this."

Turning away from her was one of the hardest things he'd ever done, but he forced his feet to move, ordered his legs to carry him down the hall, out the door, and into the parking lot. His strength nearly gave out on him before he made it to the van parked at the end of the lot. Climbing inside, he stabbed the keys into the ignition. The engine responded with a throaty rumble. He put the vehicle in gear.

But there was nowhere to go. Every single place in Heart's Landing held a memory of Jenny and him. Together, they'd visited the shops on Bridal Carriage Drive. They'd ridden bikes along the cliffs overlooking the ocean, had a picnic at his favorite beach. He'd watched her try on wedding gowns at Dress For A Day, dined with her at Bow Tie Pasta, and grabbed sandwiches for them from the sidewalk cafe. He couldn't even retreat to I Do Cakes. With her carefree smiles and ready wit, she'd invaded his kitchen, the one place he kept private from the rest of the world. He'd never again make cupcakes without thinking of the time they'd spent together there.

He might as well stay right where he was until he decided where to go from here. He had fallen in love with Jenny. Even now, he couldn't deny it. But could their love survive the lies she'd told? Because she *had* lied. There was no doubt about that.

Was she still lying?

No, he'd seen her face when the newscaster had broken

the story about Karolyn and Chad's wedding. The news had shocked Jenny more than it had the reporter.

Could he forgive her?

He had to, didn't he? In going along with her cousin's plan, she'd been supporting her family. He couldn't hold that against her.

Did he love her still?

Yes.

Despite everything else, he knew the real Jenny. The feisty brunette who'd snapped at him when they'd collided outside the bakery—that was the woman he'd fallen in love with. The sad and broken woman he'd comforted on the porch of the bed and breakfast—that was the woman he wanted to protect for the rest of his life. The carefree visitor who'd walked the beach beside him, who'd skipped shells across a tidal pool with him—that was the girl who'd stolen his heart. If it were up to him, they'd always be together.

But would she leave him?

She might. As angry as she was with her cousin right this minute—and rightfully so—he had no doubt the two of them would patch things up eventually. Karolyn Karter, despite her faults, was family. And if he knew one thing about Jenny, it was that family trumped everything else.

The question was, was there room in her heart for a new family?

There was only one way to find out.

Jenny stood stock still, unable to move, unable to breathe, while Nick slowly trudged down the hall, turned the corner, and disappeared. She really couldn't blame him for leaving. Though he'd tried to hide it, she'd seen the shock waves roll across his face when he'd learned she'd been lying—to him, to everyone—all this time. He'd never forgive her. That night at the bakery, she'd thought she couldn't feel any worse when he rejected her. She'd been wrong. Seeing how disappointment in her had rounded his shoulders and weighted him down—especially now that she'd begun to think they might be friends again—that hurt worse.

A lot worse.

But the sooner she accepted that she'd blown her only chance at happiness with the man she loved, the sooner she could move on with what was left of her life.

And to do that, she had to face the music.

People were waiting for her. Friends she'd wanted to make her neighbors. They'd probably never want to see her again after tonight, but they deserved to hear the truth. From her. Not thirdhand from some reporter who'd stumbled over a story. Because, if there was one thing she'd learned in the years she'd spent in L.A., it was that secrets didn't stay secrets very long. This ruse of Karolyn's would come to light. It might not happen tonight or even next week, but some reporter somewhere would eventually figure out she'd been planning a Heart's Landing wedding. A wedding that never took place. When that happened, Jenny didn't want the news to hurt anyone in the town that went out its way to give every bride the wedding of their dreams.

Even if everyone in the conference room turned their backs on her like Nick had.

She stood where she was for a few minutes while she drew courage and strength around her like a cloak. When she thought she was ready—when her sobs had died to soft hiccups—she blotted her eyes and blew her nose a final time.

Then, her head held high despite her aching heart, she forced herself to take the longest walk of her life.

A low buzz of conversation died the moment she stepped across the threshold. She squared her shoulders. "Sorry for running out like that." Now that she'd decided to do this, she needed to get it over with. She crossed swiftly to the front of the room where she cut the power to the TV. Turning, she faced the people she'd hoped to work and live beside for the rest of her life.

"I have a confession to make. But first, I need to tell you how grateful I am for all you've done for me these past few weeks. I know I haven't been the easiest"—knowing it would be the last time she'd ever have to say it, she stumbled over the next word—"bride you've ever dealt with."

"We've had worse," Alexis or Ashley piped.

"No, we haven't," her counterpart corrected.

She let a spate of laughter die down before she continued. "I've asked a lot of you, and you've delivered one hundred percent. More than that, you've been kind to me when I didn't deserve it. You've helped me when you didn't have to." She gestured toward the reception hall and the waiting gift bags. "You've treated me like a friend. I'd hoped we'd continue to be friends—and possibly neighbors." Her gaze flitted about the room, landing on the faces of the people who'd come to mean so much to her in such a short amount of time. Mildred. The twins. Alicia. Marybeth. Cheri.

"But that's probably not going to happen." She held up a hand, silencing the few, scattered objections. "There's something you don't know. Something I need to tell you." She paused. This was the hardest speech she'd ever given. Not so much because of what she had to say, but because once she did, she'd be surprised if anyone in the room ever spoke to her again. She forged forward. "I—uh, I'm not engaged to Bob." She aimed a wan smile at Marybeth. "Or Tom, either."

Shock electrified the room. On its heels, dismay spread like a puddle of dark molasses.

Alicia spoke for the others when she asked, "You mean, you two called off the wedding?"

"No, I—" She stopped, her attention drawn to the door that whispered open.

"Hold on to that thought for a minute, will you?" Carrying a bouquet of red roses, the man she least expected stepped inside.

Jenny shook her head. She had to be seeing things. "Nick?"

"Jenny." He crossed the room, coming to a halt a step or two away from her. "I'm not sure what you've told these good people, but I have something to say before you say another word."

Her gaze landed on the flowers Nick held. Roses, her favorite. Of course, Nick knew that, but why would he bring them here? To her? Her heart in her throat, she nodded.

Nick shifted closer. His gaze captured hers. "Jenny, I've loved you from the moment we collided outside my bakery. From that instant, I've known we were meant to be together. The only thing was, I thought you were engaged to someone else. Now that I know you're free, there's a question I need to ask you."

A collective gasp sounded in the room when Nick went down on bended knee. As for her, Jenny was certain her heart had stopped beating.

Taking her hand in his, Nick stared up at her while everyone went utterly still and silent. "Jennifer Longley, will you marry me and let me love you forever?"

He loves me.

The torn and tattered pieces of her heart stitched themselves back together. An incredible sense of wellbeing radiated outward from her center. Despite it all, she shook her head. Tears pooling in her eyes, she pointed out the one reason they could never be together. "I lied. I haven't earned your trust."

"I trust you with my heart," came Nick's instant response. His signature grin spread across his face. "One day, this will make a great story to tell when our grandchildren ask how we met."

"Our grandchildren," she whispered. "And our children."

In the blink of an eye, she saw the future Nick held out to her. The house with the white picket fence. Little League games and dance recitals. Best of all, she'd spend the rest of her days in the arms of the man she loved. She and Nick would build a life together. They'd grow old together. They'd spend their twilight years sitting in matching rockers on the front porch of a quaint little cottage, surrounded by their children and grandchildren…and love.

"Yes," she whispered. More than anything, she wanted to spend her life, her future, with him.

"I didn't have time to shop." Undaunted, Nick took something from his jeans pocket and slipped it on her finger. "This'll have to do until I can get you a real one."

"I don't need a ring as long as we're together," she said, glancing at the plastic trinket he must have pulled from the one of the bins in the bakery. Designed as decoration for a cake, the oversized bauble winked in the glow from the overhead lights. "Oh!" She pressed the toy to her heart. "I'll treasure it always."

Rising, Nick closed the distance between them. Her heart stalled again at the tender brush of his fingers. He cupped her jaw, nestling her chin in the palm of his hands. She met him halfway as he leaned forward. At last their lips met, and she knew, once and for all, she'd come home.

She could have gone on kissing Nick forever, would have, if she'd had her way. But moments later, applause rang out around them. His eyes filled with promise of more kisses to come soon, Nick smiled down at her. He slipped his arm around her waist and, together, they turned to face the sea of happy faces.

Congratulations and well-wishes flowed for a while before someone declared that the situation called for a toast.

"Here's to a Heart's Landing love for the ages!" Matt lifted his paper cup while he hugged Marybeth.

"The best is yet to be," added Roy.

"To the marriage of a one of our favorite sons and a true Heart's Landing bride," Jason said, holding his cup high.

Jenny looked to Nick. One day, she'd ask him to explain Jason's comment. For now, she wanted nothing more than to have Nick's arms around her and more of his delicious kisses.

"Have you set a date?" Ashley wanted to know.

Nick chuckled. "Give us a minute, will you? We haven't exactly had time for that conversation. But soon." He snugged Jenny closer to his side. "I don't want a long engagement. Do you?"

Looking up into the slate-blue eyes of the man she loved, she knew one thing—she didn't want to wait a minute longer than necessary to walk down the aisle and marry the man of her dreams. "I hear the Captain's Cottage is available tomorrow."

Nick's eyes flared while his famous grin widened. "Alicia," he called without lifting his gaze from hers. "What do you think? Can we do this?"

"Why not? The place is yours for the entire weekend."

One by one, the others chimed in.

"We have the flowers."

"And the perfect gown."

"We're all set for the reception."

"Gift bags. Check!"

"Photographer. Check! Check!" JoJo snapped a picture.

"But no guests." A frown niggled Nick's brow. "Don't you want your family here?"

Jenny looked into the face of the man she adored. There were truths she still needed to share with her friends, her new neighbors, but she was certain of one thing. "You are my family," she whispered. "Now and forever."

And with that, Nick swept her into his arms again for another kiss.

Epilogue

In the end, they decided to wait six months before walking down the aisle. Jenny and Nick put the delay to good use by spending every available moment together. Not that they had as much time on their hands as they would have liked. Business was up at I Do Cakes. Even with Jimmy's help, Nick worked long hours filling the orders for weddings, birthdays, and celebrations of every kind.

As for Jenny, her new position as Alicia's second-in-command occupied most of her days. She'd expected to be good at her job—and she was. The work was demanding, but seeing the happy glow on the faces of the brides she helped more than made up for the long hours.

No matter how busy she was, though, Jenny took a break at two o'clock sharp each day and wandered down the hill from the Captain's Cottage to I Do Cakes. There, Nick greeted her with a kiss and one of the specials he'd set aside just for her. Over cupcakes and coffee, they swapped stories about their day before they each dashed back to work until dinner time.

On weekends, they studied real estate ads and dropped in on open houses until they found an older home in Cathedral

Heights they loved at first sight. A wide front porch and a big backyard made the Cape Cod the perfect place to raise the family they hoped to have one day. Once the current owners accepted their offer, they spent weekends prowling estate sales for furnishings so the house would be ready to move into when they returned from their weeklong honeymoon in Newport.

And so it went until, finally, the day they'd been waiting for arrived.

Jenny buried her nose in the mixed bouquet of red and white roses and inhaled the rich floral scent. Next to the aroma of cakes fresh from the oven at Nick's bakery, the smell was her all-time favorite. A soft smile tugging at her lips, she smoothed a tiny wrinkle in the satin wrapped around the stems. She broke away from her musings as Karolyn rushed into the bride's dressing room on the first floor of the Captain's Cottage.

"It's almost time," her cousin gushed. "Any sign of those cold feet everyone warns about?"

Jenny grinned while Kay searched her face. "Not a one. In fact, if you don't step aside, I might run you over in my rush to walk down that aisle."

"That wouldn't be hard to do, considering I'm still half blind from the camera flashes that went off in my face on my way in here." Like they did everywhere the star went, news vans and reporters had tracked her every move from the moment her plane had touched down in nearby Providence.

"Should we ask the police to make them leave?"

"You wouldn't dare! Having the camera crews here is worth a few spots before my eyes. Think of the free publicity Heart's Landing is getting. By tomorrow, pictures of Chad and me walking into the Captain's Cottage will be on the front cover of every tabloid in the country. You couldn't pay for that much exposure." Karolyn tapped a perfectly manicured finger to her lips. "I may have even let it slip that the Cottage employs not one, but two, first-class wedding planners, who are ready to give every bride a perfect Heart's Landing wedding."

"Kay, you didn't!" Jenny eyed the woman who'd become the town's unofficial spokesperson. Over the past six months, Kay had sung the praises of America's wedding capitol at every opportunity. As a result, bookings across the board were up over last year's.

Kay's brows lifted while her lips shifted into a knowing grin. "It's the least I can do to make up for all I put you through last summer."

The stunning diamond drop earrings she wore swung gently when Jenny shook her head. For one solid week after Kay and Chad had slipped off to Vegas, she'd blocked her cousin's calls. The two of them might still be at odds if it hadn't been for Nick. He'd insisted that Kay was family, and as such, deserved a second chance. When Jenny had finally relented and checked her phone for messages, she'd taken one look at the long list of her cousin's voicemails and had known Kay was serious about repairing their relationship. She'd had no choice but to forgive her. But her cousin hadn't let it go at that. Not only had she paid every bill for the wedding-that-never-happened, she'd tipped each vendor generously and had insisted on covering the costs of Jenny and Nick's special day as her wedding gift.

"The ballroom is amazing. It's like a fairyland," Kay whispered.

Picturing the grand room draped in white with touches of gold and red, Jenny smiled. In keeping with the snow on the ground and the sharp nip in the air, she'd settled on a winter theme when she and Nate had decided on a December wedding.

"It makes me wish Chad and I hadn't run off to Vegas to get married." Karolyn twisted the rings on the third finger of her left hand.

"You'll have to come here to renew your vows on your tenth anniversary." Jenny lifted her gown's voluminous skirts as she turned so her cousin could fasten the satin belt at the back. "I happen to know a great event planner who could handle the arrangements for you. Although you'll have to sign an iron-clad contract guaranteeing there won't be any last-minute changes."

Her fingers making swift work of the task at hand, Karolyn gave a wry laugh. "Okay. I deserved that. Chad and I put you through the wringer, didn't we? There"—she straightened the belt at Jenny's waist—"all set."

Slowly, Jenny rotated. A last-minute doubt shimmied through her midsection as she waited for Karolyn's reaction. Would her cousin approve of the choices she'd made for this, the most special day of her life?

Time stood still for a long second. At last, Karolyn gave a breathy, "Ohhhh!" Real tears welled in her eyes. "Jenny, you look like a princess in that dress. Nick is going to lose his mind."

"Thanks, Kay." Jenny expelled a breath she hadn't known she was holding. "I knew this was the gown for me from the first moment I tried it on." And it, like the rest of the details of their wedding, had fallen into place just as easily. From the invitations she and Nick had sent to their small families and their not-so-small group of friends, to the flavor of their wedding cake, they'd created a simple, but elegant, celebration of their love for one another.

"Nick and the minister were standing up front when I checked. We probably shouldn't keep them waiting much longer. Do you have everything? Something old, something new?"

"Right here." Jenny traced the edges of the pendant Nick had given her as a wedding present. Fashioned from a chip off one of Captain Thaddeus's handmade carvings, the miniature stone heart hung from a chain around her neck where it served as both her something old and something new.

"Something borrowed?"

Jenny touched one finger to the dangling diamond earrings on loan from Kay's private collection. "You never did tell me how much these are worth."

"That's because you'd never wear them if I did, and they're perfect for you. So, something blue?"

"Alicia embroidered blue flowers on my handkerchief."

Careful not to crush her dress, her cousin leaned in for a quick hug. Kay's fingers actually trembled as she lowered Jenny's veil. "You're the most beautiful bride I've ever seen. Nick is a lucky, lucky man." She blotted her cheeks. "Give me two minutes to get to my seat, then you're all set." She blew a kiss as she hurried off to join Aunt Maggie and Chad in the ballroom.

Warmth ripped through her when, standing just beyond the entrance to the ballroom a few moments later, Jenny caught a quick glimpse of the waiting guests. Practically everyone in Heart's Landing had shown up to help her and Nick celebrate their love for one another. From beneath her veil, she tracked the red petals scattered along the runner that ran between the rows of folding chairs. Avery, Nick's four-year-old niece, had done her job as flower girl perfectly. The child's crinolines rustled as she emptied the last flowers from her basket and slipped into place beside her mom. Decked out in miniature tux and tails, six-year-old Mattox stood proudly beside his uncle. Matching gold bands glinted from the satin pillow balanced in his small hands.

"Are you ready?" In full Captain Thaddeus regalia, Jason Heart extended his arm.

The grin she'd worn practically nonstop ever since the moment Nick had proposed deepened. "More than ready," she whispered. She'd been dreaming of this moment from the time she'd first read about Heart's Landing in her aunt's magazine.

From the front of the room, the stringed quartet reached the end of Pachelbel's "Canon." She slipped her hand into the crook of Jason's arm and rested her fingers on his forearm. Her grip on the round bouquet of roses tightened. A nervous thrill passed through her, but one look at Nick—standing tall and handsome, his unwavering focus on her—and her nerves steadied.

He was the love of her life. With him at her side, she felt loved and cherished like never before. He tempted her to try new things, step out of the norm, become more than the person everyone expected her to be. Though she hadn't known it at the time, he was the reason she'd come to Heart's Landing. He'd always be the reason she stayed.

Fabric rustled. Chairs creaked as friends and family rose to their feet. The stringed quartet played the opening notes of "The Wedding March." It was time. Eager to start her new life, Jenny took her first step down the aisle toward her very own Heart's Landing love for the ages.

The End

Lemon Bars

A Hallmark Original Recipe

In *A Simple Wedding*, life hands Jenny a few lemons. But her visits to Nick's bakery—and her conversations with him—have a way of making even the sour moments sweet. These lemon bars are so easy, they'll look and taste like they came from a professional bakery, and they'll add pure sunshine to anyone's day.

Yield: 24 bars (24 servings)
Prep Time: 15 minutes
Bake Time: 50 minutes
Total Time: 65 minutes

INGREDIENTS

- 2 cups all-purpose flour
- ½ cup granulated sugar
- 1 pinch kosher salt
- 2 sticks (1 cup) unsalted butter, softened
- 6 large eggs
- 3 cups granulated sugar
- ¾ cup fresh-squeezed lemon juice
- 1 cup flour
- as needed confectioner's sugar
- as needed, candied lemon peel (optional)

DIRECTIONS

1. Preheat oven to 350 degrees F. Coat a 9-inch by 13-inch baking pan with non-stick cooking spray.
2. Combine flour, ½ cup sugar and salt in food processor; pulse to blend. Add butter and pulse until mixture resembles coarse crumbs and pulls away from sides of processor bowl; press shortbread crumbs into baking pan. Bake uncovered for 12 to 15 minutes.
3. While crust is baking, combine eggs and 3 cups sugar in bowl and whisk to blend. Add lemon juice and flour; whisk until blended. Pour filling over warm crust.
4. Bake for 30 to 35 minutes, or until filling is set. Cool; cut into 24 bars. Dust bars lightly with confectioner's sugar. Garnish each bar with a piece of candied lemon, peel if desired.

5. To prepare candied lemon peel: using a vegetable peeler, slice the outer rinds of 3 lemons into thin strips. Combine with 2 cups water. Bring to a boil, drain and repeat. Combine drained lemon peel with 2 cups sugar and 1 cup water; bring to a boil, reduce heat and simmer for 45 minutes. Drain and cool candied lemon peel; toss in sparkling sugar.

Turn the page for a sneak peek of

Hallmark
PUBLISHING

Chapter One

Jason Heart tugged on the door of I Do Cakes and stepped into the bakery. A sea of voices rolled over him like a wave, drowning the merry tinkle of the bell that announced his arrival. He brushed an unseen fleck from his starched white shirt while he took a second to regroup. The noisy crowd had thrown him off-stride. Even though he was right on time, owners and managers of the town's businesses already crowded the dining area. Chairs at the small tables were filled. Along the back wall, people had already laid claim to the best spots for leaning against the pink-and-white striped wallpaper. No matter. Unlike previous meetings that had gone on for hours, this one was just a formality—a final review of the agenda in preparation for the arrival of the Executive Editor for Weddings Today. He headed for the closest empty space.

"Jason. Here. Sit by me." Mildred Morrey beckoned with an age-spotted hand. "It's about time you got here," she groused, though the lines in her face softened into a smile. The owner of Forget Me Knot Flowers removed a gargantuan purse from the chair beside her. "I've had to fight off three people who wanted this seat. One more, and you were out of luck."

"Sorry. I meant to get here earlier. I was waylaid by an anxious bride on my way out the door." Jason bent his long frame into a pretzel and squeezed in between the woman who'd taken him under her wings ages ago and Cheri Clark, the owner of the area's premier bridal salon.

"Are you ready for all the chaos?" Mildred asked once he'd gotten settled.

"You don't really expect it to be as bad as everyone says, do you? After all these months of preparation, I'd expect everything to go pretty smoothly." For a town that put on more than two hundred weddings each year without a hitch, playing host to one woman ought to be a snap, even if she was one of the most influential people in the industry.

"I keep forgetting that you've never been through one of these."

Jason's throat tightened with a familiar ache. He coughed dryly. During the last review, his dad had still been in charge of the Captain's Cottage. At fifty-five and otherwise healthy, David Thaddeus Heart had complained of indigestion in the weeks leading up to the editor's visit. The diagnosis—pancreatic cancer—had been handed down at a doctor's appointment shortly after Heart's Landing had once again been named American's Top Wedding Destination. Over the course of the last two years, Jason had learned a lot about running one of the country's busiest wedding venues, but every once in a while, something came up that he'd never handled, like the magazine's biannual competition.

"We all miss your dad." Mildred played with an earring that dangled among her silvery curls and cleared her throat.

"He was a good man," added Cheri.

"Thanks. He was always sprucing up something. I bet he'd have enjoyed all the changes we made this spring." Jason glanced out the bakery's front window. With the magazine's evaluation looming, practically every storefront in town had been treated to a facelift. But the heart of Heart's Landing was, as always, the Captain's Cottage.

Jason's mouth tugged to the side in a wry grin. "Cottage" was hardly the word for a house the size of the one his great-

great-great-grandfather and the town's founder, Captain Thaddeus Heart, had built. Fourteen bedrooms and two enormous ballrooms took up only a small portion of the home a scant hour southeast of Newport, where wealthy families like the Astors and Vanderbilts had once vacationed on their own enormous estates. Many of those mansions had fallen into disrepair, but the Captain's Cottage looked better than it ever had. Working around a schedule crowded with weddings and celebrations, the housekeeping staff had polished the one hundred twenty-five-year-old hardwood floors, carefully dusted every globe in chandeliers the size of small cars, vigorously shaken out rugs, and repaired even the tiniest nicks and smudges. Outside, white masonry walls gleamed in stark contrast to black shutters and trim. The season's roses had been trellised along the veranda, and every plant on the acres surrounding his family's ancestral home had been carefully manicured.

Mildred nudged his shoulder. "The pressure to retain our number one ranking is intense. Then, there's the fact that Regina Charm is handling the evaluation herself this year. She isn't the most pleasant person to deal with."

"Humph. You can say that again. A cold fish, that's what she is."

Jason smiled at Cheri. "Don't hold back, now. Tell me what you really feel."

The woman's face colored. "Oh, I shouldn't talk about our clients like that. But Regina pushed all my buttons."

"Mine, too." Mildred's voice dropped to a whisper. "She has that whole New York vibe working for her—aloof, snooty. Nothing was good enough for her when she was planning to get married here. And once her dreams of having a Heart's Landing wedding hit a snag—"

"When did that happen?" And why was he just hearing about it now? Jason threaded his fingers through hair that brushed his collar. It sounded like Regina Charm was a real piece of work. No wonder everyone in town was on edge.

"A year ago this spring. Remember the leak at your place?"

How could he forget? He'd taken a rare weekend away from his responsibilities at the Captain's Cottage last April. While he was in Boston, a bad storm had taken out one of the estate's massive oaks. To make matters worse, the uprooted tree had broken a pipe. Water had backed up into the Blue Room, causing severe damage. Among the many phone calls he'd swapped with Alicia, the venue's event coordinator, he seemed to recall a vague reference to a bride who'd been less than pleased that her ceremony had been shifted to the larger, more beautiful Green Room. But by the time he'd arrived back in town, Alicia had worked everything out. Or at least, he'd thought she had. "You're saying that was Regina's wedding?"

"It would have been. She and her fiancé called the whole thing off." Mildred sighed heavily. Though the breakup had nothing to do with Heart's Landing, the town prided itself on delivering a perfect wedding to every bride. On those rare occasions when they weren't able to meet that goal, it hurt. Even a year later. "Let's just say, I don't think she'll be looking at us through rose-colored glasses."

Jason stifled a groan. "I hope we're up to this."

Thank goodness repairs to the Blue Room had finally been completed. He'd hired Ryan Court, the best restoration contractor in the business, and had personally overseen every detail. Not that he'd needed to. Ryan had done an excellent job of painstakingly restoring the wainscoting to its original beauty. Refurbished with new drapes and paint, the second-largest ballroom had once again become a popular spot with the brides who chose the Cottage for their ceremonies and receptions.

"You'll do fine." Mildred patted his hand. "I'm sure you dealt with your fair share of CEOs and celebrities in Boston."

She had a point. He'd started out as the booking agent for a small comedy club and moved up to manager of one of the area's largest convention centers. Over a span of ten years, he'd worked with the most popular bands and artists on the music scene. But all of that paled in comparison to the importance of the next ten days. Placing second or third in the Weddings

Today competition was not an option. Maintaining their spot as the first choice for brides from one end of the country to the other was critical to the success of every business in town.

At the front of the room, Mayor Greg Thomas rapped firmly on the hostess stand. The low buzz of conversation died down.

"If I can have everyone's attention." Greg hitched a pair of khakis higher on his round belly. "We'll run through the agenda, item by item, and get this over with. I know you all want to get home to your families, and I don't want to keep you a minute longer than necessary. Let's dive right in, shall we?" He glanced at the notes he'd spread across the makeshift podium. "Regina Charm is due to arrive at three PM on Friday afternoon. She'll go straight to the Captain's Cottage. Jason, why don't you take it from there?"

"Yes, sir." Jason unfolded his legs and stood. Around him, the familiar faces of people he'd known his entire life nodded their encouragement. Everyone in the room shared one thing in common. Their livelihoods depended on a perfect score from Weddings Today. Determined to do his part, he cleared his throat.

"Much like it was done in the Captain's day, the entire household will turn out to greet Ms. Charm. I'll assume Thaddeus's role, as usual, but I've asked my girlfriend Clarissa to fill in for Evelyn." Well, not exactly. He and his cousin Evelyn had appeared at quite a few weddings and receptions dressed as the Captain and his wife, Mary. But when Clarissa had heard that the Executive Editor for Weddings Today would be in town, she'd begged to play a leading role. Which reminded him, he needed to confirm Clarissa's travel plans. He jotted a mental note and continued. "We've set aside the Azalea Suite for Ms. Charm's use while she's in town. It's the largest of our bridal apartments and has been recently updated. Once she's settled in, we'll turn her over to you, Mr. Mayor, and get ready for the meet-and-greet at six that evening. It'll be in the Green Room. You're all invited, of course."

He took his seat as the mayor nodded. "That's good. My

only concern is in the timing. Since Ms. Charm opted to drive up from New York, rather than take the train, I'd be watching for her to arrive any time after noon. She's known to throw things off schedule a bit. Shows up early for interviews. That sort of thing. She likes to test people's reactions."

When a murmur of agreement passed through the room, Jason nodded. So, Regina Charm liked to spring surprises on her hosts, huh? Well, she wouldn't catch him napping. He'd post one of the house staff on the widow's walk bright and early Friday morning. They'd sound the alarm the moment a car turned onto the long, curving driveway that led to the Captain's Cottage.

Greg cleared his throat. "Everyone should have Ms. Charm's agenda." From a list that included practically every business in town, the editor had selected the places she'd like to see, as well as events she wanted to attend. It was more than enough to fill a crowded schedule. "Like I told Jason, Regina is prone to surprises. If your shop isn't on her list, she still might pop in for a quick visit. Stay on your toes."

One by one, the mayor called for brief reports on the plans to entertain the editor. From Something Old, Something New on Bridal Carriage Way to the bed and breakfast on Union Street, owners had arranged for tours of their businesses. Restaurants in the area had signed up to host Ms. Charm and her party at so many breakfasts, lunches, and dinners that the woman was in danger of needing an entire new wardrobe before she headed back to the city. Invitations to several weddings had been issued by brides who were eager for the opportunity to have their special day mentioned in Weddings Today. Plus, plenty of leisure activities had been planned in case the editor wanted to take advantage of the warmth of early summer. Last, but certainly not least, Regina would be the guest of honor at a special presentation of the Heart's Landing pageant. Usually performed in the fall, the play portrayed the time Captain Thaddeus had braved a hurricane in order to make port in time for his wife's birthday.

"I guess that sums it up." Mayor Thomas rubbed his hands together. "I'll be on call to serve as Ms. Charm's escort and answer any questions she might have throughout her visit here. One final word. I don't have to tell you how important this competition is for our town. With ceremonies taking place 365 days a year here in Heart's Landing, we pride ourselves on delivering the perfect wedding to every bride. But hard times lay ahead if we lose the designation of America's Top Wedding Destination. If anything goes awry, and I mean even the smallest hiccup, I'll expect to hear from you right away."

Greg scanned the room, his blue eyes meeting and registering agreement everywhere. Satisfied that his team knew what to do, he grinned. "All right now, we've got this. Let me hear that good old Heart's Landing spirit. What do you say?"

Jason, along with everyone else in the room, lifted an imaginary glass of champagne. He chimed in with the rest in the familiar toast. "The best is yet to be!"

"Yes, it will." Greg ran a hand over his bald pate. "Okay, folks. Time to head home now and get some rest."

Jason couldn't agree more. If Regina Charm was half as difficult to deal with as Mildred and Cheri said she was, everyone in town would need to keep their wits about them during her visit.

Read the rest! *A Cottage Wedding* is coming soon!

Thanks so much for reading *A Simple Wedding*. We hope you enjoyed it!

You might like these other books from Hallmark Publishing:

The Secret Ingredient
A Country Wedding
October Kiss
Sunrise Cabin
Dater's Handbook
Moonlight In Vermont
Like Cats and Dogs

For information about our new releases and exclusive offers, sign up for our free newsletter at hallmarkchannel.com/hallmark-publishing-newsletter

You can also connect with us here:

Facebook.com/HallmarkPublishing

Twitter.com/HallmarkPublish

About the Author

Leigh Duncan, an Amazon bestselling author and a National Readers' Choice Award winner, has written over two dozen novels, novellas and short stories, including *A Simple Wedding, A Country Wedding,* and *Journey Back to Christmas* for Hallmark Publishing, the Glades County Cowboys series for Harlequin, and her own Orange Blossom series. Leigh lives on Central Florida's East Coast where she writes complex, heartwarming, and emotional stories with a dash of Southern sass.

Leigh loves to stay in touch with readers through social media. Find her at www.facebook.com/LeighDuncanBooks, or visit her website at www.leighduncan.com.